AND THEY WERE ROOM MATES

Also by Page Powers
The Borrow a Boyfriend Club

PAGE POWARS

AND THEY WERE ROOM MATES

HODDER CHILDREN'S BOOKS

First published in Great Britain in 2025 by Hodder Children's Books
First published in the United States in 2025 by Roaring Book Press

3 5 7 9 10 8 6 4

Text copyright © Page Powars, 2025

The moral right of the author has been asserted.

*All characters and events in this publication, other than those clearly
in the public domain, are fictitious and any resemblance to
real persons, living or dead, is purely coincidental.*

All rights reserved.
No part of this publication may be reproduced, stored in
a retrieval system, or transmitted, in any form or by any means, without
the prior permission in writing of the publisher, nor be otherwise circulated
in any form of binding or cover other than that in which it is published
and without a similar condition including this condition being
imposed on the subsequent purchaser.

A CIP catalogue record for this book
is available from the British Library.

ISBN 978 1 444 96837 8

Printed and bound in Great Britain by
Clays Ltd, Elcograf S.p.A.

The paper and board used in this book
are made from wood from responsible sources.

Hodder Children's Books
An imprint of
Hachette Children's Group
Part of Hodder & Stoughton Limited
Carmelite House
50 Victoria Embankment
London EC4Y 0DZ

The authorised representative in the EEA is Hachette Ireland, 8 Castlecourt Centre, Dublin 15, D15 XTP3,
Ireland (email: info@hbgi.ie)

An Hachette UK Company
www.hachette.co.uk

www.hachettechildrens.co.uk

*FOR SHANNON, MY
CLASSMATE-TURNED-VALENTINE.
WILL YOU MARRY ME?*

Chapter 1
THIS SIDE OF PARADISE
TUESDAY, SEPTEMBER 3

"A *roommate?*" My heart races as I glance back at the waiting line full of frowns and tapping feet. I'm taking too long. Day one, and the spotlight is already on me. The exact situation I need to avoid as long as I'm at Valentine Academy for Boys.

My accidental nervous outburst forces my fourth-year orientation leader to finally glance up from his clipboard. He rules above me from a cocktail table at the back ballroom wall. Of course this academy hosts orientation in a literal ballroom. His plastic smile and dress shirt are properly buttoned to the neck, and his name tag claims he's called Maverick.

"Room 503," Maverick says, leaning forward to hand me a key. I instinctively take a step back to maintain the space between us. "You've been assigned to a double room. You're in Philautia Residence Hall. My floor."

I push my glasses farther up my nose to inspect the key, which is the size of my fist and made out of brass. "Your floor?"

"Yes, I'm your residential retainer."

"Sorry, my what?"

"Residential retainer," Maverick repeats. No explanation. Second years should know this by now. An RA, maybe, but for fancy schools?

"I apologize for the inconvenience," I try to say calmly, setting the key back on the table, "but I believe I paid the extra fee to reserve a single room."

It's a fact. On top of studying nonstop for Valentine's entrance exams and crafting a perfect portfolio for their Excellence Scholarship application, my summer break consisted of tutoring nearly every elementary schooler in Queens to afford the extra fee for this room. Hard to forget that.

From his cocktail table throne, Maverick scans the parents and students waiting behind us. "It'd be best to discuss this with your caregivers."

Today would be easier if Mom were here. It's not like I chose to be alone after my four-hour train ride to middle-of-nowhere upstate New York—Au Sable Forks, population 55. But some parents can't miss work if they want to pay rent, Maverick.

"She didn't come with me," I say.

"Remind me of your name again?"

"Charlie."

"Last?"

"Von Hevringprinz."

"Quite a long one you got."

Never heard that one before, *Maverick*. "Mhm."

"If you had paid for a single, then that would be marked here." He holds up his clipboard and points at my name. "I, too, apologize for the inconvenience."

Second year and *double* are marked on the spreadsheet.

Then there's been a huge mistake. "Would you mind double-checking with the office?"

Maverick rapidly rips a sticky note off a nearby stack like I struck a nerve by questioning his authority as a measly underclassman. "I'll note it. Large requests like these can only be approved by the principal. What was the reason you listed for requesting a single?"

"Um. Personal reasons."

His impenetrable smile falls a centimeter. He's heard that excuse a hundred times, but I'm not about to tell him or anyone else here the real reason. "Since all other rooms have been reserved, you'll need to stay with your assigned roommate in the meantime."

"How long will it take?"

Instead of answering, Maverick pulls a wicker basket of phones out from under the table and slaps it down in front of me. "All electronics, please."

Delilah warned me about the phone ransack. I just didn't realize it would be so soon. I hesitantly drop in my phone. "I don't get this back until winter break?"

"If there's an emergency, the office will happily accommodate you."

"Right, but—"

"As you should know, we have a history of celebrating Saint Valentine's lifelong passion for love through our own passion—for learning. This academy is for traditional, intensive study, and all electronic and internet access is limited as such." After his clearly rehearsed speech, Maverick takes a long look at my basic black T-shirt and jeans that are still too long for comfort despite being cuffed. "And, once checked into your room, students must change into proper uniform."

"I didn't know," I mutter, crossing my arms enough to cover my chest.

How could I? Most people don't know what goes on behind Valentine Academy's ivy walls. The outside world only knows that students from here end up in top-tier universities.

Even with Mom and Delilah's combined wisdom, I feel lost.

"All campus guidelines are in your package." He hands me a bound stack of paperwork with my full name sticky-noted on top. "Class schedules will be delivered tomorrow morning. Welcome to Valentine."

♦ ♦

Philautia Residence Hall is the missing piece of a castle.

Rather, a cobblestone tower with turret-like domes that screams early 1800s. Seven metal statues of Saint Valentine, the celebrated man himself, guard the front arch. Some pose with palm branches. Others outstretch their arms in cleric robes. A sign beneath is inscribed with LOVE IS PATIENT, LOVE IS KIND.

A chill rushes through me as I head into the lobby. Thankfully, there aren't more statues of old men advertising love to the academy's underage population. Just cedar benches that belong in a glamping cabin and tickle my nose with their faint earthy scent. Chandeliers twinkle above me as I follow a path made by a mahogany rug to a vacant winding staircase at the back.

After five flights, I stand before an absurdly long hallway punctuated with thick wooden doors. The stone-tiled floor is adorned by yet another rug, and the embossed art nouveau wallpaper effortlessly reminds me that this academy was resurrected in 1899. Once I reach the end, I spot the placard I'm looking for.

ROOM 503.

On the door is an intricate engraving of the same crest printed on half of Mom's sweatshirts. Gold paint accents the VALENTINE ACADEMY FOR BOYS and NAM AMOR TRADITIONALIS EDUCATIONIS running along the top and bottom, and red fills the inner heart design. An arrow brutally stabs through the center.

Beyond this hallway is my roommate. Someone who could discover the truth easier than anyone else here.

"But, man, the blockade."

"You think G cares?"

I look toward the voices. Two classmates wearing Valentine crest sweatshirts step out of Room 506. As they pass by, one spots me staring and goes in for a handshake. A bro kind.

My panic takes over, making me nearly black out as I floppily twist my hand around his own. He stares a beat too long to be considered normal before he silently continues to the staircase with his friend.

Awesome. Great work.

Re-collecting myself with a breath, I shove my room key into the lock.

The door creaks open, revealing twin beds with the crest on the quilts, cedar wood dressers and desks, and dome windows with velvet red drapes. What's most jarring is the wallpaper—a repeating pansy bouquet pattern, casting the room in shades of pink and puke green.

No roommate.

The knot in my stomach unravels. He isn't here. Yet.

Although one side has already been claimed. The bigger side, flaunting a longer wall that allows the bed, dresser, and desk space to spread out, unlike the other. Of course.

Three stacked suitcases of increasing size are beside his bed. No, *trunks*. Old-timey and leather with brass hinges and everything. Books are scattered along his desk and the floor, flowing onto my side.

Who is this guy? Is he eighty?

Kicking his books out of the way, I toss my five-pound package detailing all the school's guidelines on the desk that's apparently mine, then roll my suitcase up to the accompanying bed. When I throw myself on top, my body sinks deep into the ridiculously plush, thousand-dollar mattress. I try to adjust so I don't drown in my own bed but eventually give up.

I'm alone. In my new room. I cast an arm over my face to block out the world. The fears I've shoved down since orientation rush to the surface. My plan to lie low like Mom suggested was already nearly ruined by a handshake.

A *handshake*.

I feel like I'm twelve again, back when Mom first took me to Valentine's brother campus for their *Hamlet* production. The boys who sat beside us used words I'd never heard, messed with each other in ways they innately knew how to, like a magic spell. All I could think was how much I wanted to be put under it too. At first, I assumed since Mom had been an Excellence Scholar on their nearby sister campus, that unshakable feeling was because I belonged at Valentine too. I went to their Shakespeare and Classics camp two years later. Stayed in the sister campus residential hall and fell in love with how much I learned. And realized the truth. I didn't only want to go to Valentine because of Mom or the education.

I'd been drawn to those boys because I wanted to be a boy. Because I was a boy.

A burst of orientation chatter beyond the window brings the world rushing back around me. Lifting my glasses to scrub my face, I open my eyes again.

A poster of a white teenage boy on the ceiling smiles back.

I jolt and grip the bed. He wears an aloha shirt with half the buttons undone, and a parrot perches on his shoulder. Large cursive text placed across his chest reads *Sexiest Poet of the Year*. That face is familiar. Too familiar.

My pulse spikes as I hop on top of the mattress to get a better look.

He looks older than when we met at fourteen. His hair is longer, flowing to his shoulders, but I could never forget those blazing blue irises and upturned nose. I check the ceiling above the other bed. Another poster of the same blond, smirking in a tuxedo.

He became a model in the last two years. Or a famous poet. Or both. He *was* the most talented student during that poetry workshop I was forced to take at Shakespeare and Classics camp. Subjectively, at least. To others.

I'm trapped with a roommate who's his diehard stan? Him, of all obnoxiously vain people?

Vain. The word clicks something into place for me.

He *was* the vainest at camp. He *would* hang up posters of himself.

Maybe this isn't a stan.

I rush over to my roommate's desk and rummage through the stacked composition notebooks. A name, an address, something to identify the person I'll spend every night with for who knows how long? When I open up the third notebook, I go still at the name on the corner.

The only name who would know the truth regardless of how well I hide. Who stole my first kiss and shattered my heart, and who can expose whatever he'd like as soon as he sees me.

Jasper Grimes.

Chapter 2

PARADISE LOST

TUESDAY, SEPTEMBER 3

Delilah spits out her energy drink. "A *roommate?*"

I grimace at the regurgitated green liquid on the grass. "That's what I told them."

"You paid for a single room," she says, raising her bumpy nose at me, the only physical similarity we share as best friends. While I can barely control my dark curls, she complains about her blond hair lying too flat. While I have boxes for brows, she's never had to pluck hers. While Delilah was taller than me by an inch when we met at camp, my shoe inserts shoot me up enough to be the tall one now.

"I also tried to tell them that," I say.

Digging her stiletto acrylics so hard into her drink that the aluminum crinkles, Delilah leans against the soaring brick wall dividing our brother and sister campuses.

A few parents and students passing through the wall's gate stare at Delilah's palpable dark aura the longer she emanates her fury.

My shoulders tense. The focus isn't on me, but still. "People are watching."

"Enjoy the show," Delilah barks at the setting sun and courtyard, where an unsettling séance circle of cupid statues inside a marble fountain shoot water from their arrows. "How dare they shove a roommate on you?"

I haven't even told her the worst part: It's Jasper Grimes, the asshole who had me bawling my eyes out to her at the end of summer two years ago.

Delilah has "accidentally" committed arson on oak trees in the surrounding Au Sable Forks woods more times than I've seen her in person since camp—twice. Both were a result of her angrily monologuing about Valentine's strictness and chucking around sparklers that she snuck into camp. Since she's upset now, I need to assess that anger on a range from tree arson to whole planet arson before I tell her the entire story. As far as I can tell, she doesn't have any sparklers handy. But with Delilah, you never really know.

"I can't even help you," Delilah goes on. "My academy is right there, but it's basically not with this cockblockade in the way."

"The what?"

"This wall between us! We all call it that." She smacks the palm of her hand against the brick wall.

Yet another word I don't know. Delilah already informed me that summer campers never learn the real campus slang, like how both academy courtyards are the Halos due to their circular shapes and the chocolate-caramel lattes sold at the coffee stands are Jesuses because they taste as good as him. Or something. Cockblockade, however, evaded me.

At least I was familiar with how traditionally the academies operate, even after the recent *Saint Valentine's* to *Valentine Academy* rebrand—an attempt to separate from its religious-focused origins. At camp, everyone attended workshops on the sister campus but slept in their respective residential halls on very-most-opposite map corners, split by this wall. As students now, we only get free rein today and during some winter mixer—which Delilah claims is our sole time to celebrate after months of studying, and which I'll unquestionably avoid.

Delilah smacks the wall again for dramatic emphasis, pulling me back.

Whole-planet-arson status it is. The best course of action is to wait to share the details on my roommate situation. "My residential retainer said he'd check with the office about a single," I say. "It'll be fine."

"Good. Or I'll set them on fire."

"Do not."

"We'll see."

I tug on my left suspender strap. The fact that we need to be in uniforms the moment we're assigned to rooms—a black-and-red plaid blazer with the Valentine crest on the lapel, matching plaid slacks, bright red button-down shirt, and black ties spawned from the depths of ugly Hell—is cruel. "Do I look like a guy in this uniform?"

"You are a guy."

"But like." I wiggle the dress shoes hanging off my feet, which I purposely ordered a size too large. Not my smartest move, but fearing that everyone would notice I have the smallest feet on campus beat my logic. "You know."

Delilah crosses her arms in her much more aesthetically pleasing uniform. While I look drenched in fresh blood in my suit, she gets a pastel blazer and a plaid skirt that falls to her knee-high stockings. The reminder of how aggressively the brother and sister uniforms play into stereotypes isn't a thrilling one.

"I thought you finally felt good about this stuff," she says.

"I did. I do. Sort of."

"You deferred your acceptance here for a reason."

I did. To take online classes for a year. To figure out guy clothes and guy hair and other ways to survive, all in the privacy of my bedroom. But. "I guess."

"No one's gonna find out. How would they know?"

Jasper Grimes would know.

If he tells anyone, it's over. The guidance package doesn't mention transgender students, but that's the problem. They only use the old church as a bell tower now, but when Mom studied here, going to church was mandatory on Fridays at nine o'clock. She took religion like other students took math. And whenever I visited Valentine before, not a single student struck me as someone who may need updated guidelines for the same reason I do.

Hence, keeping my head down.

"I just have a bad feeling all this will pile up," I say. "And I'm worried I might not rank top five of my class."

"Please, you're the smartest person I know."

The compliment only briefly warms my chest. Delilah could never understand the fear of losing a scholarship. Although both our parents went to Valentine, hers are doctors drowning in money. Mom was also an Excellence Scholar and now owns a bookshop that, although it's a cornerstone of the Queens community, is drowning in debt—an anomaly when Valentine alumni get an unofficial fast pass to any Ivy they wish. But Mom wished for her dream instead. "My scholarship depends on it."

"I mean, I get that. If I want to be able to run for the student council board this year, then I have to rank within the top fifteen of my own class."

I nod, even though I barely take in what she says.

Delilah sighs, and it comes out a bit irritated and short. A piece of me wants to ask what's going on, but she distracts me by continuing to talk. "I'm just trying to say that I hear you. About the pressure. I'd back out now if you don't want this."

"No," I say, playing with Mom's varsity Valentine ring on my finger. "I want it."

Even more than that. When Grandma and Grandpa were alive, they would ramble about how proud they were of Mom to have scored this scholarship—and when she wasn't around, how it was "wasted" on a tanking bookstore.

And then there's Mom. At first, I applied without telling her, assuming the odds of being chosen as one of their Excellence Scholars were microscopically low, and that she would be crushed if I got her hopes up. Once they emailed me that my scholarship was still on the table after I deferred and came clean to her, though, she didn't cheer like I expected. She only frowned, knowing full well that I would need to stay on the boys' campus for reasons that might not thrill administration. She insisted there had to be other Ivy feeders in the region besides the one she went to—that I could apply elsewhere, to a place that wouldn't pose as much risk.

But Valentine is where I realized I was a boy. It's called out to me all my life, insisting I belong here. It had to be *this* campus. *This* academy. After four attempts at explaining this to Mom— alongside reminding her how this life-changing education pointed her toward her love of books and, ultimately, mine—she let go of enough worry to give a hesitant seal of approval.

Yet I'm already facing problems one day in. Exactly like Mom worried about.

"But look how terrified you are," Delilah says.

"I'm not *terrified*."

Delilah points at my hand. It's shaking.

I drop my arm. "I've dreamed of studying here forever.

Academics that'll actually challenge me, and on the boys' side of campus. I never thought I'd be able to..." I trail off, recalling the worst roommate I could've been assigned who might blow up this dream.

How do I keep Jasper Grimes silent? A bribe?

Bonging noises resonate through the courtyard. I startle and cover my ears.

Delilah rips my hands down. "Bro, relax, it's the ten-minute warning bell till lights-out."

I glance down the brick wall—cockblockade—where a bell tower sticks out of an otherwise unused church. I hadn't noticed it in the dim sunset.

Instead of the bro handshake I faced in the residential hall, Delilah goes in for a basic hug. I've never been more thankful.

"If you start panicking or sobbing at any point, contact me," she says. "Since I'm your emergency contact, my residential retainer can send me to the office to take the call."

"I won't sob." I pause. "But thank you."

Delilah disappears through the open cockblockade gate to the sister academy, and I head toward the residence hall. The sidewalks are crowded with families rushing their goodbyes, but I barely perceive them. Too much is on my mind.

Tonight, I have to sleep in the same room as another boy. One who kissed me and walked away like I was nothing.

My *first* kiss.

I shove my hands deep into my pockets as if that'll punch the nerves out of me. The second Jasper sees me, he'll have questions, and I won't know how to answer any. I need to have a speech ready, and that bribe, but I don't know what I'd offer.

I'll just ask. He never had a problem taking whatever he wanted.

Chapter 3
THE TIME MACHINE
TUESDAY, SEPTEMBER 3

I press an ear against the door to Room 503, listening for signs of life.

A clang here. A shove there. He's back.

Where's that speech, Charlie?

Yes, I'm the person you met at Valentine's Shakespeare and Classics Summer Camp two years ago. Yes, we kissed by the lake. No, I'm not that person anymore, but also, I am. What would you like in order to stay silent?

That'll do.

As I reach for the handle, my hands lock up. *Do it. Just do it!*

Adrenaline surges through me, and I yank back the handle. The door whips open and slams against the wall.

"Oops," I mumble.

At the end of the room, a slender figure in the same plaid blazer and tie as me jolts. Although my uniform loosely hangs in all the wrong places, his cinches in all the right ones. He loses his grip on a glass object—a heart-shaped paperweight—and fumbles three times before catching it.

The Sexiest Poet of the Year poster boy with glistening blue eyes and blond hair pulled into a stubby ponytail. In real life. Staring back at me.

The speech I prepared drains out of my head.

Jasper Grimes is really here.

Jasper tosses the paperweight despite saving it seconds ago.

The glass cracks against the windowsill and falls to the floor in chunks. "Charlie von Hevringprinz!"

Even though he's never spoken this full name before, everything about the way he says it sounds so familiar.

Next thing I know, he dashes across our room—or, rather, with so many books in the way, he hops—and snatches my hands. His flowery fragrance swirls around me, and his touch is as freezing as I remember it being. The cons of having a heart secretly made of ice.

He smiles so wide I worry his whole face will crack like the paperweight. "It's an honor to meet you."

As if he hasn't recognized me. Yet.

I take in his fluttery pale lashes, the ever-present red tint to his cheeks, and the frayed hairs that have escaped his ponytail. It's all the same as two years ago.

Keep your head down.

I abruptly step back. How sharp is my face in this lighting? I haven't checked how my arms look in this blazer yet. "P-pleasure."

"A shame that we lost our single rooms."

"You got screwed over too?"

"Yes, but what a plus. Now I'm roommates with the second-year Excellence Scholar. The fact that you beat out thousands and stand before me now. A genius!"

"Oh, I'm not a genius." My focus drifts toward the first three buttons of his red dress shirt left undone, showing off his collarbone and chest. He's always been just toned enough—not too muscular or slight—to appear as if he casually plays an after-school sport. Obviously, the Sexiest Poet of the Year, whose hobbies include posing for cameras, charming every woman within a mile radius, and punching hearts to death has to look good.

I mean, he does look good. But that has nothing to do with me anymore.

"Of course you're a genius," Jasper says, yanking my focus up again. "Did you not start that English tutoring program in New York City? The one that gained thousands in nonprofit support in a single year?"

"I did..."

"See?"

Admittedly, the compliment touches me. After I decided to defer for a year, my Excellence Scholar spot was replaced. Only four are here at a time, chosen as a first year to represent their class until graduation. When I was later told my replacement left after his first year, I assumed I was dreaming. At least until I realized no one would leave that honor behind willingly. There were two possibilities:

One, he got kicked out for breaking guidelines. Maybe even for a reason like mine.

Two, more likely, he couldn't handle the pressure.

I refuse to be like that replacement. I *will* last until graduation.

"How do you know all of this?" I ask Jasper.

"My aunt told me. Have you considered tutoring here?"

Rewind. "Your aunt?"

"I suppose you know her as Principal Grimes."

"Your aunt is the principal?"

Jasper's memorable laugh trickles off his lips. Soft and bubbly. "Pretending not to know. You're funny, von Hevringprinz."

I return a laugh, but it's frail. Of course. The sole woman who has the power to send me home, and who will either approve or deny my single room request, is Jasper's aunt. Of course I somehow never came across that memorable last name through my application process. *Of course* Jasper was supposed to have a single. As her nephew, probably the fanciest.

And he, without a doubt, doesn't recognize me.

I should be relieved, but the tip of my tongue burns with what rages within me instead. *How did it feel to kiss me while writing poetic love letters to three other people during camp? You couldn't have cared enough to even remember my very memorable mess of a last name?*

"Your aunt is letting you stay stuck in a double?" I ask, trying to stay calm.

Jasper shrugs and walks toward his desk. "I didn't file a complaint. I've heard a roommate can be fun. With an Excellence Scholar like yourself, I bet our conversations will be stimulating. A blessing in disguise!"

"Right," I mutter. "A blessing."

As he rummages through books scattered across his desk, a silver bracelet jangles against his wrist, competing with the cricket chirps filtering through the cracked-open window for most obnoxious, high-pitched sound. "I assume you'd like my autograph? I've never offered this to anyone before, so please keep this hush-hush from my followers."

"Wait, what?"

Jasper holds up a paperback book like a trophy. *Love Is a Broken Party Clown* curves around a poorly drawn crying clown printed on the cover. The title isn't what makes my brow furrow. It's the author's name. *His* name.

"You published a book?" I ask, and I fail to hold back my sass this time.

Jasper's head tilts like he almost recognizes it. Like this was definitely how I spoke to him when we first met at camp too.

My whole body tenses.

"Poetry collection," he finally says, slowly and curiously. "My most popular posts online." He signs the inside with a permanent marker and hands me the copy. "For you, roommate."

My brain glitches as I hold the very real signed book. What about him could be impressive enough for him to have followers? Books? Posters?

It must be because of his looks.

"Thanks," I mutter despite the gift being wasted on me. The only reason I met Jasper at camp was because I was forced to take that poetry workshop alongside my lectures and reading hours about the greats. What's the point of writing poetry if you're not one of those greats? Regurgitating your own overemotional, gushy soup?

Jasper steps deeper into the room, outstretching his arms, his bracelet jingling again like an annoying bell. "Do you appreciate what I've done to the place?"

I've been so overwhelmed by his presence that I didn't notice. A crystal vase is on a new side table, a candle collection is set on the windowsill, and a freaking life-sized cardboard cutout of himself is propped between our beds. Mardi Gras beads hang from his cardboard neck.

I would've rather enjoyed a bookshelf.

Jasper clasps his hands together. "Do you?"

I don't know. Do you remember who I am? I clench my fist to compose myself. Jasper forgetting is beneficial. As long as I can prevent him from remembering, then he can't report who I am to his aunt.

But being able to keep my burning hatred toward him a secret?

I glare at the poster of Jasper on the ceiling, the cardboard cutout, and then back to the real Jasper. "You've made yourself a prominent focal point."

"Thank you."

"That wasn't—" I force a smile. "You're welcome."

"I'm just brimming with questions about you, roommate," Jasper says, clasping his hands together. He inspects me with big, expectant eyes. "Do you have pets? Any hobbies? What's your family like? Do you have siblings? Please, don't hold back."

My insides shrivel into a prune. "I. Well—"

Jasper waves a hand. "Apologies, I'm getting ahead of myself again. You deserve to settle in before we start learning more about one another."

"Yeah. Yes. Thank you."

"Of course. After you rest, that is when you will answer all my questions."

I try to hold in a grimace.

"We must spend some intimate time together soon, then," Jasper says, ever oblivious to my discomfort. "Tomorrow. Let's meet for lunch between classes."

"I'm bus—"

"Wonderful," he says. He heads to his dresser, squatting to dig through his unfolded pajamas shoved in the bottom drawer. Conversation over, apparently. He tosses plaid pants over his shoulder.

I frown and walk to my own dresser, pulling out one of my folded Valentine-branded pajama sets, then turn back around. "Sorry, but I really can't meet you for lunch—"

Jasper's shirt is off. His pants, barely on.

"Jesus—!" I spin to face any other direction. My elbow knocks my dresser so hard that a textbook falls off and smashes my foot. I yelp.

"What's wrong?" Jasper says. Totally calm. At least I assume he is from his typical singsongy voice. No way I'm looking over to verify that.

"N-nothing."

He chuckles in the face of my breakdown. "Have you forgotten we're both guys?"

Being told I'm a boy should feel good. Amazing.

All I feel is crushed.

"I'm gonna—" I point toward the bathroom. "Bye!"

The door shuts beside me. My legs collapse, and I land on the floor, my blood pumping through me. Jasper's fancy glass containers of shampoo and conditioner are visible through the translucent shower door next to my two-in-one. Rose scented. Bright pink.

We'll share a shower.

Sitting there, I take deep breaths to stop myself from having a heart attack in my teens. Then, only a few seconds later, I pick myself back up. Because Excellence Scholars don't nearly throw up their dinner on the first day of school. They excel.

My residential retainer will talk to the office. I'll escape soon.

Chapter 4
BRAVE NEW WORLD
WEDNESDAY, SEPTEMBER 4

CHARLIE VON HEVRINGPRINZ | ID: V183019
Zero Hour: Homeroom
First Hour: Physical Education
Second Hour: Advanced Chemistry
Third Hour: Advanced English Literature
Lunch C
Fourth Hour: Advanced Calculus
Fifth Hour: Advanced World History
Sixth Hour: First-Year Civics

Physical education burns my eyes like acid.

I whip off the class schedule taped to my door and inspect the list closer. First-year civics should take up one of my two extracurriculars—a requirement I missed as a transfer. But when I submitted my desired course list over the summer, I nearly passed out when I saw all the literary options: Factual Journalism, the Art of Persuasive Writing, History of Chinese Literature, Intro to Poetry. Who wouldn't kill for those? Well, minus poetry.

I had marked the first three down with enthusiastic interest, happy to get into any.

So why physical education?

Playing sports with other guys. Being compared to other guys. Showering with guys.

"No way in hell" shoots out of me so loudly that my voice echoes down the hallway, my filter annihilated after being awake until two a.m. last night.

Jasper doesn't snore, but he does read. Loudly. Deep into the night, he leaned against his headboard, reading a book thicker than my head. Each page turn crinkled. His lamp buzzed. And, of course, he just had to vocally react to every stanza. *Oh, wow. My goodness. Unbelievable.* What could be that interesting? Ten bucks it was his own poetry.

I glance at Jasper's made bed, which has a whopping eleven extra throw pillows and a decorative patchwork quilt patterned with knit ambrosia flowers. The posters of himself still hang from the ceiling. All that's missing is the real Jasper.

He was gone by the time the bell tower woke me up, which allowed me to dig through my suitcase to ensure nothing could identify me as somebody he used to know. I ripped up my favorite photo of me and Delilah posing in front of Au Sable Forks Lake as campers.

Maybe Jasper is sneaking off to the sister academy to see his girlfriends. Wouldn't be the first time he's had more than one.

I glare at my schedule again. PE is a mistake like my single room. I'll fix this before I even reach class.

⋄ ⋄

"All men, rise!"

That's the first thing I hear while stumbling onto the Pragma Recreational Center field, sweaty and gross and dying for a sports drink. Of course, even after a thirty-minute hunt, I couldn't find Maverick the Residential Retainer in his room nor in the communal lobby space. The five gravel paths that sprout out of the courtyard like appendages turned me into a rat in a torture maze for thirty more, trying to find this center. The limited signposts did not help. I check my watch. Ten minutes late. The way an Excellence Scholar should not act.

At least there's no Jasper. Just a plot of grass so freshly cut that I smell it in the air, surrounded by oak and maple trees, perfectly and evenly planted around the perimeter. An instructor in a red Valentine-crested tracksuit stands before lines of students. They vary widely in height, facial hair, and bulk, ranging from pre- to post-puberty. A multiyear class. They all wear the same tracksuit as the instructor.

I pluck at my tie. There's a separate uniform?

The instructor starts explaining the locker room rules, flipping through her clipboard paperwork. A chance to join the crowd undetected. I claim a spot in the back row, behind someone a whole head taller whose tracksuit can barely stretch around his bulging biceps. A shield until I can figure out my schedule.

"Banks got a detention," the human shield whispers to a guy beside him.

"For what?" the other asks.

"Out past lights-out. By three minutes."

"That's nothing compared to Richards. I heard he's getting *expelled*."

"Seriously? How? It's only been a day."

"Told his roommate he was planning a party in their room, and he snitched."

Detention over three minutes. Expelled over a plan. I signed up for this life, but my stomach still twists.

At least I found some reliable informants. "Hey," I say, tugging the tracksuit hem of the human shield. He turns. I instinctively step back to maintain enough space and lower my face. "I think my residential...re..." What was that called? "Retainer. He gave me the wrong schedule."

His towering body leans over mine to read my schedule, shattering that space within seconds, and I go rigid. When I told Delilah I was confident enough in my appearance at orientation, I meant from a *distance*. Every student shoving their nose into my business wasn't on my bingo card. He points at the top of the page. "Here's the name and student ID. You Charlie?"

"Yeah."

"Then this one's yours."

"But I didn't sign up for PE," I say, trying to deepen my voice to deflect his closeness.

"Every grade level is required to. You new here, bro?"

"Um, a bit. They make us?"

"'Cause Valentine doesn't offer sports. They gotta make sure everyone keeps up with their fitness. You get it."

I do not.

Defeat hits me hard. This really might be my schedule.

"Does everyone remember what first-day fitness testing is?" the instructor shouts with so much vigor that her dark brown braids wrapped in bows bop against her tan cheeks.

A resounding *Yes, Ms. Nallos* floods the field.

"To recap, you'll be paired up. Every minute, you'll rotate to different stations around the field. Signs will tell you what exercise to test each other with."

I scan the outdoor exercise equipment. A few signs taped to orange cones are marked with PULL-UPS and PUSH-UPS.

Today?

"Halfway through the term, we'll check again for improvements. Questions?" Ms. Nallos's sneakers crunch against the tended-to grass as she meanders between rows to check.

The moment she locks eyes with my tracksuit-less body, it's over.

She walks up, studying my outfit. "You're quite overdressed."

I obscure my hands into fists and lower my chin so my curls shroud more of me. "I didn't realize PE was on my schedule, so I didn't buy the tracksuit set. Is this class really required for every student?"

"It is."

"Ms. Nallos, I didn't sign up for PE either," a nasally voice whines one row over. Some white guy with a foot for a face, his chin overpronounced and bedhead sticking up in chunks.

Snickers come from another row.

"Quiet, Cody," Ms. Nallos yells, then smiles at me oddly before checking her clipboard. "I've never taught you. Are you the Charlie von...Heavy Prince...I marked absent?"

Close enough. "Yes, I got lost on the way."

Ms. Nallos returns to the front of the field and digs through a workout bag on a bench. She pulls out a clump of red clothes and chucks them over the lines of heads. "Catch!"

The clothes land in a pile at my dress shoes.

"Luckily, I've come prepared to help those who *forgot* their uniform." Ms. Nallos points toward Pragma Recreational Center. "Locker room. Go. Five minutes to change."

Spotlight number two.

Murmurs hit me from every angle as I swipe up the clothes and make my trip across the field, then search for the locker room in the center, mortification crashing through me. My feet are too small to wear just socks, I wear dress shoe sole inserts for a reason, I *can't*—

My back slides down the locker room door until I hit the freezing tile. The pants and shirt are marked with *L* on the tags. Could mean *Loser*. But probably just means *Large*. Now my body will look even narrower compared with everyone else's. I check my watch again. Four minutes left. Maybe it's already time to use my emergency phone call to Delilah. Why didn't she warn me that physical education is mandatory? She should've known this would blow up my life.

Yet I sit there, frozen in place, letting time pass by as the fears I've swallowed since yesterday consume me. I haven't gotten a second to breathe, let alone process everything already falling apart. Maybe I can't pull off hiding here.

I *have* to. For Mom. For *me*.

I rush into a stall to change. Of course the joggers hang over my feet by an inch, and two watermelons could fit between me and this undershirt. By the time I'm back on the field, testing has begun. Ms. Nallos is listing off partners.

She recites a slew of names I don't recognize before shouting, "Xavier Nguyen and Charlie von H, begin at pull-ups."

From a group of muscular guys huddled in a friend circle, one steps forward. The six-foot-tall monster I cowered behind earlier.

My stomach drops as the walking mass of muscle named Xavier Nguyen approaches. I didn't notice before, but unlike everyone else's buzz cuts and short hair, the black bangs draped over his forehead are at least parted with a bit of style. He stops before me, and his meaty fist comes flying at my face.

I squeeze my eyes shut, but the blow never comes. I open them.

Xavier shows a crooked smile, waiting for his fist to be bumped. "We meet again, man."

My nerves flip as I knock his fist back lightly—but not too much. Be manly. Was it too much? "Y-yo." I cringe internally even as I say it. End me.

We walk toward a square expanse of asphalt marked with PULL-UPS, where three metal bars increase in height. Xavier zips off his tracksuit jacket, only leaving behind the undershirt, and pulls a spoon from his pants pocket. He kisses the curved back.

I blink at the spoon.

He returns a blink like I'm the problem. "What? Gotta beat my personal record from last year. This spoon's lucky."

It's not even a miniature collector spoon for grandmas or a special trinket one could find in an antique store. Just a normal spoon. "How do you know it's lucky?"

"My friend's an expert in the dark arts."

Okay.

Ms. Nallos blows her whistle. "One minute. Go!"

Xavier latches onto the tallest bar and pounds out pull-up after pull-up, keeping a perfectly parallel angle. I stare in awe. His muscles are bigger than I even imagined. If I stole his lucky spoon, would I sprout muscles like that?

The whistle goes off again, and Xavier's feet hit the asphalt. His cheeks are flushed, but there isn't a drop of sweat on that chiseled face I could only dream of having. He twirls his spoon over the top of his knuckles before shoving it into his pocket. "Verdict?"

"Um," I say. "You had nice form?"

"No, my number of pull-ups."

My shoulders hitch. I forgot to count. "Fifty?"

Xavier's head tilts. "The pull-up world record for our age is forty-four."

"Switch partners!"

I approach the medium-height bar. Maybe someone like Jasper Grimes, who magically achieves success at everything he touches, could hit the same number as Xavier. Not me. But if I don't, will Xavier figure it out?

The whistle blows.

A fire ignites within me. I pull myself up as Xavier watches.

Then I come flopping back down like a dead fish. Stomach first, then head, a sharp pain zapping through me. I flip onto my back and squeeze my eyes shut. How many human sacrifices do I need to make to pass PE?

Ms. Nallos does the rounds with her clipboard, asking each pair for their numbers. She reaches us quicker than I'd like.

"I got twelve, I think," Xavier tells her. "Charlie got two."

Ms. Nallos inspects my limp body that very much got zero, then moves on to the next pair. Once she's gone, Xavier offers to help me up.

My instincts warn me to decline so he can't compare our hand sizes, but I'm in such a daze that I accept, only for my oversized tracksuit sleeve to get in the way. Slapping the sleeve back up to my shoulder, I try again. "Thanks."

"You know they sell our gym uniforms at the campus gift shop, right?"

"We have a gift shop?"

Xavier's brow pinches. Naturally, a gift shop was built since I was a camper, and I still know nothing about Valentine. "Yeah?"

"I didn't know," I mutter. "Why did you lie? About my score."

He studies me in a way that makes my heart race. "Hey, we all took a break during summer. Let me know if you're ever looking for a trainer. I train mornings and nights in the workout rooms here."

On top of PE? "Thanks...," I say again.

"Either way, I'm sure you'll make some gains back soon, man."

How am I supposed to *make gains back* when I never had gains to begin with?

Chapter 5
THE PRINCE
WEDNESDAY, SEPTEMBER 4

The universe does me a favor by keeping my new roommate away from my PE class, but the favors run dry after that.

"Charlie von Hevringprinz!" Jasper waves from the back of my chemistry classroom. No blazer or tie on him—only a red dress shirt with three buttons undone like last night. Already breaking dress code on day one. A mural of the periodic table of elements stretches behind him. *Ge* for germanium, *Ni* for nickel, *U* for uranium, and *S* for sulfur are bolded above his head.

He chose that seat on purpose.

Two people hovering around Jasper follow his wave toward me at the door. Must be his friends. A few others by the whiteboard stare. Spotlight number three.

Jasper picks up a hardcover book—that one he kept me awake with—and slaps the chairback of the unclaimed spot beside him. "I saved you the best seat in the house. Right by me, the perfect start to getting to know each other so intimately."

The stares turn to snickers.

My face heats to a boil. I puff out my shoulders. These stares are fine. I look fine.

What's not fine? No seating chart. Maybe at an academy ranked fourth in the nation that costs more to attend than Mom makes in a year, they don't need one to behave. If I reject Jasper, these lurking, judgmental eyes will witness it. My spotlight will shine brighter. So will every little bit of me.

Sitting near Jasper for a whole period, though, will spotlight me worse. I wiggle my glasses. "Bad eyesight. Need the front row."

Jasper's hand wilts out of the air, the book in his grasp accidentally knocking his friend in the head. I swear, the constant red tint to his cheeks fades to a dull gray.

I walk toward a vacant front desk, my worries subsiding only somewhat. That felt polite enough, yet the sensation that I'm being watched persists. As the instructor goes over roll calls, icebreakers, and a borderline-threatening syllabus, that feeling grows worse. Am I holding my pencil right, or do guys hold them like they're stabbing someone? Are my legs splayed out enough to seem casual but not so spread out to be inconsiderate?

The bell finally rings.

Thankfully, I don't need to hunt too hard for my English lit class since I'm already in the Storge Academic Center, but I need the third floor. After rushing up a winding staircase, I locate the room at the end of a hall.

I open the door, then freeze.

"Charlie von Hevringprinz!"

Jasper, in the front row. This time, he's stacked the desk beside him with a tower of objects. A messenger bag with *JFG* embossed in silver on the leather flap, his hardcover book, and a whole-ass globe. "I saved us better seats."

He got here before me. *How?*

Why is he trying *this* desperately to get to know me?

I rack my brain for another excuse to sit far away. I'm the Excellence Scholar; I should be able to. The longer I take, the more eyes land on me. Trapping me.

No escape.

Slowly, I walk toward the reserved desk. "You didn't have to," I grumble.

"This is what roomies are for." Jasper grins brighter than the silver JFG on his bag. He transfers the objects on my desk onto the floor, starting with the book—my enemy. Last night, his quilt blocked most of the cover, but now I see the author. PIERRE-MARIE LAFRAMBOISE.

Not his own poetry. Shocking.

More students trickle into the classroom. Now that I've marginally calmed down after the chaos of PE, I'm able to actually observe them. Each one wears the same red-and-black uniform as me, yet they somehow look cooler. Their plaid slacks cuff at the ankles, and their blazers are rolled to the elbows. At an academy with a twenty-page guidelines package, I suppose an unspoken list of rules *would* form to challenge them.

Totally casually, I roll up my sleeves.

Unspoken Guideline 1: There's the traditional uniform, and there's the real uniform.

The classroom door whips open.

"'I CALLED MY LOVE FALSE LOVE,'" a low, bold voice bellows from the hall. A Black man with a dark complexion who must be young on the adult scale. His locks fall to the shoulder pads of his floral-print blazer, and his navy slacks are as tight as plastic wrap.

I gawk at his outfit, expecting everyone to do the same. They watch, bored, as if he's explaining a conditional clause.

Unspoken Guideline 2: Students are forced to blend in with the traditional uniform, but instructors certainly are not.

"'SING WILLOW, WILLOW, WILLOW,'" he bellows on the

way to his desk, then slams down the briefcase with so much force that his blazer tail flaps behind him. Even his voice sounds like he didn't graduate from college yet. "'IF I COURT MORE WOMEN, YOU'LL COUCH WITH MORE MEN.'"

"*Othello*," Jasper shouts beside me. "Shakespeare."

The instructor grins so widely that his eyes crinkle at the sides. He pushes his chunky glasses higher up his nose. "Context?"

"A woman is being killed. It's one of the few moments where women speak authentically to one another despite their differences within a play centering on male manipulation and violence."

"Mr. G did his summer reading." The instructor tosses him a lollipop from his briefcase.

Jasper catches it as voices pop up around the classroom.

"Of course it goes to Jasper."

"The legend."

"Bro should go on *Jeopardy!*"

My brow furrows. People here actually like this high-and-mighty know-it-all?

Jasper's "mysterious, confident poet" vibe did wow the guest speakers at our camp workshops. He could recite every poetic device and form before day one—which I denied impressed me despite my stuttering heart rate. Other campers, however, weren't as subtle about their attraction to that intelligence. Jasper received no shortage of romantic interest from girls. That's why, when he walked up to me and asked to work on our first dramatic mode assignment together, I assumed it was a twisted prank.

But now Jasper is trapped at an all-boys academy. He shouldn't have a leg up anymore. Yet even though he can't use his romantic charms here, he's *still* well-liked.

Unbelievable.

The instructor shushes away the compliments about Jasper. "Thrilled to have you for another year, Mr. G. In the front row for once."

Jasper kicks his feet onto the desk like an animal. "I need the best seat for your education, Mr. Stern."

I flick my gaze between the odd poet and the odder instructor. Jasper doesn't get a *where are your blazer and tie?* No *put your feet down*. He gets a *thrilled to have you*. Because he's the principal's nephew? A famous poet? Because he's friends with the so-called Mr. Stern? These two do give off concerningly similar energy.

Great. One Jasper was plenty.

Although, Valentine does boast about hiring the most intelligent instructors in the nation, which means Mr. Stern must be as passionate about literature as I am.

When he starts our *Othello* discussion, my theory is proven. As he breaks into more monologues by memory, quizzing us on which character spoke what line, a breeze blows through the open window, carrying the scent of the lavender bushes and the trickling fountain beyond, where the major academic buildings encircle the courtyard like a small town. Instead of being surrounded by silent, sleeping, potentially dead students at online school, hands fly up around the room. These students are like me.

I'm like *them*.

I catch myself smiling as I take notes. I really have left behind online school, where class discussions barely existed. And Twenty-Eighth Avenue Middle School before that, where I had so little confidence that I didn't make a single friend until Delilah at camp.

"'Doting on his own obsequious bondage,'" Mr. Stern announces, a hand raised toward the ceiling, "'wears out his time, much like his master's ass.' What does Iago mean?"

Easy. *Othello* is one of my favorites. The perfect play about betrayal. I raise my hand.

A voice comes behind my shoulder. "If you value obeisance too much, you'll reach the end of your life with nothing to show but service. This, of course, plays out for Rodrigo later. Though, ironically, it's Iago who he ends up being of service to and dies."

The explanation was so eloquent that it must've been read from a textbook. I glance back to see the boy who stood by Jasper at the start of class—exceptionally put together, not a wrinkle on his dress shirt. He's Black, on the lanky side, and has a drop fade with dark curls on top. On top of his overfilled organizational binder is a copy of *Othello*, sparkly bookmark with a horse on it sticking out. *Robby Walker* is written on the corner.

"Excellent, Mr. W," Mr. Stern says, tossing him a lollipop over my head.

This is the intelligence I'm up against.

A crackling noise comes from my left. Jasper, tearing paper out of a leather journal. He holds a note my way. In the front row. Right before Mr. Stern.

Does he have a single brain cell?

I focus on taking my notes, but Jasper coughs. Again. *Again*. Now that he's set his journal on the desk, I can make out the cover clasped by an ocean-blue crystal, and a bright red strip of fabric slides down the inner spine. Like on his cross-body bag, *JFG* is embossed on the cover. The typeface is the same too—an elegant serif font with the three letters overlapping. His initials? Does he imprint them on everything like a designer logo?

Jasper holds the note out my way again. His lopsided dimple pops.

Maybe it's important.

I irritably snatch the folded note and peel back the corners. The paper is freakishly white due to the likely million-dollar price, but between smeared red ink and his scribbly penmanship, it's barely legible. Just like his writing from camp.

Mr. Stern is the most inspiring sunrise of knowledge, is he not?

All that effort. For this.

I crumple the paper and shove it into my backpack. I'm an Excellence Scholar. He dares to distract me?

Jasper frowns. At least this makes him back off. He spends the rest of class with his feet still kicked up, twirling his fountain pen—which looks even pricier than his gold-plated journal. He observes the encircling academic buildings out the window, lost in his own world.

I remember that look. The way his blue eyes would soften when he'd gaze at the lake bordering campus, silently pondering a poem by my side. Compared to the way he'd run his mouth during workshops, this look felt like a truer part of him that he showed no one else, like I was special. It forced me to stop denying my racing heart any longer.

The only problem is, he shouldn't be lost in his own world during *class*.

At least I know he won't be top five competition.

More questions come and go over the hour. Hands shoot up to answer Mr. Stern, and I'm consistently a second too late. The competition is fiercer than the Olympics.

"Yes! Mr.—" Mr. Stern bends sideways to check his class roster on the desk. "H. V? H."

The question melts out of my brain. *I gave her such a one; 'twas my first gift.* "Right! Uh—Othello. The gift is a handkerchief.

Desdemona's. Othello is attached because it's the first gift he gave her. But he later cares for its familial value."

"Correct!" Mr. Stern hurls a lollipop at my face.

I catch it with a grin.

The bell rings, and Mr. Stern recites a farewell speech. I snatch my *Othello* copy off the desk and toss my backpack over my shoulder, accidentally kicking Mr. Stern's globe—which Jasper left on the floor—but still feeling on top of the world it so humbly depicts. I head out of the classroom.

Until Jasper shouts after me like he's drowning in the courtyard fountain.

I spin around and clench my book so hard that my nails dig into the cover. "WHAT?"

Jasper stutters to a stop, classmates dodging him in the doorway. He's sucking on his winning lollipop now, and the stick tilts as his face crinkles with offense. Only then do I realize how sharp I was toward someone who is supposed to be a stranger.

"Sorry," I say quickly. "Did you need something?"

He pulls the lollipop out of his mouth, casually spinning it in the air. "Shall we go spend our intimate time together?"

A startled noise chokes out of me.

More stares for the millionth time that day. Spotlight number four.

Jasper doesn't stop rambling about us *getting to know each other intimately* until I smother his mouth with my hand, and so abruptly that he drops the lollipop. "You can't keep shouting stuff like this," I snap. I don't even care how close our faces are as long as he shuts up.

"Why?"

"People will misunderstand."

He plucks my hand off like a used moist towelette. "I only meant having lunch."

The idea to shout that I can barely spend three more seconds with him compels me, but my logic remembers the stakes. Keep my roommate—the principal's nephew—on my good side in case he realizes anything he absolutely cannot. "I'm a bit busy." I continue down the hallway.

He follows. "Too busy for Dix?"

"What'd you just say to me?"

"Dixon. The dining hall." Jasper makes a face like *I'm* weird. "It's by the Halo."

Right. The courtyard is the Halo. Dix is the dining hall. I filter through my memory bank, trying to recall if I've embarrassingly referenced either incorrectly to other students yet.

We reach the exit of the academic center, and he rushes to open the door for me. I skipped breakfast, knowing I would sit alone in the dining hall like a loser, and didn't feel hungry all morning. Now that's rapidly fading.

Still, better to be hungry than sit with my new roommate who ruined my life once and could do the same again. "Sorry," I say, walking down the steps, "I need to study whenever I have free time, being the second-year Excellence Scholar."

Jasper's mouth twists as he reaches the base step. The sun brightens his blond hair a shade and forces his sensitive blue eyes to squint. "Shame. I'm still so excited for us to learn more about each other, roommate. Rain check?"

I try and fail to hide my wince. "Maybe."

"Wonderful! Until then."

With that, Jasper wanders deeper into the Halo.

I want to feel like I won, but my stress only builds. When I return to my room tonight, we'll be forced to spend that *intimate time* together. He'll keep pestering me with those icebreakers from yesterday, demanding to know my favorite color and hobbies and siblings that don't exist. I barely kept my identity hidden last night. How can I survive that again?

Glancing back at Jasper, I see that two plaid figures have already replaced me at his side. Sleeves rolled, slacks cuffed, charming faces that read *rich parents* and confident auras that signal *popular*. Maybe Jasper falls into the same bracket.

Another comes, shyly rubbing the back of his neck. He's only as tall as Jasper's shoulders, and his ripped, knockoff-brand backpack matches mine. Maybe a first year. Jasper gives him attention, throwing my deductions off.

If I'd gone with Jasper, I could've gotten to know all these people.

Regret pulls through me, but I shake it away.

Too risky. No friends.

◆ ▶

While I'm searching the campus for a food source on my own, Laney's Bean Shack catches my eye first. The outdoor coffee stall advertises the infamous chocolate-caramel "Jesus" lattes for double-digit prices, as if I can afford them. Nearby is a building with a gift shop sign, where a vending machine sticks out by the entrance.

Pulling my embarrassingly thin wallet out of my pocket, I survey the options behind the glass. Dining hall food is covered by the Excellence Scholarship, so this move is impressively devoid of intellect. But how can I go in when Jasper is there too?

Gradually, my attention is pulled toward the gift shop door, left open, and the burst of bright red beyond. Valentine-crested backpacks priced in the hundreds. VALENTINE DAD mugs. Academy slogan sweatshirts bragging about how old the campus is with EST. 1899 written in bold lettering. Behind the cash register, the classmate who sits in front of me during calculus wears an anthropomorphic, heart-shaped sandwich board sign. A costume.

So, some students do sacrifice their self-worth to afford lattes. Even during lunch hours.

I focus back on the vending machine, where chip bags are so faded from the sun that they look older than Mom. My void of a stomach forces me to select one.

"Are you serious?!"

Four guys surround a nearby sign under an awning. One is groaning, and he's wearing his blazer sleeves rolled to his elbows, reminding me to fix my drooped one. "Why do ranks carry over from last year?"

"The rankings barely changed," another responds.

"I wish it was the mixer already. I need a dopamine hit."

As they drift away, I take their place at the sign titled WEEKLY GRADE RANKS. It's divided into four columns, one for each class year. Under SECOND YEAR, full names are paired with numerical grade averages ranked from one to forty-six.

All our grades. Publicly shown.

Unspoken Guideline 3: Students perform the best in the nation because they fear humiliation in a public forum.

My insides twist. I must be ranked first. Second. My gaze zaps to the top of the second-year list. The first five names are marked with heart stickers.

Jasper Grimes (100/100)

That's not my name.

I slap my palm against the sign and lean closer, squinting hard. Jasper is first. Yet he didn't pay attention during classes. To receive a perfect hundred, he could never get a point off. Not even on a subjective essay. Clearly, I underestimated him.

Deep breaths. My name must be close.

> Robert Walker (99.89/100)
> Bingo A. Dixon (99.13/100)
> Frankie Schultz (99.05/100)
> Andrew Parker (98.98/100)

"WHERE AM I?" I shriek at the sign.

A few heads turn my way.

Straightening and stepping away, I clear my throat. In my online classes, grades were weighted out of 4.0. Advanced classes could bump us higher. But at Valentine, where everyone gets all As, they must have to readjust us out of a hundred for there to even be a competition. Here, it comes down to the tenths. I look closer at the board. No, the hundredths.

If they didn't readjust the ranking system I bet I'd be flying past a hundred. Past *Jasper*.

I scan the list until I hit the bottom.

No Charlie von Hevringprinz. There's only one explanation. My name isn't here yet because my online grades never carried over. Relief crashes through me like a tidal wave, nearly making my legs collapse beneath my weight.

Next week, I'll make the top five. I have to, or else I'll say goodbye to my scholarship next term. Even though I could barely raise my hand in class today before someone else was already answering. Even though the competition is fiercer than I ever expected.

The relief twists into nausea. I grip my stomach to try to make it go away, to pretend like everything isn't going wrong for one second.

"Mr. V! Mr. V!"

I spin around, clutching my copy of *Othello* to my chest.

A mash of floral prints and tight pants that could only belong to Mr. Stern rushes toward me, his briefcase jostling against his leg. "You exited my classroom in a dash."

I swallow away the burning in my throat. "I didn't mean to."

"It's fine. Just didn't expect you of all people to want to leave my lesson so fast."

"No, I was fascinated. Especially when you went deeper into iambic, trochaic, spondaic, anapestic, dactylic, and all the stress patterns in comparison to Shakespeare's meter and length. Anapestic tetrameter has my whole heart—" I'm talking too fast. Embarrassment hits me so hard that I cover my face with *Othello*. "Sorry."

Mr. Stern lowers the book. "I was a faculty member who reviewed your Excellence Scholar application. Your personal statement was the best one I've read since I was hired."

"Really?"

"Yes, I'm eager to read your *Othello* essay due next week."

I smile back. Maybe I can reach close to Jasper's Rank One. His perfect hundred may be impossible, but Rank Two must be on the table.

Mr. Stern holds out a red note stamped with the Valentine

crest. "Anyway, I chased after you because Principal Grimes called to ask you to her office. Here's an excused pass for your next afternoon class."

My blood runs cold. "Did she say why?"

"Just that it's confidential. And time-sensitive."

Confidential. Time-sensitive.

That's it, then. Jasper realized who I am. He told his aunt the truth.

I'm already being kicked out.

Chapter 6
THE WOMAN IN WHITE
WEDNESDAY, SEPTEMBER 4

The office is deserted during lunch, but it is packed with gnomes. *Stuffed* gnomes, which invade the lobby tables and wall shelves. Heart-patterned pointy hats hide their faces except for their blobby noses and gray-yarn beards. Each has a name stitched on the stomach. DeMario, Kennedy, Ignacio...

I approach the counter cluttered with university prep pamphlets, trading careful looks between the gnomes and the vintage gramophone in the corner. "Für Elise" plays from its aluminum horn. The peaceful melody is a cruel counterpoint to my heartbeat. "Excuse me?"

"Just a moment!" a high-pitched voice calls from the back room.

I fold my hands on the counter to stop them from shaking. Maybe Principal Grimes doesn't need to kick me out. Maybe she'll convince me to leave on my own. She'll explain how hard everyday life will be, that I should've never expected my residential retainer to get back to me about my single, and that I'm a total failure. She'll tell me that Mom did just fine as an Excellence Scholar and I'm the family disappointment.

A white woman in a rolling chair finally slides into view. The heart-patterned bow holding together her curly ponytail looks bigger than her head and makes her seem as young as a first year, even though she must be in her twenties. "What can I help with?"

A loaded question.

I straighten my shoulders. "I'm here to see the principal. But I also want to inquire about switching to a single room?"

"I'll warn you now, they hardly indulge these requests unless it's serious, love."

"It is serious."

She rolls toward the counter, better revealing her sweatshirt with VALENTINE NAM AMOR TRADITIONALIS EDUCATIONIS on the chest, and boots up the ancient desktop computer. Her manicured nails—also heart-decorated—clack along the keyboard, punctuating the air out of sync with the piano music. As I wait, I read more gnome name tags. Colton, Leandro, Becca, William...

"You watch *Gnome in Love*?" The woman's pupils practically sparkle.

"Huh?"

"You seem interested in my collection."

"They're yours?"

"They're from a reality dating show I adore. The contestants fall in love dressed as gnomes. I collect their stuffed toy line." She sighs sadly enough for her hair bow to droop. "I assumed you knew. For an academy of love, the students don't care much about romance."

Unspoken Guideline 4: Valentine attracts people obsessed with love. Because of the heart branding? The cupid statues in the fountain?

Or in the middle of these woods, maybe she feels as alone as I do.

"I'm in the system, love," she says. "What's the serious roommate sitch?"

"I paid extra for a single on the housing application," I say. "But my residential retainer said there was a mix-up."

"We've never had that kind of mix-up. You're sure?" More scrolling and clicking. "I don't see any fees paid in your file. The academy must've randomly assigned you to a place."

"I gave my mom the check," I blurt, my brow spiking. "She sent it in the mail." Although I never technically checked if the money left my account. Too many other venturing-off-to-boarding-academy purchases were happening at the same time.

"I apologize, love," the woman says. "Apply once you're a third year? All singles are occupied until the end of the academic year."

End of the year rattles me to my core.

If I manage to stay here, no way can I be trapped with Jasper that long. I promised Mom that I would keep my head low no matter what, but these last two days have been fighting to break that.

"Is Charlie here, Ms. Lyney?" a voice calls from farther down a hallway. It belongs to a woman with the same wispy blond hair and delicate features as Jasper. Her pantsuit is white on white, since someone like her can afford the torturous upkeep, and the badge of her heart-themed lanyard reads PRINCIPAL NATHALIE GRIMES.

"Yes," Ms. Lyney says, eyeing me expectantly.

Trying to stay calm feels impossible, but I force myself to walk steadily through the hall lined with portraits of old, esteemed members of Valentine society, and follow Principal Grimes into an office marked with a PRINCIPAL plaque. As she claims a seat at her glossy executive desk, I take one of the two leather love seats facing her. The towers of manila folders on her desk block her head from view completely.

Muttering under her breath, Principal Grimes shoves the

towers to a corner of the desk, barely avoiding a Jenga-style collision on the floor. Then she smiles, folding her hands like she's praying. Maybe a signal that I should be. "Welcome, Charlie."

I stare at the paperwork. "Hello."

"On behalf of the board of trustees, we're overjoyed to welcome you to Valentine Academy for Boys as our new second-year Excellence Scholar. And, selfishly, I'm thrilled to meet my nephew's roommate!"

The sole mention of him reels dread through me. But if she's thrilled, does this mean Jasper didn't spill my secret?

"I'm so glad he's decided to stay in the residential hall with you like a normal student this year," Principal Grimes goes on. She doesn't have the same dimples as Jasper, but she does have too much light in her eyes, even with that workload on her desk making stress seep out of her. "That boy needs down-to-earth time."

"Actually—" I stop. Principal Grimes, the one person I need on my side, *wants* Jasper and me to be roommates?

"Right...," I say. For now.

"We heard your mother was also a Scholar." Principal Grimes motions toward a framed painting of the Valentine crest behind her. "We cherish these moments that highlight our passion for tradition. Did your mother tell you how we have the largest secondary-education library collection in the nation? Or about our student-beloved mixer each November? Although I want to make it clear, you were not chosen because of legacy. Your accomplishments are your own."

First the familiar electric hum to her tone. Now the persistent topic changing. This must be Jasper in disguise. "Thank you."

"Anyhoo, sorry for pulling you out of class, but this is a bit time-sensitive."

"Okay," I say, folding my hands so tightly that my knuckles burn.

"Have you heard of the Student Tutoring Remediation Interdisciplinary Program run by a few of your classmates?"

"I don't think so."

"Although other students volunteer as tutors, I've noticed a lack of improvement in those who use this service lately. Would you assist our members?"

She's asking for a favor.

Relief floods through me. My secret is still a secret. Jasper didn't sell me out. He doesn't know who I am.

"The previous Scholar for your class used to help many of our students, but he"—Principal Grimes hesitates—"left halfway through last year. That's what we believe changed."

From that hesitation, he didn't simply leave. Maybe too much pressure *was* the reason.

My relief twists into something less so. "Thank you, but I should focus on study—"

"This would reflect wonderfully on your college applications." She hits me with another too-bright smile. "This program is another long-standing tradition, and that's important to the board of trustees, you see. I'm admittedly in a tough spot the longer this continues."

The board of trustees again. Some omnipotent power who must have puppet strings on Principal Grimes. Maybe they lay the groundwork for the guidelines. I can't say no to them.

My heart sinks, the words dying in my throat.

"I get it," I say slowly, twisting Mom's varsity ring on my finger.

"Excellent! Please speak with the members after class." Principal Grimes whips out a notepad and scribbles something down before handing me it.

Student Tutoring Remediation Interdisciplinary Program
Scholar Research Library 3 p.m.–5 p.m.

Chapter 7
PERSUASION
WEDNESDAY, SEPTEMBER 4

When I pull back the library door, the hinges shriek louder than Delilah when she'd chuck her shoes at bugs during camp. Yet no students glance up from their textbooks. After a long day of classes, they remain absorbed at desks that stretch back to the stacks. A few play on marble chessboards at the center of each, but most have books loaded so high that they touch the green-shaded antique lamps curved over them.

My footsteps echo as I walk through the middle aisle, keeping an eye out for a sign or group marked with TUTORING. The farther I venture, the more a familiar scent of ink and paper chemical breakdowns floods my nose, transporting me back to Queens. Mom always said her used books section made her store smell sweet, like acidic vanilla.

Two students rush past and through a high arch leading into the stacks, so quickly their backpacks jostle against their backs.

"—we won't get any help," I barely hear one hiss to the other.

Tutoring help? Back in the stacks?

I follow them through the arch, only to go still from awe. No matter how far back I tip my head, the bookcases rise. A forest of stories lives back here.

The two students round the corner. I catch up, dodging rolling ladders and step stools until I reach a section marked TRAVEL & TOURISM.

A figure stands at the end. Blond hair pulled into a short, messy ponytail. Red-and-black-plaid blazer slung over a shoulder. Crossbody bag with a sparkling JFG emblem. Jasper, trailing a finger along a spine of books.

I freeze. What is he doing here?

Murmurs come from the next aisle. The last thing I need is Jasper noticing me while I'm in the middle of a chase. Tiptoeing past him, I pass by CRUISE LINES, TRAVEL AGENTS, ECOTOURISM, and HOSPITALITY INDUSTRY, before I realize the two students have stopped. One reaches toward the right side of a shelf and tugs on a green spine.

The bookcase swings inward. The two slip through, and it shuts again.

I'm hallucinating. Clearly. Or there's a secret door. In the library.

I inspect the green spine. A thin booklet of *Cupid and Psyche* by Lucius Apuleius Madaurensis. In the travel section?

I tug the spine. Slowly, the bookcase reveals a small, office-sized room split by a maroon brocade curtain. The right is too dark to make out much, but the left is lit by antique library lamps set on shelves and sandwiched between mythologies and books of fairy tales. A runner rug directs a single-file line of red-and-black bodies toward the back, where three guys stand behind books stacked like makeshift tables. A handwritten sign stretches above.

Welcome to the Student Tutoring Remediation Interdisciplinary Program!

The tutoring program *is* back here.

As I wiggle my way around the line, the vanilla-like tang in the air grows muskier, more like dirt and mothballs, and I scrunch my nose. Eventually, I reach the three guys seemingly in charge, who must be tutors. I recognize two of them.

Xavier Nguyen, who saved my life in PE, writing names in a notebook. Seeing his muscles stuffed into the typical plaid-on-plaid uniform instead of a tracksuit is jarring. An enamel pin of the number three is fastened above the Valentine crest on his lapel, the gold material carved with flower petals, flaunting its price tag.

Robby Walker, aka Rank Two on the second-year grades, stands on his right. Another enamel pin is on his blazer: the number two. He shuffles cards with sparkles on one side and illustrated drawings on the other, but his rapid hand movements shield details. Trading cards? On his makeshift table, a horse-riding helmet is flipped upside down, full of more cards.

Not average tutor behavior.

Still, my nerves settle. I know them. I know *someone* here. "Hi—"

"Cutting is for the weak," a third tutor beside Xavier interrupts. His low voice sounds forced to the back of his throat, yet it's still higher in pitch than all the other competing conversations. His dress shoes, marked with spikelike symbols, are kicked up on his book stack. Between his narrow shoulders and shortness—he's no taller than five feet—he looks younger than a first year.

I tilt my head. Most of his face is shrouded by bangs that crinkle like seaweed and look too black to be natural. The guidelines don't allow dyed hair. "Excuse me?"

"You hearkened me." The boy looks up, his bangs splitting and revealing such a pale complexion that his hair looks even darker now. He flashes a ring on his thumb—a ruby varsity gemstone that matches Mom's varsity ring on my finger. "Or shall I eradicate you myself?"

I glance around, expecting everyone to acknowledge the middle schooler who has broken into Valentine to threaten me.

Only Xavier stops writing in his notebook. "Oh, Charlie."

My chest leaps. He remembered my name.

Except no one is supposed to remember who I am. No spotlights. I push down my excitement. "Yeah. Hi."

A slamming noise strikes behind us. I startle and look over my shoulder.

Fairy-tale books tumble off a shelf where Jasper's shoulder is pressed now, like he rammed into the thing at full force. His breathing is heavy. "Is someone named Charlie here?"

I stare at him in horror. Does he have the hearing of a hawk?

"Who's holding up the line?" someone complains.

Bobby signals those impatiently waiting to shift farther down, moving them away from our conversation. Once the crowds split enough for Jasper to spot me, he rushes to the front on a blast of his sneeze-inducing floral fragrance, shampoo, and soap—*all* of it.

"I see you couldn't resist spending intimate time with me today, roomie," Jasper says through a grin. He wears an enamel pin too—a gold number one fastened to his red dress shirt, weighing down the neckline and exposing his collarbone more than usual.

"Why are *you* here?" I ask, keeping my eyes firmly on his face.

"STRIP."

I clutch my blazer. "Excuse me?"

"Student Tutoring Remediation Interdisciplinary Program," Xavier says, who's returned to jotting names and numbers in his notebook. "STRIP for short."

There's no way Jasper, Rank One, needs tutoring. Logically, there's only one reason why he's here.

I struggle to stop my expression from contorting. "You're a tutor."

"Welcome to the most helpful program on campus," Jasper says.

"Here to assist with all your"—he tosses up air quotes—"'tutoring needs.'"

"Do those numbers mark you as tutors?" I ask, gesturing at the pin on Jasper's collar.

He glances down. "No, these are our top five passes."

"Your what?"

"Didn't you check the weekly grade announcements today? Did you see an instructor sitting around with a basket?"

"No?"

"They hand these out at noon every time on both campuses. Well, to any student who ranks top five of their class. As long as we keep our rank, we get special access to the equestrian center that's half on their campus and half on ours, Friday through Sunday."

Another part of Valentine I never knew existed. "An equestrian center is our perk? Who cares about horses?"

"Who cares about horses?" Robby repeats farther down the line. His eyes are wide with shock. Almost offense.

I bite the inside of my cheek for failing to blend in once again. Must be a weird rich-people thing. "Right. Sorry."

"It's not only about the horses," Jasper says. "Whenever the top five visit the equestrian center, they also get to see the top five *girls*."

Of course. "The academy allows that as a perk?"

"Well, that perk, in particular, isn't written on paper. It's more like a glitch in the system. Faculty claims the whole arrangement is to encourage friendly competition. They'll do anything to make sure we stay the best private academy in the nation."

That's almost more screwed up than having a public grade board. Delilah and Mom never mentioned this. "Is everyone who ranks in this thing?"

"Some ranks change too often. Rank Fours and Fives, really. But most refuse to get involved."

Most refuse. Yet I'm supposed to join this. "Why?"

Jasper twirls a finger in the air, his bracelet jangling so obnoxiously that I debate ripping it off. "Because we are not here to tutor, von Hevringprinz. We—"

"*Jasper*," Xavier mutters warily from his table, then faces me again. "Sorry, man, but we shouldn't share too much since you're, well, new."

A piece of my heart cracks. Still a transfer. An outsider.

"We can trust Charlie about us being non-tutors," Jasper insists, walking over and swatting Xavier's shoulder. "He's an Excellence Scholar."

"Yeah," I say, admittedly appreciating Jasper sticking up for me. If everyone else knows, then I need to, especially since Principal Grimes expects me to fix this. "You're...non-tutors?"

"French for not a tutor," Jasper answers. "Apologies, this may be confusing for you since you don't speak the world's most romantic language like moi. Really, we deliver love letters."

"*Love* letters?"

"Oui. Although some simply use the service to keep in touch with their girlfriends beyond the wall, I offer a much more popular, secondary option of writing love letters on their behalf. I am a renowned poet, after all. Then the other members bravely deliver them to the sister academy each week and pick up whatever the sister academy wishes to send back. Blaze delivers, mostly. Robby and Xavier step in, too, to avoid suspicion."

My shock quickly turns to anger.

Somehow, writing to three other girls behind my back at camp wasn't enough to knock Jasper's love letter obsession out of his system.

"Why waste time on pointless love letters?" I say too sharply. I can't help it. Now my principal-assigned job is impossible. These guys don't tutor at *all*.

Jasper's mouth hangs open. "Pointless? How else will these heartbroken souls stay in touch with their crushes and lovers across the cockblockade that divides our academies?"

People really do refer to that wall as a cockblockade. "They won't?"

"Exactly! Saint Valentine would weep over so many young lovers being ripped apart." He passionately clasps his hands together and looks to the ceiling. "Isn't that right?"

Saint Valentine doesn't respond. Neither do I.

Xavier does. "We operate under the tutoring program so that the academy doesn't suspect us of breaking their biggest guideline—no talking to the sister academy. That's why we only allow top fives to join." He points at his number-three pin. He wasn't top three of the second-year class, so he must be an upperclassman. "We aren't seen as rulebreakers. Plus, we're the only ones who can access the equestrian center that connects to both academies. Our way in to trade letters with a few other top fives who have their own long-established system."

I glance around at the shelves, then the door. Maybe only the brightest of Valentine could pull this off. "How has this stayed a secret?"

"Before Jasper? No clue. It's been tradition for years." Xavier points at Jasper. "Nowadays, we rely on the principal's nephew's powers."

Beside me, Jasper beams.

Unspoken Guideline 5: Principal's nephew's powers beat the guidelines.

"According to legend, when the academy was established in 1899, the administration set up the Student Teaching Remediation Interdisciplinary Program as a real tutoring program," Jasper explains further. "Only a few months later did our brave forefathers start to set up a communication method with the sister campus instead. Allegedly, the librarians forgot this janitor closet existed, so it was usurped to keep their meetings about their letter deliveries a secret. We so valiantly carry on their mission—and continue to improve and grow."

My mind sparks. I already wished that Delilah had forewarned me of several dreadful surprises since showing up here, but this might be the biggest one. Students on both campuses have seriously risked expulsion for being involved in this for a hundred years. All in the name of tradition.

Maybe I'll never be able to understand the others at this academy. I pull out Principal Grimes's note from my slacks. "Well, the principal asked me to join since no one's grades are improving. They're getting suspicious."

The four non-tutors stare at the letter with fiery intensity.

Jasper sways so much that he stabilizes himself against a shelf. The waves of hair escaped from his stubby ponytail cast across his face. "My aunt? It's over for us?"

"Nay," says the short seaweed-bang boy from earlier—Blaze, apparently—who I now notice has tied his blazer sleeves around his neck, the rest fluttering behind him like a childish dress-up cape. *Is* he a student here? If he is, he must be a first year. "We won't be defeated. I propose we outsource a face to keep the enemy off our trail. A courageous warrior who tutors at the study

AND THEY WERE ROOMMATES

desks daily, in full view of the librarians, while we operate back here."

"You came up with that quickly," I say, impressed.

"We've already needed a new one for a while," Xavier says, rising from his seat behind his book stack and tossing his pen on his notebook. "Sometimes first years come for real tutoring and threaten to complain to instructors, so we'd sic them on the previous Excellence Scholar you replaced. Jasper filled his shoes for a while but was..." His face scrunches.

"He told people they had brain damage," Robby finishes from down the waiting line.

Jasper frowns. "They waste my time. I'm busy back here."

"And we've been turned down by everyone we asked since," Xavier adds.

I'm still stuck on *the previous Excellence Scholar you replaced*. I want to inquire more, but Blaze points his varsity ring at me so aggressively that I flinch.

"This eight-legs can be our face," Blaze announces, pointing directly at me.

I glance at my legs. Only two. "Me?"

Jasper snaps off the shelf he's been slumped over. Next thing I know, he's slinging an arm over my shoulder and bumping our hips, his fragrance blasting my nostrils all over again. "Charlie even started a tutoring nonprofit in Queens. A fantastic idea!"

A piece of me longs to keep learning about this secret piece of Valentine, even though Jasper is among the crowd welcoming me into it.

But I also made promises to myself. Don't make friends. Study. I have enough reasons to be kicked out.

"I don't want to break the guidelines," I say, and keep it at that.

"You won't," Jasper says, palm to his heart. "If we get caught, say you never knew our true operations."

"How can you promise that?"

"Would I lie to you?"

Well, he has before.

I grip my forehead, as too much keeps getting thrown my way at once. Even with Excellence Scholar to my name, I can barely tell the difference between the truths of this program and Jasper's regularly flawed opinions. There's no way I can join.

Except. Jasper's principal's nephew powers might be enough to get me what no one else can.

Standing before him, I square my shoulders to look more like his. It's a risky idea. He's the one person I should avoid. Every second we spend together helps him remember who I am. But I nudge my head toward a corner of the room where no one can overhear, then walk in that direction. He gets the hint and follows.

"I'll consider being your face," I say. "If you do something for me."

Jasper leans forward curiously. "Yes?"

Just one word, but he speaks with such a balanced blend of confidence and judgment that it holds as much weight as a speech. I struggle to not let it get to me. "Convince your aunt to move you into a single room so I get the double to myself."

Jasper's expression flickers with shock, like he had a list of possible answers I'd provide, and this didn't match any. A weak, almost hurt chuckle trickles from his lips. "You dislike me that much, von Hevringprinz?"

"Ah, no," I lie, feeling a twinge of guilt myself. "I requested one before I even knew we'd be roommates. You said you never complained to your aunt, right? Doesn't that mean you have the power to?"

Jasper nods slowly.

"Is that a yes?" I ask.

"I want more from you. Help me write letters until the winter mixer in November."

"What?" I say. "How is that fair?"

Jasper shrugs. Because he holds the power, and he knows it. "More students in every grade keep finding out my poetry is award-winning, so the demand for me to write letters on their behalf keeps rising. On top of that, I write all the confessional love letters for anyone who wants to ask their sister-academy crush to the mixer. I could use another hand. Although we should keep your involvement from the other members a secret. Especially from our visitors. They come here for my brand, you see. Not yours." He places a hand to his chest. "After, I'll ask my aunt."

"No way," I say. "Ask now."

"If I ask today, what forces you to hold up your end?"

November is better than an academic year. Still, my heartbeat thrums in my neck. The idea of me, who hasn't dated anyone since my lips touched Jasper's, writing love letters is laughable on its own. But helping Jasper write what he once used to break my heart?

"I won't be good at it," I mumble, even though Valentine would expect me to excel at anything this campus presents me, including poetry. Insecurity burns in my chest for admitting this, but it's the truth.

"Of course you won't be as good as me," Jasper says, tossing a hand. "There will always be someone better at fine literature than you. *Such is the circle of artiste life.*"

I stare back, stunned by how big his head truly is.

How did I ever consider striking a deal with him?

"Forget it," I say through a huff. "Figure out a new face on your own."

Jasper's brow lifts in surprise, but I'm already heading for the door, leaving him and this deal behind.

Chapter 8
THE REMAINS OF THE DAY
WEDNESDAY, SEPTEMBER 4

At least, until I return to our room that night.

When I arrive after a solo study session in the Halo, Jasper is digging through his desk drawer, tossing aside dog-eared books and half-drank coffees from Laney's Bean Shack. He spins around in the dress shoes that he didn't bother taking off—animal. "You're back!"

I blink from the doorway. Everywhere smells like cinnamon and hints of smoke from his guideline-breaking fire-hazard candles. I sneeze. "You're making a mess."

"For good reason."

"And that is?"

"I'd like to convince you to assist me with my letters."

I rush to shut the door behind me before Maverick the Residential Retainer can overhear. If Jasper were anybody else but the principal's nephew, I'd throw the door at his face. "I already told you that I wouldn't do a good job."

"And I humbly offer a solution." Jasper picks up a pile of pens, pencils, and notebooks, then strides across our room, dodging the books strewn along his side. His ponytail is barely holding its shape after a full day, hanging loose around his cheeks. "For you to write with the quality STRIP promises, you need a love tutor. I will so graciously be yours."

My heart rate spikes so sharply, I swear, it rattles all my bones. "Love tutor?"

"Please, call me Tutor Jasper. Per your previous stated terms, I'll convince my aunt to find me another room."

I stare at the three moles below his thumb shaped like a constellation. The last hand in the universe I want to touch.

"Please choose the inscribing instrumentation that resonates with you most." Jasper shoves the pile of writing materials into my arms. I grunt. "One lesson with me. That is all I ask. Then you may decide if we make the brilliant team that I believe we would."

Two pens slip out of my grasp and hit the floor, where Jasper's books have spread to the door. I look to the ceiling posters of Jasper, then the cardboard version of him between our beds. "You really chose to bring your life-sized cutout? Out of everything?"

"It was a gift from *Poetic Fortune Digest*. What else was I supposed to pack?"

"Gee, I don't know." I kick one of his books. "You have stacks of a certain something all over your desk. And your floor. And my floor."

Jasper blinks. Potentially genuinely.

"A bookcase," I say through clenched teeth.

Jasper surveys the empty space between our beds. "Oh. I see, von Hevringprinz."

"You know you can just say my first name, right?"

"But your last name is beautiful."

Spit lodges in my throat. I cough it out. "It's long."

"Could be longer. Consider Oscar Wilde's real name."

I thought I was the only one who knew this. "Oscar Fingal O'Fflahertie Wills Wilde?"

Jasper's dimple pops. "Not as beautiful."

I grin back until I realize what I'm doing. A serial heartbreaker like him has called a hundred other people beautiful too. We could never make a *brilliant team*.

But a bedroom of my own. Logically, that may be worth sucking it up and writing love letters with the one boy who broke my heart—and who can't figure out who I am.

Jasper's face falls. "Something the matter?"

"N-no," I say quickly.

He squints back at me, like he's trying to find an answer in my body language or facial features instead. "You're quite evasive, you know that?"

"What do you mean?"

"Evasive. It means not straightforward. Avoidant. Hiding your thoughts."

"I know what it means," I snap, but my voice nearly warbles from the nerves shooting through me. One day in, and Jasper can already tell how desperately I'm trying to avoid him.

If I keep running from Jasper, that may only look more suspicious. Knowing him, he might try to dig deeper into my life than he already has.

"One lesson," I say, even though it's the last thing I want. "I'll try it. No promises."

Jasper's face lights up again. "Wonderful!"

I bend over to spread the writing materials along the rug. What did Jasper say? To find what resonated? Well, no resonation detected. I follow my head instead of my heart when I avoid the pens and pick the first mechanical pencil I spot—how is Jasper confident with permanent ink?—and a standard composition notebook. When I look back up, Jasper's arms are crossed.

"Write a poetic love letter and recite it," he says. "Within five minutes."

This is happening. I'm being told to recite a love letter to my long-dead crush. My stomach tightens. "Don't I get a prompt?"

"You need one?"

"It'd help?"

"I see." My desire to strangle him over how confused he sounds intensifies. "Imagine what typical adversities a couple would face when split by such an evil, towering, gated wall."

That's barely a prompt.

I go sit at my desk with my chosen pencil and notebook. I scribble down a first line, but the curtains rustling in the breeze are too distracting, and the scent of fall leaves mixing with the room's explosion of cinnamon and floral fragrance is too overbearing. My brain floods with camp memories of Jasper, raising his hand with more meaningful questions and gaining more praise from guest speakers than I ever did.

Jasper snatches my pencil. I reach for it, but he tucks it behind his ear. "Time's up."

I glare at his wrist, devoid of a watch, even though Valentine repeatedly told us to bring one. "How would you know?"

"It felt like five minutes."

"How are you surviving here?" I gesture to his empty wrist. "All we have is the bell tower. Neither of us even brought a clock for our room."

Jasper points toward the curtains. "I can tell based on where the sun or moon is in the sky. You can't?"

"No?"

He hums. Judgmentally. "Stand and read."

I look down at my paper again.

Roses are red, violets are blue
/

Pushing in my chair, I debate lighting one of Jasper's candles and setting the notebook on fire. Jasper is Rank One. He can't see me fail already.

Think, Charlie. "Roses—"

"Look at me. I want to feel the emotion."

I do, and the pressure skyrockets. Jasper's eyes are such a familiar piercing blue, gazing back the same as when we'd write by the lake and he'd ask me to recite what I'd written for workshop. He always wanted to hear mine.

"You can trust me with your emotions," Jasper says. "We're roommates."

Strangely, my first instinct is to believe him. Although Jasper has been as obnoxious as predicted since I got here, he's also been oddly kind to me, constantly asking to be my dining hall buddy and trying to learn more about me so we can bond. Maybe it wouldn't be the end of the world if he remembered.

"Jasper?" I say.

He watches me just as brightly as he did two years ago. It's enough for my senses to come roaring back. Jasper showed me the same *kindness* then. The only difference is that I was still naive enough to believe it.

What am I thinking?

"Never mind." I take a breath. "Roses are red. Violets are blue. I…" I rack my mind for something. Anything. "If only… this wall… weren't between us, our love could… grew. Grow. Wait. Roses are red—"

Jasper yanks away the notebook. "You will attend love lessons with me daily."

I must've heard wrong. "But I have to study!"

"This is a race against the clock, von Hevringprinz. On top of our usual demands, the winter mixer is nearly here. Our busiest event of the year."

Delilah claimed the mixer is the only time Valentine students are allowed to have fun. I never believed her, though, since the word *mixer* only evokes a sense of cringe within me. What would she advise me to do if she knew I was being asked to break the rules? Would she encourage me to screw the Valentine system with a tossed middle finger in typical Delilah fashion or to keep my head down like Mom?

All I want to do is hunt down my phone locked in the depths of campus and message her updates like I did throughout school last year, even though she couldn't read any until her own phone was released at the start of winter break. Now that I'm enduring this phone-less life, I get why she nonstop messaged me all day and night—which I admittedly slept through—until she returned to campus. Maybe I should've tried harder to stay up.

"Is the mixer that huge of a deal?" I ask Jasper, since he's all I have instead.

"It's everything. A tradition as ancient as STRIP itself. A celebration of every Valentine couple, new and old. We'll serve hundreds of lovesick souls."

I still don't understand. STRIP can't be worth all the risk that comes with it just for the sake of tradition, and it causes my biggest anxiety spike of the night.

It must be obvious because Jasper closes the distance between us to clap my shoulder. I instinctively lower my face. "I need one week to prepare a lesson plan," he says. "You'll start as our face in the library then. We'll hold your lessons after. Agreed?"

Will I have the time? Create a strict study regimen, wake up early, and stay up all night to please a poet who only respects himself? Besides, spending more time with Jasper outside our trapped room would only give him more chances to look at me closer.

But it would give *me* a chance to keep an eye on *him*. Stop him from investigating into who I am on his own. Give me a small bit of control.

And the room. I *need* this room to myself.

"Fine, Jasper."

"Tutor Jasper." He grins.

I clench my jaw. "Tutor Jasper."

Chapter 9
THE TROUBLE WITH BEING BORN
TUESDAY, SEPTEMBER 10

Ms. Nallos blows her whistle from the bench she's leisurely sitting on during PE class. "Great laps! Head to the showers!"

I lean over myself on the track, gripping my thighs as sweat drips down my forehead. An impromptu twelve-minute run on the hottest, most sweltering day of the year so far, according to the locker room thermostat. A real-life curse after my weekend of sleepless nights glued to textbooks to make sure I rank tomorrow. One world history group project. Two forty-question-long calculus assignments. Two free-response papers. It all has to be perfect.

But we had to reach at least ten measly laps today. I got six.

Will my PE grade drop?

Laughter booms down the track. Xavier, lucky spoon between his fingers, high-fiving two others. Since they kept whizzing past me, I recognize the back of their stubby buzz-cut heads. They must've gotten quadruple my laps.

I barely summon enough strength to walk to the locker room. A sea of drugstore colognes attacks me, and fluorescent lights cast a grim glow, because the concept of a boys' locker room wasn't terrifying enough. I approach the lockers to search the bottom row for VON HEVRINGPRINZ, stepping over two used towels, a mound of plaid clothes, a bruised banana, and a few sparkly trading cards that look like Robby's from the library. One is overturned, showing off artwork of an illustrated spotted horse.

Boys' locker rooms are stranger than I thought.

Splashes echo from around the corner. Showers, probably, and ones I've never used. Last week's PE classes left me tired, but not too sweaty. Today, though, I'll spend the next seven class hours drenched if I don't rinse off. Grabbing the towel that I've left untouched all week, then my uniform, I follow the splashes.

Then I freeze, my uniform slipping out of my hands.

Naked bodies. Facing shower heads. No privacy curtains divide them. Mirrors stretch along the walls, doubling them. They laugh with each other as if they're at a baseball game.

Not showers. One communal shower.

Another one of Xavier's buzz-cut friends reaches for a shampoo bottle, glancing my way. Presence detected. No towel covers him. Not even a washcloth. "You good?"

I try to form a sentence. A word. All I manage is a honk. I sprint past the lockers and into an empty bathroom stall. As I bundle my uniform and towel against the scars on my chest, my insides clump into knots. There's no time to shower in my room. Calc starts in eight minutes.

The stall door rattles.

"You done yet?" a voice calls.

"Just a second!" I say so unnaturally oddly, I sense the guy back off entirely.

I scramble to change. Even though I wipe my face with toilet paper and layer on six days' worth of deodorant, an obvious workout stench seeps from my oil-clogged pores. I bust out of the stall, keeping my head low, and walk onto the field.

Ms. Nallos passes by me on the sidewalk. Her even breathing

and perfectly symmetrical braids make me even more painfully aware of my uncontrollable panting and messy hair.

"Ms. Nallos?" I say.

She stops, eyeing my greasy body up and down. "Yes?"

"Can I verify how many laps you put me down for today?"

She checks her clipboard before looking back with a frown. "You were trying your best?"

Ouch.

It's not like my body *can't* conceivably handle the same number of laps as everyone else's. But while I was sitting at a desk all year during online school, they were apparently running like gerbils. "If your concern is that I didn't put in genuine effort, I promise, I did."

Ms. Nallos sighs. "Valentine's grading stance is strict about this. As long as you don't have a doctor's note from Health Services, it's about results."

Even if this is a private academy, this has to break some law. At least an ethical one.

Unspoken Guideline 6: Valentine can do whatever the hell they want.

I ask the dreaded question. "How much will this drop my grade?"

She rechecks the clipboard. "As of now, you're at a C."

Chapter 10
GREAT EXPECTATIONS
WEDNESDAY, SEPTEMBER 11

SECOND-YEAR LISTINGS

1. Jasper Grimes
2. Robert Walker
3. Bingo A. Dixon
4. Nicholas Burton
5. Reese Collins
6. Frankie Schultz
7. Gabriel Acosta
8. Frederick Brown Jr.
9. Andrew Parker
10. Alessandro Beasley
11. Uriah Clayton
12. Ishaan Kapoor
13. Joseph M. Briggs
14. Kamari Barrera
15. Cody Wilson
16. Liam Yun
17. Sebastian Mitchell
18. Gideon Mittelman
19. Edward Lobb Jr.
20. Alexander Davis
21. Luis Gabriel García Perez

22. Jackson W. Zang
23. Matthew St. Paul
24. Isaiah Lim
25. Kade Cervantes
26. Alexander Young
27. Zachariah Wilson
28. Samuel Baker
29. Jack Reid
30. Derek Gonzales
31. Michael Aguilar
32. Lucas Banas
33. Carson Giles
34. Zain Chang
35. Jacob Christensen
36. Eiji Nakahashi
37. Patrick Kennedy
38. Leonardo Evans
39. Emilio O'Hare
40. Andrew Huang
41. Thomas Shaw
42. Xuan Ma
43. Matthew Davidson
44. Griffin Li
45. Charlie von Hevringprinz
46. Aiden Alston

Chapter 11

BORROWED DREAMS
WEDNESDAY, SEPTEMBER 11

Less than an hour after the weekly grade announcements, Maverick the Residential Retainer informs me that Mom would like to have a word.

Over the backdrop of Mozart's "Rondo alla Turca" playing from the gramophone, Ms. Lyney hands me the phone over the counter. "Five minutes. Communication with family outside of emergencies is unfortunately supposed to be kept to a minimum, love."

I take the phone. "Hel—"

"You're second to last on the grade rankings?"

Arrow to the heart. "Hello, Mom."

"Hi, sweetie. How are you doing?" From her warbling voice, I can already picture her sitting behind the Bibliobibuli Bookstore register, tugging on a blouse she bought from Q Train Vintage two blocks from our apartment.

I clutch the phone harder to keep my emotions together. After coming in at forty-fifth place, I expected the sensation of failure to eat me alive during this call, but not only two seconds in. "I'm fine."

"The top five scholarship requirement is for each term. That's coming up soon. Are you still thinking you'll be able to handle this? You can always come home and visit on a weekend, you know. We can even reconsider this."

I wince. "I know. How did you hear about my grades already?"

"A notification was sent to my email."

Unspoken Guideline 7: Technology is only used to snitch on students to their parents.

"Are you having a hard time?" Mom says when I don't respond, only to pause when a yawn overtakes her. A con of never taking a day off from the bookstore. "Or are you just not adjusting to living alone?"

I'm not living alone.

I could never tell Mom. Her worry would soar through the roof. As long as I can avoid that, I'll hopefully make it out of this call alive. "That's not why. I said, I'm fine."

"All right. Oh, that reminds me, you've read the guidelines package? You're making sure to follow it? I know from personal experience that it's a lot to memorize."

"Yes." The guilt for lying hits hard. I don't even know how she'd react, knowing I'm breaking the number one guideline with STRIP. On *top* of what I'm hiding.

"Good. As an Excellence Scholar, I remember having to be an example for the rest of the students. And you know what I always say—breaking rules always spirals."

"I know."

"Did I tell you about Samantha? My friend I lost touch with because she copied an algebra problem of mine during class and was sent home?"

"I get it, Mom."

She sighs. "I know. I know. I'm trying to be supportive like you asked. Just promise you'll let me know the second you have doubts, okay?"

Ms. Lyney shows two fingers. Two minutes.

My conflicting feelings that have built up since stepping on campus sizzle on my tongue. That hiding who I am, let alone at an all-boys academy, is starting to feel impossible. That maybe Mom easily ranked top five because she didn't fear her own roommate, and she could make friends because there wasn't any risk of them looking a little too closely and figuring out a hidden truth. That maybe she was right all along, and this is too risky. But Ms. Lyney is here, listening.

"How's the store?" I ask to change the subject.

A beat passes over the line. Then the sound of shuffling papers, as if this reminded her to keep working behind the cash register that's always cluttered with mail and administrative files. "Sales have been slow this week. But back-to-school season should bring in our usual local teachers soon."

It's not like I expected much change after twelve years of her struggling to keep the lights on after my dad cheated and caused their divorce. Especially now that I'm away from Queens and can't help. Maybe that's also why she's so stressed. "You think?"

"Absolutely. And the Fall Book Club for Young Readers kicked off yesterday. We have more kiddos signed up this year than ever. Sixteen!"

That pulls a small smile out of me. Mom has always focused on putting our community in Queens over profits. Maybe most Valentine alumni make change in the world as doctors and lawyers and professors, and maybe Grandma and Grandpa expected that from her, too, but she's doing the same in her own way.

"That's great," I tell Mom. "I gotta go, but I'll get my name to the top. Promise."

"Okay, sweetie. I hope you will."

◆ ▶

Standing in front of Pragma Recreational Center's workout room door feels like a crime. At least when it's me. But PE isn't going to pass itself.

I roll up the sleeves of my new tracksuit from the gift shop, which I could actually afford since my single room check awesomely never cleared. People like Xavier will be in here. Well-liked, high-ranked, textbook-example boys. If they don't judge me for invading their territory, they'll judge my lack of mass. Time to blend in.

The second my foot is through the door, my mouth hangs open at how far back the room stretches. Valentine crests border the casement and the top of the walls, watching like surveillance cameras, and everywhere magically smells of lemon disinfectant instead of sweat. The metal machines that could crush me dead are endless. More importantly, abandoned.

I make my way more confidently through the empty room. Treadmills line one wall, but weights are stacked by another. I need muscles to run better. Maybe?

A clink comes down the row, and I jump.

Xavier is bench-pressing, lifting a barbell with two plates on each side. Okay, not alone. The only signs of perspiration are on the collar of his undershirt and his prominent forehead, even though the weight is triple my head size.

If I could become 5 percent as strong, I'd get an A+ in PE.

Xavier glances to the side, sensing my lurking presence. His eyes widen. "Christ—!" The bar slips through Xavier's grip and nearly squashes his neck.

I rush to spot him, only to end up tossing my hands upon

realizing that I do not know what spotting is. Xavier pushes the bar back into place by himself.

He sits up from the bench, shoving his floppy dark bangs out of his eyes. "You scared the juices out of me, bro."

"Sorry."

"Not your fault. There's just never anybody in here."

"Why?"

Xavier smirks like it should be obvious. "Everyone else is always studying."

"You're Rank Three for third years. Shouldn't you be?"

"Just gotta be smart about time management. Training takes an hour out of the day. Plus, I eat on the go." He taps on his temple. "Were you watching me?"

"No," I say. "Well, yes. Not because I'm weird. I'm here to train too."

"You know how to?"

"You just lift stuff, right?"

"If you plan to live at Health Services. Want help?"

For a PE grade this dire, help is what I need. But to have Xavier stand too close? *Look* too close? I wave a dismissive hand. "That'd be a huge favor."

Xavier digs through his gym bag on the floor. He whips out a sports drink and cracks open the lid. "Aren't you STRIP's face now?"

"I guess."

"You're technically doing us a favor, yeah?"

"Do you care that much about STRIP?"

"Hell yeah, I do." He chugs his drink so fast that his Adam's apple bounces like a pinball. "I was so done with the cockblockade last year. Couldn't talk to my girlfrie—er, ex-girlfriend—at the sister academy. That's what led me to STRIP, and then I saw how happy it makes everyone. I got why this was a tradition for a hundred years, and that's why I've stuck around to continue carrying it on. It's the right thing to do."

I eye him curiously. "Was that Jasper's situation too? Having a girlfriend?"

Xavier wheezes so loudly that it echoes through the workout room.

I'm not sure what's so funny. Jasper trying to win over someone from the sister academy, let alone a hundred, seems likely.

"Not really," Xavier says. "But Jasper always loved the tradition of it all, so he eventually became a self-appointed leader. It was all P.M. who got Jasper to join. He's the one who came up with offering a love-letter-writing service within STRIP instead of just a delivery service."

"P.M.?"

"Pierre-Marie. The previous Excellence Scholar for your class."

A book cover flashes to mind. It can't be. "The famous poet?"

"You know him? If you haven't already noticed, I'm the oldest member since everyone else graduated. I sort of went on a spree, recruiting anyone I could. Got P.M. first with the whole spreading-love-via-the-written-word angle."

My heart pounds as I recall what I've assumed about the previous Excellence Scholar. That he likely left due to the pressure.

They knew each other.

For some reason, that irritates me most. "Why didn't Jasper bring up that I replaced him? He's constantly reading his books."

"Well, they spent every day writing letters at STRIP together. They got so close that P.M. even boosted Jasper's work on his platform. Then they had a ... falling out, I guess."

"Oh. That's not why P.M. left, right?"

Xavier awkwardly rubs the back of his neck. "Sorry. I promised P.M. that I'd keep it all to myself. Probably best not to touch it with Jasper."

Plenty more questions pop into my head—did P.M. confide in Xavier about why he left? About Jasper?—but Xavier stands and lifts his hand for a fist bump/handshake concoction. He towers over me, and I ignore how small I feel.

"Let me show you how to use the machines at least," Xavier says. "I'm here to train regardless. It's not a favor. Come three days a week? After STRIP stuff?"

As I clumsily bump him back, a small smile rises to my face, even though I'm stuck on what I learned. In addition to the pressure P.M. must have faced, getting too close to someone as dangerous as Jasper seemingly pushed him out of Valentine. I'm walking in those shoes too closely for comfort. But I'm also outsourcing help. I have Xavier. If only I could tell Delilah the good news. Her whole-planet-arson status over my relentless struggles on this side of campus would turn down a few notches for sure.

"Wait," I say, a possibility hitting me. "So you guys can deliver a letter from me to the sister academy too, right?"

Xavier shrugs. "Why not? Just bring your letter to our meeting room so Blaze can pick it up before his weekly runs. He usually goes on Friday or the weekend."

My chest fills with hope. Maybe I can talk to Delilah despite this wall, after all. Although a piece of me wonders why she didn't offer this as an option during orientation. Maybe, somehow, she doesn't know about STRIP. Even though everyone seems to...

"Great. Thanks," I say anyway, only for my smile to twist once I replay what Xavier said a moment ago. "Oh, I can't train with you after STRIP. I have"—my mouth squirms more—"love lessons. With Jasper."

"Repeat that?" Xavier says, brow pinching.

The fact that I wasn't supposed to tell anyone jogs in my memory bank, and I bite my lip. "Jasper told me not to tell you guys, but I'm helping him write letters alongside being your face. Only until the mixer in November, though. Then I'm gone."

Xavier stays silent.

"You good?" I ask unsurely.

"I'm just surprised. People have offered to help Jasper write love letters since P.M. left, but he always sent them away."

"Really? Why?"

"Jasper claimed he never saw anything special in them." Xavier shrugs and walks toward the nearest pull-up bar. "At least, until you."

Chapter 12
LETTERS FROM A STOIC
THURSDAY, SEPTEMBER 12

Hi Delilah,

I found out about the love letter program. I'm giving this to someone named Blaze Alpha Destroyer, who apparently delivers letters to and from our campuses every week, so we'll see if this gets to you.

You told me to call you if I start sobbing, but I don't want to waste my emergency contact use already. I waited to tell you this, but I need to talk to someone about it: Do not set anything on fire, but I never got a single room. My roommate has already gotten naked in front of me. Knowing I was there. Do guys seriously do that?

Also, I haven't reached top five on the second-year ranks. Not even close. Just wanted to tell you because I miss you.

Charlie

Chapter 13
THE TRIAL
FRIDAY, SEPTEMBER 13

Thankfully, Ms. Nallos spends the remainder of the week of PE teaching volleyball, which requires minimal strength. I only have two exams in my other classes, which is actually a reprieve after the rigor of the past couple days. And English literature introduces a unit on Edgar Allan Poe, who apparently published exactly sixty-nine poems and married his cousin. We never work independently and call it a day like in online school. We read aloud, and Mr. Stern even assigns us a project to present on how each event of Poe's life—bad and good—affected every word he wrote.

Then there's Jasper, whose schedule I'm finding ways to work around, thanks to a Saint Valentine miracle. A terrifying morning person like himself showers before the bell tower startles me out of my sleep, which I still struggle to get enough of due to his annoying buzzing bedside lamp. He begs to get breakfast together, despite me declining nine times now, until he surrenders. After lunch, he swaps his morning and afternoon class materials, so I swap mine before. He then only ever returns at least ten minutes *after* lights-out. My curiosity wonders where he is, but I can't complain if he's out of the room and his buzzing lamp is off.

As long as our deal works out, he'll be gone forever.

A week later, I'm forced to be the face of STRIP.

I stare down the intimidating rows of desks, antique lamps, and chessboards in the near-silent library, only light pencil scribbles and chair squeaks to be heard. Since I've been able to study in my room, thanks to Jasper's absence, I haven't visited here since I came to hunt down STRIP in the stacks. Just like last time, nearly every station is claimed. Only lights-out forces everyone's brains to stop.

Jasper's instructions flood my head. *Sit in front of the librarian. Place the STRIP sign on the table. Make sure employees witness you being a real tutor to get them off our trail. Is that too much for you to remember?* How does his well of arrogance never go dry?

But then his instructions are replaced by Xavier's words that have replayed nonstop in my head. *Jasper claimed he never saw anything special in them. At least, until you.*

A strange tingling takes root in my chest. I hold my textbook tighter to make it stop, then check the double doors. Last night, Jasper said he'd join for moral support until our love lesson. Maybe he's running late.

I claim a table. From my backpack, I pull out the STRIP TIME paper sign folded into thirds and shove aside the chessboard to make room. Step one. I spot the librarian at her desk and wave. She stops scanning a book to return it, confused. Presence detected. Step two. Finally, I sit, take out my textbooks, and start my chem homework.

A metallic bang comes at my left. Chair legs scrape against the floor.

Down my row, four upperclassmen hover over a water bottle spilled on their homework. One elbows another in a half-rough, half-playful way I've seen guys do before. A few quiet laughs pop up from other tables.

A sinking feeling pulls through me as I sit at my empty one-person table. Still very much an outsider.

I shake away the feeling. No one showing up is good. More study time. It's unlikely visitors would come anyway. Every student knows STRIP is a love letter scheme.

"Bro," a whisper comes above my head. "Please tell me you're that new second-year Excellence Scholar."

A guy no taller than me and with a medium-tan complexion stands by my table, a cross necklace dangling between his plaid blazer lapels. His dark curls are familiar—the same ones in my view during calculus class.

I put down my pencil and inspect his face clearly for the first time. It's on the rounder side, and his cheeks are soft in a cute, attractive way. "I am."

"I'm Luis." His voice cracks. "Listen, I bombed my calc exam last week. Differential equations. You know anything about that garbage?" Another crack.

I try to ignore his voice for the sake of his ego, but my mouth crooks at the charm to it. His constant up-and-down modulation is one I briefly had when mine went through changes. Being reminded that I've gone through the same mortification as every other boy here admittedly dials up my pride meter. Then I realize why he looks familiar. "Yeah. You work at the gift shop? In that heart-shaped costume."

He groans. "Say something else. Anything else."

"You're in my class too?"

"Oh yeah! Charlie with the never-ending last name." Luis plops down in the seat beside me with so much force that the table rattles, echoing through the silent library. Three pieces on the chessboard fall, and heads around us turn. Luis doesn't care, just tugs on his curls. "Charlie, I got in trouble with my parents. 'Just go to that tutoring program!' they shouted. But they don't know STRIP is really, well, you know."

"Right," I say, leaning back and scattering my bangs over my own face.

"But then Jasper Grimes showed up to our homeroom to say that the new second-year Excellence Scholar joined STRIP."

"He did what?"

"No one told you? At first, I thought Jasper was telling us in code there's another new love letter deliverer, but then he emphasized *real* in *real good tutor*. I cried. *There's a real tutor now?* It felt like a sign." Luis gestures a Father, Son, and Holy Spirit across his upper half.

I mirror him until I remember signing the cross doesn't operate like a handshake. "That exam *was* tough."

Luis pulls his calculus textbook from his bag. *Luis Gabriel García Perez* is written in permanent marker on the fabric. "I bombed the slope field portion. Got a B-plus."

"Oh."

"Super embarrassing, I know. My parents are demanding I get my grade back to a ninety-eight or higher ASAP. What'd you get?"

"A-minus," I mumble.

"Rough."

Unspoken Guideline 8: An A− everywhere else is an F− here.

"At least a rough start for you makes sense," Luis adds, barely keeping his voice low. "You're new. You gotta figure out a whole new campus on top of locking in."

Is Luis the first person to acknowledge how hard transferring has been for me?

I smile. "Yeah. Thanks."

Tugging on his curls more, Luis opens to our 3.2 homework questions due in two days. A lesson I haven't gotten a free moment to review yet. "An Excellence Scholar like you must pick up this stuff mad quick. Walk me through these?"

If I can't solve simple calculus, Luis could tell everyone that the second-year Excellence Scholar is a joke. Outgoing plus attractive like him equals lots of friends, just like Xavier. This could get back to STRIP. No more being their face. No more double room to myself.

No backing out.

I flip to the introductory section of 3.2. After several *place short line segments* and *xy plane* phrases later, I'm only more lost. Still, I swipe up his calculator. "Let's solve number one together first. In drawing the slope field for the differential equation—" I plug in numbers that seem right according to the page. "At the point (−1,1), you'd draw a short segment of slope..."

I write down *= 1−2(−1) = 1 + 2 = 3* on scrap paper, then check in the back of the book for answers, squinting in preparation to be wrong.

$$= 1-2(-1) = 1 + 2 = 3$$

My eyes widen. I was right?

Luis groans loudly enough to pull the librarian's focus, but not enough to get shushed. Yet. He points at the *(−1, 1)* on the page. "Because you substituted both. I only used this one."

The double doors squeal open.

Jasper? I whip my head around. Three upperclassmen I don't recognize.

Why am I waiting for him?

Focusing on Luis, I guide him through the nine remaining questions. Every time he answers correctly, he hugs me in full view of the librarian. More STRIP reliability points. Once we're done, my head brims with equations I suddenly understand. I had *fun*.

Was I paying attention to my face? My hair? Were we sitting too close?

I can't remember.

"You're the best guy in STRIP, for real," Luis says as he packs his belongings. His curls have doubled in size. "No offense to Jasper. He does write awesome stuff."

"You think?"

"STRIP, in general, is how Emilio has stayed in touch with his girlfriend every week for the last year. But I guess the two were fighting all through summer break. Once he told Jasper about it and got a love letter written by him, they instantly made up. He's a wizard."

"What are Jasper's letters like?" My face burns once I realize what I asked. I shouldn't care, but I still can't figure out Jasper's social standing. A part of me wants to know others' opinions. When he speaks in class, he's cheered on. During passing time, others swarm him. Although same for Xavier. Either they're popular, or their top five rank is. If it's the latter, ranking may come with being seen more than I expected. Being watched.

If I join them, that could be a problem.

Luis hums, twirling a black king piece from the chessboard. "I'm not an artist, but there's something sparkly about Jasper's writing. It's basic but relatable."

Not the answer I predicted. Everything that leaves Jasper's

mouth is so flowery and long-winded. He *smells* like flowers. His letters should be the same.

"At least that's what my friends say," Luis adds, setting down the king.

"You've never asked him for a letter?" I ask.

"I don't have the same barriers as my friends. 'Cause, you know, they're into girls."

"Oh."

"And I'm—"

"Yeah—"

"—into guys."

"Yeah. Got that."

Luis isn't straight. At an all-boys academy. More surprisingly, he isn't stress-yanking his curls while telling me that.

"You're not worried?" I ask, swallowing my nerves over discussing anything related to this here. "When traditional is literally in our slogan?"

"I'm careful, for sure. You just gotta find your people, you know?"

I nod, even though I don't know. Minus Mom and Delilah, I had no one to lean on when figuring myself out. Especially no one like me. Besides, how can I figure out who *my people* are without first telling them who I am and risking they won't be?

Luis pokes my chest. "You going to Dix now?"

I glance toward the zigzag paths of the Halo beyond the double doors, where Jasper should've shown up an hour ago. The longest I've spent in Dixon Dining Hall is a record five minutes. I've only awkwardly meandered the perimeter to snag bagels and breadsticks, never sitting down and instead shoving them in my bag to sneak by the check-in workers who have made it clear that removing any food from the dining hall is expressly forbidden. This was my genius plan for dinner again. "In a sense."

"Wanna join me?"

My heart leaps at the chance to sit without looking like a loner. But this could count as making a friend. People have too-big eyes and mouths. Does Luis? Could he count as finding my people?

A throat clearing interrupts us.

Jasper, smiling at our conversation, but his typical lopsided dimple doesn't accompany it. Late, of course, because when has Jasper ever cared enough to be on time? He holds a coffee cup from Laney's Bean Shack and wears tortoiseshell glasses that I've never seen in our room. Behind the lenses, his gaze is strangely glazed over. "Apologies, Charlie and I have plans. Unless you'd like to keep making me wait?"

My mouth parts in shock. "Jasper."

Shockingly, Luis laughs. He even tosses a playful thumb toward Jasper. "This guy. Let's do lunch some other time, Charlie." Then he's out the double doors.

I check if the librarian is at her desk. Nope. I slap Jasper on the arm, and he nearly drops his coffee. "You're lucky people like you, or they'd beat you up."

"*Like* me?" Jasper grumbles, rubbing away the pain.

"Don't they?"

He ignores the question. "Whatever did I do to you?"

"Did *I* do something?"

"I'm surprised to see you accept Luis Perez's lunch invitation."

I *have* declined Jasper in the past, but why would he care? To him, we barely know each other. "The last person you should be upset with is me. Have you forgotten I was your face for hours?

Helping *your* program? Which went well, by the way, thank you for asking."

"Good." He sips from his coffee. *Black* and *Plain* are checked on the side.

Black coffee. I never noticed during camp. Considering how disgustingly flowery he is in life, I'm surprised he doesn't guzzle the chocolate-caramel Jesus lattes towering with whipped cream and fifty packets of sugar.

Jasper's coffee and glasses aren't the only unexpected additions. For once, his dress shirt is buttoned to his neck and accompanied by a tie. He even wears the plaid blazer instead of casting it over a shoulder, gold number-one enamel pin on the lapel. To anyone else, Jasper would look like an average student, but after witnessing him ignore the dress code for weeks, he looks more distinct somehow. More handsome.

Well, not handsome. He *is*, objectively, as a poet famous for his looks. But not to me.

Does he really think I'm special?

"You look interesting today" splutters out of my mouth.

Jasper's brow rises. "Is this your attempt at flattery?"

"No. You're just." What am I *doing*? "Proper-er."

"This is my first day as your love tutor." Jasper sits across from me, setting down his coffee and kicking his dress shoes onto the table. "Thought I should act more *proper*."

"Right," I mutter at the dirty soles.

"Before I can assign you love homework, we need to cover basics. Ready?"

No. But I still grab the mechanical pencil and composition notebook I *resonated with* from Jasper's stash last week.

From the chessboard shoved to the side, Jasper picks up a black pawn and points at my notebook with it. "First, take records of my EROS."

"Your what?"

"Essential Requirements of Seduction."

My insides recoil. I have no clue what he's talking about, yet I already know this is the last thing I want to learn. "Go on."

"The first EROS is to use different handwriting for every letter."

Nothing to do with seduction so far. "Why?"

"What we sell is an illusion"—Jasper sets the pawn on my notebook—"that the patron has written the letter himself. I sign them with his name, not mine." He sets another black pawn by the other. "If every letter we sent over to the sister academy used the same handwriting, that illusion would shatter."

"I guess."

"Plus, think about if the letters were caught by the academy. Worse, my aunt. What could happen if we used our real handwriting?" Jasper picks up a white queen from the chessboard, grinning. A challenge.

But this is easy. "We could also get caught. Even if we sign these letters with different names, they could trace our handwriting back by comparing them to our assignments."

Jasper's forehead wrinkles in a playful way. Satisfaction courses through me, knowing that means I won. He holds up the black king and queen pieces together. "Aren't you clever, Excellence Scholar? Yes, I don't want to be traceable. And now, you." As his final move, he knocks over the black king and queen with the white queen. A reminder that I could get sent home for two reasons instead of one now.

After, he casts aside the chess pieces and pulls my notebook toward himself. "There are three more EROS. Second, write in an environment that will never sway your feelings."

"Okay."

"Third, remember that love does not have to make sense; neither do your words."

Side-eye. "Okay."

"Fourth, craft for yourself—not your audience—for true connection."

Double side-eye. "Okay."

"Once I assign your first homework, make sure to apply these four points. Before I can, though, you need to take part in STRIP's weekly one-on-ones."

"Am I supposed to know what that is?"

Behind his glasses, Jasper's eyes flick around the busy library. "Not in public. You'd be surprised how many eyes and ears lurk. Visit STRIP after your tutoring next Thursday. That's all you need to know."

Chapter 14
THE GIVER
THURSDAY, SEPTEMBER 19

"**MAINTAIN HORSE HIERARCHY**," Blaze commands, standing upon a stack of books. He shows off the ruby varsity ring on his thumb, then gesticulates something like a fluttering butterfly. "FOR THE RING OF ANCESTRAL DARKNESS COMMANDS YOU."

Everyone in STRIP's back room goes still and stares.

I do the same by the moving bookcase door. I've just entered, and I'm already confused. But there are as many red-and-black-clothed bodies as there were the first time I came here, so I can at least piece together that a weekly one-on-one must have also been taking place then.

I weave through the crowd made up of—what I've learned over the last week—all levels of Valentine standing. Ishaan and Frankie, Ranks Twelve and Six, who raise their hands quickest in calculus and come from enough money to sport bank-breaking Valentine-branded backpacks: high standing. Matt, Rank Forty-Three, who interrupts with roughly one joke per class period: at Twenty-Eighth Avenue Middle School, high standing, but here, low. And lots of in between.

Behind Blaze's chants of darkness, Xavier and Robby sit on the floor, the upturned horse-riding helmet full of sparkly trading cards on display. They're too swarmed by visitors to notice me.

One non-tutor is missing.

I detour toward the brocade curtain splitting the room in two and look inside, spotting Jasper's mop of blond hair in a corner. Of course everyone else works during a rush except him. He sits cross-legged on his blazer to fight off the dusty floor, using another stack of books as a table to scribble in his JFG journal. What are his initials, anyway? Jasper Fucking Grimes?

I struggle not to roll my eyes. "Jasper."

A nearby antique lamp casts shadows across his startled demeanor, which flips to a lopsided dimple. "Tutor Jasper."

His fingers. They're red. Covered in blood.

I run at him, kicking aside some books on the floor, and swipe up his hand. Not blood. Red ink from his leaky fountain pen.

Jasper's grin widens. "Worried about me?"

My cheeks burn, and only then do I realize we're still touching. I chuck his hand onto his lap. "No. Buy a new pen."

"I will not. This is my cherished six-hundred-dollar fountain pen. Limited edition. Only ninety exist in the world. I'm eighty-nine." Jasper points at the black resin barrel where *89* is engraved. "Any other pen would render my life a feckless charade."

"It's leaking."

"All fountain pens *smear*."

I inspect the barren room more. A handwritten NO LIQUIDS sign is on the wall, a bucket tucked in a corner is sparsely filled with cleaning supplies, and a single shelf is over Jasper's head, where there's a row of the same red-and-white-striped paperback book spines. *Love Is a Broken Party Clown* by Jasper Grimes. Compared with the other side's musty, concrete scent, there's something familiarly floral in the air, like Jasper is here all the time.

Let me guess. "This side of the room is your office or something?"

"From your tone, I take it you're not impressed."

"I thought the place you'd write would be"—I shrug—"a garden of roses."

"Are you forgetting EROS Two?" Jasper is still writing, his number-one enamel pin gleaming on his collar. Is this the type of brain I'm up against for Rank One? One that can simultaneously handle full conversations and craft prizewinning prose? "I could accidentally think my writing is romantic enough due to the romantic environment."

As if I expected to understand a poet's mind.

Jasper points his broken pen at another makeshift book table. "Are you staying?" he asks, his tone undeniably eager and hopeful that I am. It's the same way he sounded when he approached me the first time all those years ago, asking to work on our dramatic mode assignment together, and it makes my chest lurch in a way I can't place. "You can use a tome table as a seat."

"Tome table?" I ask.

"A tome is a type of book. A large, heavy, scholarly one."

I hold myself back from throwing him into Au Sable Forks Lake. "I know what a *tome* is. A tome table?"

"A table made of tomes, naturally. What we call them in the STRIP Crypt."

"Where?"

"This whole back room. On days like today, I wait on this side of the crypt or in the stacks until I'm needed to provide my gift of poetry to them all." Over his shoulder, a cobweb slung along a corner catches my attention. An insect scurries across.

Jasper must notice because he stops writing. Hooking the clip of his pen onto his shirt pocket, he grabs a duster from the cleaning supplies bucket and knocks the web.

I grimace. Crypt, at least, is accurate.

"*Welsh pony originating from southern Wales!*" Robby announces from the main side of the room—crypt. "Number two!"

I peek through the curtain. Every visitor groans except one, who stands before Robby's riding helmet full of trading cards, holding his own. It's the same type that was passed out during my first-ever visit to the crypt. From a distance, I vaguely make out a picture of a brown horse with a bushy tail on one side.

"Every week, our patrons draw horse trading cards to determine the order they'll be served by me," Jasper whispers, standing so close that his breath tickles my ear.

I startle and take one firm step away, my face heating up all over again. His personal space issues will give me an ulcer. "By served, you mean get their love letter written by you?"

"Precisely. This is what we were busy with on the first day you came here. It's luck of the draw."

So I was right. "But there are no numbers on these cards."

Jasper points beyond the curtain, toward a new patron drawing from the hat and then showing Robby the card.

"Akhal-Teke," Robby announces. "Number nineteen."

The so-called patron sighs and retreats.

"Robby is a"—Jasper switches to a bad French accent—"*horse aficionado*. He has a breed tier list—his most favorite to least favorite. Akhal-Teke is apparently his nineteenth-favorite horse right now. It mostly stays the same week to week, but there are some wild cards. His feelings toward the Welsh Cob change almost every time."

Just when I thought these fake tutors couldn't get weirder.

Although STRIP's tradition as a whole is already weird. And so are the rest of Valentine's real academy rules. Maybe it's a product of their environment. Or maybe it's simply that they're some of the smartest students in the nation. That alone means their brains aren't exactly typical.

Still, I can't help but ask: "Why not use something normal to draw names? Sticks?"

"Robby can run our admin how he pleases. We trust him as the second year's Rank Two. He's aiming for MIT's biochemistry program."

My brow furrows up to my hairline. "An MIT hopeful is involved with this?"

"Of course. To MIT admissions, he's tutoring at one of the smartest academies in the nation—the top one percent of smart. From the outside, at least, this is one of the most prestigious programs our academy has to offer. Blaze is also a supergenius; he skipped several grades and still landed at Valentine. He's twelve."

"Twelve?"

"You couldn't tell from the—" Jasper gestures vaguely at Blaze's five-foot stature across the crypt, where his uniform turned cape flows behind him.

"I guess," I say.

Unspoken Guideline 9: Everyone is aiming for the stars, and I'm just trying to pass PE.

Jasper passes through the brocade curtain on a gust of his fragrance that's growing more familiar by the day. He waves to gather the crypt's focus. "Attention, patrons!"

The patrons wave back. A few even cheer. He really *is* liked.

"Welcome, as always, to the tradition our Valentine forefathers bravely founded over a hundred years ago to deliver letters of the heart between the brother and sister campuses. These last two years, I have been honored by the positive reception shown toward my love letters—a new, secondary option we've added for when your own letters are feeling, well, dull. Since we've begun this, STRIP's one-on-ones have been conducted privately between me, the poet, and you, the lover." Jasper pulls me toward him, tugging on my blazer cuff. "However, now you must consent to my new student being present. Everyone, welcome Charlie!"

Confused stares are the only response.

Then whispers.

"Isn't he that Excellence Scholar who flopped on the grade ranks?"

"No way he's writing our letters."

"Be for real. We came here for an actual poet."

Spotlight number one million. My stomach twists.

Jasper holds up a defensive hand. "Since my student is in training, I promise, your letters will still be written by moi. I give my gift to you!"

Even though Jasper Grimes may be a triple threat—perfect face, grades, and poetry career—he sucks at lying. I'm not the only one who can tell. The looks around the crypt have grown more suspicious.

"It's true," I say. I won't let my classmates run me out of STRIP until my own room is secured. "I'm his loyal student, here to watch."

Jasper looks my way to send a covert *thank you*, then over to Robby. "Who's the first horse?"

◆ ▶

First, Jasper lights a taper candle in a brass fixture set on the tome table—the only light source in his office now that he's turned off the antique lamps.

Next, he leans toward our first patron sitting across from us. Faint mumbles come from a line beyond the brocade curtain, waiting to be served. "Thank you for trusting me with your love story today. What is your name?"

I sit in silence beside him, staring nervously at the candle releasing a semisweet cherry blossom fragrance only someone like Jasper would enjoy. Our bedroom was pushing it, but flammable objects in a building full of paper? Maverick the Residential Retainer would cut him like a fish.

"My name is Eli," the patron says shyly despite the office's privacy, playing with his Shetland pony card on the table. His blazer sleeves hang to his fingertips. Either he's a first year who hasn't figured out the unspoken guidelines, or even a size S is too big on him to maintain the rolled sleeves look.

"Tell us about yourself," Jasper says.

"I'm fourteen. On the debate team."

From his JFG cross-body bag, Jasper reaches for his broken fountain pen and journal to jot notes. Immediately, red ink smears across his right hand and the page. He glances at my closed backpack on the floor. "Not taking records, student?"

"You're not giving said student any guidance," I say, frowning.

"You're the second-year Excellence Scholar. Shouldn't you be capable on your own?"

I stiffen, unsure if that's an insult or a compliment, and catch myself hoping it's the latter before shutting that feeling down. I don't care what *Jasper* thinks. I reach for my mechanical pencil and composition notebook, which look mediocre next to Jasper's bajillion-dollar pen and journal. Despite what Jasper likely believes, holding a bougie pen doesn't dictate note quality. I'll take great notes. The best notes.

"When did you meet her?" Jasper asks Eli, voice repulsively soothing.

Eli stares over my shoulder as if a shimmering sunset has appeared behind me, full of longing. I turn around. Only a concrete wall. He snaps back to reality. "Sorry. Fifteen days and three hours ago."

"You met during orientation?"

"One day after. During the debate team's first meeting of the year. We got special permission to visit the sister academy's team and plan the flower sale fundraiser we held this week. She's on their team."

Jasper writes more. I don't. Wouldn't it be nice if my love tutor gave me directions?

Guess I'll go with what's always the most logical. Facts.

> Patron Name: Eli
> Date Met: One day after orientation.
> Location: First debate meeting.
> Other: Not even three weeks have passed, and he's acting like he's lost his princess to a witch handing out free apples.

"Her name?" Jasper asks.

"I was too nervous to ask."

"Her appearance?"

"She wore a braid. It was super windy. She accidentally wore her blazer inside out." The longing on Eli's face returns. "I want to learn more about her and send her a lot of letters, and then I'll hopefully get the courage to send one to ask her to the mixer—"

"Hold on." I grip my forehead. "We can't deliver letters to someone we don't—"

"We'll see it through," Jasper says, pushing a finger against my lips. A chill lances up my spine, the rest of me turning to stone.

"Thank you so much," Eli gushes before leaving through the curtain.

I rip Jasper's finger off my face and take a deep breath, attempting to slow down my racing heart. "My shoulder exists."

"Would that have been enough to stop you from talking? It appeared that you were instigating a duel with him."

"Well, I'm *right*. How are you going to find someone you don't know the name of? Isn't this extra work for you?"

Jasper eyes me strangely, like his memory is once again jogged by the sass I keep trying and failing to stifle around him. My whole body tenses until the look fades. He lazily spins the base of the taper candle around the tome table, not caring about the flame nor the melting wax. "We're not only poets, von Hevringprinz. We're cupids."

Grimacing, I spring up from the floor. "Well, I didn't sign up to be a—"

"Yo," a new patron calls, pulling back the curtain.

Jasper tugs me back down by my blazer. Our shoulders bump, and I grunt. "Come tell us about your situation, Cody."

As the patron sits, his features jog my memory. The bedhead, the foot for a face—the one from PE who thought me not wanting to take the class was hilarious. He rests an arm along a propped knee and waves my way. "Nice to meet you."

He can't even remember who he insults.

My annoyance spikes, but Jasper taps my notebook. I keep writing.

Patron Name: Foot

Jasper, who's peeking at my note taking, snorts. He covers it up with a cough.

Foot Cody pulls a sports drink out from his bag and takes a swig. Red droplets spill on the tome table. "I need to send a letter to the third-year class president over there."

Jasper stares at the Red Dye 40 seeping into the bound book page edges, then the NO LIQUIDS sign on the wall. "Name?"

"Rachel. I think."

"You think?"

"Rachel Wood, maybe."

Jasper takes the note. "How did you meet? Through your student council duties?"

"Haven't met her."

"Then why send a romantic letter?"

"She's going to be my date for the mixer after she gets this letter."

Date Met: Unknown.
Reason for Letter: The mixer, like literally everyone else.

Jasper shuts the clasp of his journal, the ocean-blue gemstone reflecting the candle flame. "Thank you. Please send in the next patron on your way out."

Cody gulps down the rest of his sports drink instead of moving. Another red droplet slithers down his chin and onto his dress shirt, which is as wrinkly as a brain. "Not to doubt your poet-ing skills, but can you write with that little info?"

"I'm not writing your letter."

My head flicks up at Jasper's sudden change in tone. The sweetness usually coating it has vanished, leaving behind something colder.

"You're denying me?" Cody asks. "You can't just do that."

"We're an unofficial, free program. So, yes, we can just do that."

"Better watch your mouth, Grimes."

Jasper calmly taps the corner of his own lips. "You should wipe yours."

Cody slams a palm against the table and lunges forward like he might punch Jasper in the jaw—but he falters and wipes the drink residue with his other hand. Maybe he recalled who Principal Grimes's nephew is. "You want the academy to discover what you do back here? How you *really* use your equestrian center privileges? Only takes one student to tell your aunt."

"Go ahead." Jasper doesn't flinch.

My mouth hangs open. What is Jasper *doing*?

Cody sneers, tosses on his bag, and passes us on his way to the curtain.

"Although," Jasper calls, still motionless, "what a shame this will be for our classmates. Their love letters will never be delivered again. Established couples who rely on us throughout the year? Future couples who haven't even had the chance?"

Cody turns around. "So?"

Jasper smiles, but it's off. His lopsided dimple is missing, and his blue eyes are glazed—I've only seen this look once before, when he was kept waiting by me and Luis in the library. He stands, readjusting the number-one enamel pin on his dress shirt, and takes calm but intentional steps toward Cody. "I hope they won't be mad at whoever tells my aunt. Maybe they'll sabotage his status as the student council president?"

"Are you threatening me?"

"You threatened me first." Jasper shrugs, still exuding a

collected aura that proves he isn't scared, yet one that has me on the edge of my seat. "It's an equivalent exchange."

"If you—"

Jasper points over Cody's shoulder, toward five other patrons peeking through the curtain to check on the raised voices. "Go on."

Cody's foot face nearly flashes red with anger. Without another word, he storms past the captive audience and out the crypt.

Sighing lightly, Jasper reclaims his spot beside me on the floor. He picks up his fountain pen and twirls the base with his pointer finger and thumb. "Who's next?"

Unspoken Guideline 10: Principal's nephew's powers include threats and blackmail.

Sweat beads on my hairline as I mentally play back Jasper's silky-smooth, authoritative tone and how strangely captivating it was. Well, not to me. To the crowd it gathered. Yeah. I'm an empath. "You threatened someone."

"I suggested he should leave."

"By threatening him."

"STRIP isn't here to harass women." His voice is soft now.

I study him in surprise and, I'll admit, begrudging respect. "You're not worried he'll tell your aunt?"

"It's his word against mine and the student body's," Jasper says. "I wish him luck."

The one-on-ones go faster than I expect after that, taking only another hour. Jasper smiles through every discussion—a real one, dimple included—and I lower my defenses. Once patron number nineteen walks out, Jasper blows out the taper candle, the runaway blond locks of his ponytail fluttering around his cheeks.

"Good work today, student," he says beside me. "Now, please write letters for all nineteen of our patrons today."

"What?" I say, pushing my glasses up my nose to reread the scribbles in my notebook. Out of the nineteen letters, five are common correspondence to their girlfriends, but the other fourteen have *Mixer* written down as the reason. Delilah was right. Students do care about this event. Maybe even more than grades. "You're starting to deliver my letters already?"

Jasper laughs so hard that he grips his stomach, his half-buttoned shirt drooping and revealing even more chest that I pointedly avoid looking at for the hundredth time. "No, this is your first homework assignment. Solely practice."

He thinks the notion of my letters being sent is a bit too funny.

I try my best to glower but fail. Despite Jasper's billions of flaws, that bubbly laugh of his is, unfortunately, not one of them. "Due date?"

"One week from today."

Nineteen love letters in seven days. The next public grade rank announcement is one day before. In addition, I'll need to ace my chemistry and world history unit exams. I'm *supposed* to handle all of this. That's my job.

But what if I can't?

"That's seven days away," I say, hoping he'll budge.

Jasper hums. "You want less time? Apologies, I didn't want to expect too much from you."

My desire for more time poofs into smoke.

I force a smile. "One week works... Tutor Jasper."

Chapter 15
IN SEARCH OF LOST TIME
WEDNESDAY, SEPTEMBER 25

One week did not work.
That's all I can think as I meet Luis at the gift shop after his shift, wait for him to break free of his sandwich-board-heart costume, and grab lunch with him in Dix for the first time.

In thirty minutes, at noon sharp, the public grade ranks update. I studied every free second between STRIP Time and my first few cardio training sessions with Xavier. Even if Jasper turned in his chemistry and world history exams twenty minutes before I did, none of the answers stumped me.

But studying also came with a price tag: zero time to write love letters from my one-on-one notes. All nineteen are due in twenty-four hours.

"You good?" Luis asks loudly through a mouthful of pad thai, competing with the lunch rush voices bouncing around Dix's cathedral-like high ceiling. He was in the middle of describing the time he snuck his cat into his room here but chickened out, especially since his roommate, Bingo A. Dixon, is allergic. I think.

I rub my thighs that are still catastrophically sore after the laps Xavier made me do around Pragma Recreational Center's field a few days ago. Which may have ended in me collapsing on the grass and Xavier promptly deciding we would wait until I healed to start our first weight training session. *No, I am not good.*

"Yeah, I'm good," I say anyway, picking at my salad bar

concoction, the only food I can stomach lately. The table Luis chose is two rows from the center, lined with teardrop chandeliers. From what I can tell as I sit down in Dix for the first time instead of awkwardly loitering around the perimeter, it's a neutral zone of popularity. The back, toward the check-in clerks, is for the less so. The front, where a maroon curtain frames headshots of seemingly influential Valentine men of the past, is apparently for foots like Cody, who laughs at a table swarmed by others in Valentine gift shop sweatshirts. Someone as outgoing as Luis probably belongs over there, but generously met me in the middle.

I wonder where Jasper sits.

Even though Dix's indoor tables are smaller than the outdoor picnic-style ones, allowing Luis a closer view of me minus the bouquet centerpiece separating us, I haven't shaken my hair over my face or kept my hands off the table runner. I trust Luis a little lately. Considering his lack of seriousness toward life that contradicts Jasper's approach, maybe he could help with my letters in a way that won't make me die. "Question."

"Bring it."

"If you got a love letter from someone, what would you want it to say?"

"I've never thought that far." Luis tugs on a curl, though, like he definitely has.

"Really? About getting a letter?"

"Getting confessed to at all. In this place, it feels impossible to date other guys, let alone if I could pull any. A love letter is, like, my step ten while it's everyone else's step one. Actually, no—first step is making sure Valentine doesn't smite me. It's like we're being watched at all times. Like." He points his chopsticks at the front of the hall. "Why's bro here?"

I follow his chopsticks toward the framed old men again, where at the center is a six-by-six painting of Saint Valentine, draped in gowns.

"He *is* everywhere," I mutter at my salad.

"My guess is, on paper, they wouldn't kick me out, you know? But there're other ways of phasing someone out. Suddenly, me sharing a room with another guy is a prob. Living in *any* res hall is a prob. PE is a prob. Principal Grimes calls me into her office to explain that there may be schools that suit me better, and I'm done." Luis tosses a hand. "At least, my theory."

"I get you." My grip on my plastic fork tightens so much that it bends. I loosen my fingers.

Luis eyes my permanently screwed-up fork. "Thought you might."

Thought I might *what*?

I guessed that Luis clocked me as *something* when we first met, but this confirms it. Fear creeps in, wondering if he's figured out what exactly that something is—and if he's not the only one. Still, the fear is milder than expected, knowing it's Luis. He may count as my people. Our issues are similar, at least.

"If I got a love letter," Luis starts again through more noodles, "then I'd want it to be heartfelt and stuff. Something I could read at the wedding years later."

Never mind.

The conversation topic is my fault, but I'm already squirming in my chair. I reach for a napkin in the dispenser instead of looking at him, only to grab a trading card with a horse on it. Furrowing my brow, I stick it back in. "You're not joking?"

"Nah."

"I assumed you'd want a purposely bad pickup line."

"Okay, not too heartfelt. *I'm in love, love, love; oh, please, baby, oh—* is cringe."

I grimace. "Don't say that again."

"Exactly. So, no cringe, but I'd make it count. Especially if it were for the mixer. It's the one thing that keeps us alive while we pull all-nighters and fail tests through the year. The love letter's gotta match the fanfare."

"How did this mixer become this big of a deal, anyway?"

Luis shrugs. "Why are the Buffalo suburbs decked out in so many blow-up inflatables and flashing lights around Christmas that you total your car? Why do we watch the Superbowl's ten minutes of gameplay when it's three whole hours long? Stuff gets hype."

I force myself to meet his eyes again. "You really think heartfelt is the most logical?"

He smiles like this topic isn't uncomfortable at all. Is this how most are about the cursed L-word? "My brain says I should care more about something like this. You get a lifetime to tell jokes, but you only get one chance to confess your true feelings."

We finish lunch and exit into a downpour, knocking the temperature down enough that goose bumps dot my arms. He leaves for the residential hall, but I head toward the weekly grade ranking board, the grip on my umbrella tightening by the second. Classmates rush past me so quickly that their raincoats flutter behind them, and their boots splash gross puddle juice on my slacks. Icy gunk seeps into my socks, but my stress won't let me care.

"*One week works, Tutor Jasper.*" I punt a chunk of gravel, imagining I'm aiming for the back of Jasper's stubby ponytail. "*That's fine, Tutor Jasper.* What is wrong with you, Charlie?"

No way can I finish nineteen letters in one day—and make

them meaningful enough to have them read at a wedding—like Luis suggested. My *true feelings*. I don't have any when I have zero experience in the art of romance.

Well, a little.

My mind flashes with memories of the only person I've kissed, looking two years younger than he does now, and my heartbeat thrums quicker. Jasper doesn't count as experience in the art of romance when he broke my heart. He's left me with *negative* experience.

Voices pull my attention. By Laney's Bean Shack, raincoated bodies swarm the grade ranks beneath the awning. Two instructors use stepladders to hang listings. A third sits with a basket on her lap. The numbered enamel pins.

My name is high enough on the ranks to make out above the crowd.

28. Charlie von Hevringprinz

Relief shoots up to my head and down to my toes. Halfway to the top five.

I have to tell Mom.

I rush through the Halo, shielding myself against the wind with my umbrella until I'm slamming open the office door. Ms. Lyney startles behind the counter, but the lifelike stuffed gnomes on the shelves stay still. She gawks at the umbrella dripping by my thigh, then the sopping coattail of my basic, non-Valentine-branded raincoat.

"May I contact my mom?" I ask through a gasp for breath.

Even though communication with family is minimal, according to the guidelines package, Ms. Lyney simply searches up my name to dial Mom and holds out the phone. My flushed face and dramatic entrance must've screamed emergency enough.

I set my umbrella by the door and take the phone. After two rings, Mom picks up.

"Hello?" Her voice warbles more than normal on that one word alone, which means she definitely saw the Valentine caller ID. Like she's already expecting the worst.

My chest sinks. Maybe, because of what I'm hiding, she always will be.

"It's me," I say.

"Charlie! What a surprise." A pause. "Did something happen? You've caught me painting spiders and ghosties on the bookshop windows, and I can't easily sit down at the moment."

I try to focus on the good news. My improved grades, even with STRIP taking up half my time and Jasper breathing down my neck at every other moment. Proving to her that I can handle this place, even if I'm on the boys' side of campus. "I'm ranked twenty-eight out of the second-year class now, and still with two months to go."

"That's a jump!"

"Yeah. I think I'll only get higher from here."

"I'm so proud of you," Mom says. "This must've been a huge challenge, especially with everything else you're adapting to there. Have you thought about taking the train down for a weekend sometime soon?"

A piece of me wants to be thankful for the recognition. Even if Mom wasn't in my exact shoes when she was an Excellence Scholar, she understands the pressure of the ranking board. Of excelling. But *take the train down for a weekend* leaves a sour taste in my mouth, like she's still waiting for me to give up.

And she doesn't even know the half of it. Right now, she thinks

I have a single room to myself. Instead, I have a *Jasper* because the check I gave her never got delivered.

How did it never get delivered?

My stomach twists as I stand there, clutching the phone.

"Charlie? Charlie?"

"Do you remember what address was on the letter for my single room check?" I ask.

"Check?"

"I gave it to you on your way to the store one morning," I say. "The office said they never got it, so now I'm in a double room. With another guy."

There's a long pause.

My heart drops. This has to be my fault. The academy's. If it isn't—"Mom."

"Oh, Charlie, I think—let me see." Shuffling sounds come from over the line. Probably all the paperwork swarming her cash register. "It's right here. I'm so sorry. It slipped my mind."

"Are you serious?"

"I can send it today. Or can you pay for it now with your card?"

A confusing mixture of betrayal and understanding swirls in my gut. Mom never takes a day off. She's exhausted. I know this.

But this was *so* important.

"Yeah," I lie weakly, even though there are no more single rooms. How can I say otherwise? She'll only worry more. "I can try with my own card."

"Good. I'm so sorry, Charlie. Really."

The clock on the wall between the gnomes catches my eye. Five minutes until STRIP Time. And—end me—Jasper's *love letters.* "I need to go. Love you."

"Love you, Charlie. I'll make this up to you whenever you visit."

Chapter 16
VANITY FAIR
WEDNESDAY, SEPTEMBER 25

When I unlock Room 503, it's empty, even though it's twelve minutes past lights-out.

Over the last few weeks, Jasper has still come home later than guidelines dictate, giving me plenty of time to shower and change without *unwanted interruptions*. But after STRIP Time, I got so caught up with distracting myself from Mom and my nineteen love letters that I didn't register the warning bell until the other library desks were vacant. I sprinted to Philautia Residence Hall faster than gravitational waves traveling at light speed and, by some cupid's blessing, didn't get caught.

Yet Jasper is gone. Again.

Unspoken Guideline 11: We can get detention for staying out a bit too late, but the principal's nephew can seemingly stay out every night. Doing what? He has *that* many friends?

My mouth twists. All these guidelines are becoming about Jasper.

As I sigh and set down my backpack, his side of the room distracts me. His floor is a bog of crumpled paper, old Laney's Bean Shack cups, and dirty clothes. But his bed is made, not a wrinkle in his decorative ambrosia flower quilt, and his Pierre-Marie Laframboise book is set on the eleven throw pillows. The only Excellence Scholar who pleases him.

Maybe P.M. is who I should emulate in my letters.

I walk over to inspect the flimsy cover. *A Craving for Champagne: Poems* is encircled by illustrated forks and knives accented by gold foil. A poetry collection. About food?

I flip to the first page.

> *a heady rush of champagne bubbles*
> *as we lose our sweetened troubles*
> *a symphony of sighs and whispers*
> *as we find each other's kisses*

I slap the book shut and hurl it at the pillows.

Not food.

I head into the bathroom to shower and try to forget that happened. If Jasper admires this stuff, then what is his like? Not that I care what his is like.

As I rip off my sweaty uniform, I catch a glimpse of my chest in the mirror. A place I try to never look. I reach for the towel on my wall hook and wrap it beneath my arms. This way, no one will spot my scars. The only way. But I could never walk around like *this* during PE.

And my training with Xavier. If I kept rushing back here instead of the locker room to shower after, would he catch on? Would everyone?

The nerves are too much, and I push them away. I toss my towel over the top of the opaque shower door, start the water, take off my glasses, and slip inside.

"CHARLIE!"

Knocking comes at the bathroom door. I screech.

"Charlie von Hevringprinz?" A shadowed hand knocks on the shower door. A bracelet jangles against the wrist. Jasper.

Blood pounds in my ears as I cross my arms and legs tight. I snatch my towel and wrap it beneath my shoulders again without thinking, water still pouring on me. I need a room to myself now. Yesterday. A year ago. "Y-yes?!"

"*I—opin—boo—!*" His voice is too muffled.

"What?!" I shout back.

Jasper opens the shower. He grips my damp shoulders, and I squeeze the towel so hard that my knuckles turn white. "Good, you're in here! I need your opinion on—"

"Sir," a deep voice calls, "where should the bookcase go?"

Jasper whips his head around so fast that his blond ponytail smacks my cheek. "Between the two beds, please."

I peek my head out of the shower. "Who's in our room?"

"Mailroom concierge." His head tilts as he processes the soaked towel wrapped around me. "Freshen up first, roommate."

In a whirlwind of red-and-black plaid, he's gone, back into our shared room. I rush out of the shower to lock the bathroom doorknob, blood pumping so loudly everywhere through me that I don't even hear the click—because, apparently, I even have to lock this when he isn't here. This is seriously how guys interact.

I can't *do* this any longer.

My legs quaver. I grip the door for stability, then force myself to attempt the rest of my shower, to keep going. I'll finish the deal with Jasper, and this will soon be a distant memory. Every bump and knock from the bedroom nearly lurches my heart out of my throat and sends it spiraling down the drain. I finish fast, then toss on my plaid pajamas and step out of the bathroom.

Whoever that concierge was, he's gone. Now there's a new bookcase rising between our beds. Half of Jasper's books that once coated the floor are organized on the shelves. He stands at the center of the rug, plaid blazer slung over a shoulder and tie missing. A walking dress-code violation, yet not a violation on his record.

I pointedly focus on the bookcase. Suddenly, I'm hyperaware of my wet hair hanging in flat clumps and exposing my face more than usual, especially after everything Jasper just saw. I lift my pajama shirt collar higher. "You *do* own a bookcase."

"Not me. We."

"Huh?"

"A while ago, you said we should."

I approach the bookcase and run my hand along the side engraved with a pansy flower pattern that matches the wallpaper. Most of the books are Jasper's poetry and romance novels, but the middle is classics. Including *Othello*. My favorite. The top frame, carved into a scroll, is adorned with doves and olive branches and more pansies. Cursive lettering is etched into the wood.

Mr. Grimes & Mr. von Hevringprinz

Jasper's lopsided dimple pops, which *does* look annoyingly charming. Unfortunately, I understand why he won Sexiest Poet of the Year, even though the existence of that award confounds me. "What do you think?"

It's ridiculous. Pointless. The moment our deal is done, Jasper and I won't be roommates, yet our names are on there like some wedding invitation.

But it also feels like an apology. I'm sort of stunned by that. "It's... Thank you."

His face lights up. "It's the least I could do for my roommate."

Warmth rises in my chest at how genuine he sounds. I cross my arms tightly against myself to smush the feeling out of me.

"Then could you do me one last favor and learn how to knock before opening our doors?"

"Oh, is this some secret roommate code I've been missing out on? How fun."

"What?"

"I have it—let's knock based on how many syllables are in our last names. I'll do four knocks for *von Hevringprinz*." Jasper punches his hand with his other four times. "Now you'll do my last name."

I punch my hand once.

"Fantastic!" Jasper pulls me into a side hug, squishing our shoulders together. "I can feel our teamwork blossoming even more."

My heart rate spikes to the stratosphere. Because I can too. Even though I shouldn't.

I can't.

Jasper lets go of me. He walks to his bed, tosses himself onto the eleven pillows, and picks up P.M.'s book. "How's your homework coming? It's due tomorrow."

As if I could forget. "Fine," I lie, my pulse still thrumming in my wrist. Whether that's due to his touch or his growing familiarity, I'm not sure.

"Is that so?"

I eye the book in Jasper's grasp. He's tasked with writing letters for the whole student body year-round yet has time to leisure read. Or P.M. is worth shoving aside his schedule for.

This is my last chance to figure out what writing pleases Jasper by tomorrow, but I need to be careful with my questions. I'd rather read P.M.'s words for the rest of my life than for Jasper to find out I'm struggling. "Why are you obsessed with that guy's writing?"

His face slackens. "You know Pierre-Marie Laframboise's work?"

"No, but Xavier told me he was our year's Excellence Scholar before me, and I've noticed you constantly reading—"

"Of course you know P.M.'s work!" He flings the book across his quilt, and the pages crumple when they hit the bedpost. He falls back and stares at his poster on the ceiling. "Who doesn't know him? That repulsive strawberry shortcake. Oh, Jasper, even your student adores your rival."

Rival. Even though Xavier barely shared what Jasper and P.M.'s dynamic was when they attended Valentine and wrote for STRIP together, I would have never guessed it'd be this. "Is he a better poet than you?"

"Worse. He gets more modeling gigs than me."

"That's it?"

Jasper scoffs so aggressively that spittle flies from his mouth. "*He's* known as the Prince of Passion in the poetry scene. Him! How can that be when I'm lying here? And as of this month, that strawberry shortcake has sold twenty-seven thousand three hundred sixty-two more copies of his pompous poetry collection than I have. At least, according to reporting sources."

"If you don't like him, why are you reading his work?"

"Because I wish to understand why people like him more!"

I blink. "Did you admit to someone being better than you?"

"I—" Jasper's lips purse, considering the question too. "No."

"Weren't you the one telling me there will always be someone better than you? *Such is the circle of artiste life?*"

"Yes, but that doesn't mean I have to be happy about it."

A laugh bubbles out of me.

Jasper sits up to get a better look at me, his wispy hair scattering across his constantly rosy cheeks—which apparently flash redder when he's worked up like this. "You—" His gaze drifts to my lips. No, my laugh.

He can't be. He didn't.

My heart pounds through me. "What?"

"Your laugh is . . ." His surprise turns into a glare. "Wait, now—what's funny about my suffering?"

He couldn't have recognized me. That was in my head.

"Nothing," I quickly say, shoving aside my nerves. Even Jasper Grimes, Rank One and famous social media poet, has someone he can't beat. I still have no hints about what writing he prefers, but this discovery was worth it. "I just never expected you to be so fussy about this."

"I'm not *fussy*."

"You are."

"I'm reading." Snatching another book on his bedside table—*Sense and Sensibility*—Jasper burrows into his blankets. He flicks on his reading lamp, filling the room with its buzzing, and rolls to face the wall.

I look toward my desk, where my love letters wait for me to stay up all night and finish them. If not that, homework. Always. But my exhaustion weighs down my eyelids, and Jasper is quiet now. A rarity. Instead, I walk up to our bookcase, pick up *Kafka on the Shore*, and crawl into bed to do the same.

As the minutes tick by, a familiar calm settles over me. One I felt whenever I hid in the aisles of Mom's Bibliobibuli Bookstore to read. I haven't experienced it since coming to Valentine. It's nice, sharing that communal silence with somebody else.

Well, *almost* silence.

"Can't you turn that thing off?" I ask him, pointing at the lamp on his bedside table.

Jasper follows the direction with his eyes. "How else will I read? By candlelight? That could hurt my eyes."

I don't know what else I expected.

I sigh and go back to my book.

Jasper stays silent too. A little too silent. Like he still really is hurt.

"P.M. couldn't handle Valentine like you can, right?" I say to him slowly. The reminder of someone so successful failing to achieve what I need to dampens my own mood, but I keep my voice level. "You're always ranked top five. You both have strengths."

Jasper huffs, his back still turned.

"And even though I haven't read your writing," I add, "I would guess it's better. I'd prefer not to understand a word of that guy's *cravings for champagne* or whatever."

"Thank you," he mumbles.

"Good night, Jasper."

"Good night, Charlie."

We stay awake together for hours, him reading and me eventually working on some love letters, filling my notebook with scribbles and crossed-out lines. Between us, Jasper's lamp buzzes until it starts to feel soft, almost comforting somehow, and lulls me into a dreamless sleep.

Chapter 17
CONFESSIONS
WEDNESDAY, SEPTEMBER 25

DELILAH!

I'M RANK 28! Just fifty-one days left to turn that into a five, but who's counting?

I told Mom. And guess what? She never sent my single room fee. She encouraged me to keep my head down, yet she's the reason why I'm stuck in a double now—the one thing that could ruin this for us both?

I hope you're okay. And that your roommate isn't walking in on you naked. Mine did. Today. But he bought us a bookcase? No matter what, though, he gives me hives. I'll get away from him soon. At least, I'm trying.

Also, I've made some acquaintances at STRIP, I guess. Don't tell my mom.

Are you getting these, by the way?

Charlie

Chapter 18
A RED, RED ROSE
THURSDAY, SEPTEMBER 26

> Roses are red
> Violets are blue
> You make me
> Say yahoo

I scribble out my hundredth love letter attempt, then return to fiddling with the STRIP Time sign on my library desk. Even if I had a million days to finish these nineteen prompts, I'd fail. I'm running on four hours of sleep and a two-day-old breadstick from Dix. Either way, an Excellence Scholar can't write about something as illogical as romance.

But they're due any moment now, once Jasper wraps up his Thursday one-on-ones with his patrons. There must be an excuse I can give so that Jasper doesn't revoke our deal. If Luis still had his cat, it could've eaten my homework.

"*Greetings, student!*" Jasper practically sings so loudly behind me, it echoes through the dead-silent library.

I jump, my hand knocking over three pawns on the chessboard. My eyes whip to the librarian, who must be armed and ready to shush us. She keeps tapping at her computer like it's none of her business. Yet another principal's nephew power.

"Today marks two weeks of your love tutoring," Jasper says, claiming a chair across from mine. He wears his *love tutoring* tortoiseshell glasses again, which I doubt have a real prescription. Maybe an old modeling shoot relic.

They do make him look good. The round frames are juxtaposed with the sharper angles of his face, and the color matches his eyebrows, which are several shades darker than his blond hair. Was his brow line always that pronounced?

"Charlie?"

"Hm?"

"I said, let me review your homework assignment."

"Right—" I push my real glasses up my nose, buying myself time to concoct a lie. "I sort of lost my love letters."

"How does one *sort of* lose nineteen letters?"

Yeah, how, Charlie? "A cat. Ripped them up."

"A cat?"

"Came out of the woods. I tried... fighting it, but it was too late."

A corner of Jasper's lip curls. His slender fingers fix the chess pieces I knocked over, one by one, his bracelet jangling against the board. "Cats don't casually set up shop in the woods, von Hevringprinz. Au Sable Forks is known to have coyotes, though."

Unspoken Guideline 12: Valentine has coyotes. Do not go in the woods.

"Oh," I say.

"Does *oh* mean you're locking in *I was attacked by coyotes* as your final answer?"

"Yes?"

Jasper points a white pawn at my very intact composition notebook.

My heart pounds harder. "I'd already ripped out the letters, so that's why my notebook is still—"

He grabs my notebook off the desk. I attempt to snatch it, but

Jasper bends too far away to reach. Holding the packet over his head, he inspects my pitiful scribbles. "What's this, then?"

"Not finished," I rush to say. A famous poet can't read that.

"Art is never truly finished." Jasper clears his throat. "*Roses are red. Violets are blue. You make me. Say yahoo.*"

A textbook page flips at a nearby desk. A cough echoes through the library.

Jasper casts aside the packet, knocking down the chess pieces he just fixed. "Might I ask why you're set on this *roses are red* pattern?"

If Jasper thought I was *special*, he doesn't anymore.

I play with the lamp pull chain beside us in a catatonic state of humiliation. "I don't know where else to start."

"Are you afraid?"

"Of what?"

"*Roses are red, violets are blue* is a cliché. Writers are told to never use them. Do you know why that is, student?"

During that poetry workshop I was forced to take with Jasper, guest speakers hammered this rule into our heads. "The more we repeat certain phrases, the more they lose emotional impact over time."

Intrigue flickers across Jasper's gaze like he's impressed. I can't deny the rush of how good that feels. "Correct. Sometimes, clichés stop a *reader* from experiencing emotions. Other times, it can also be the writer."

He wants me to write about my emotions again.

I pick at a hangnail and scowl, feigning ignorance. "I don't understand."

"You're holding yourself back from expressing your true feelings about romance. You can't write love letters if you are."

My pencil case. Now's a good time to clean it. I pick out a few pencils with dud erasers. "My *true feeling* is that I don't believe in romance."

"How come?"

I can feel Jasper's blue eyes focused on me like no one else exists. The same look that drew me in years ago. I shrug.

"You've had romantic experiences before?"

A pencil slips out of my hands. "Uh—I—"

"Why else would you feel this strongly about your lack of belief?"

My brain screams to shield my face with a textbook, to drape more hair over my eyes, to run back to Queens. If I lie to Jasper, he'll keep pestering me. If I tell the truth, his memory could be jogged.

I have to be careful here.

Shoving aside the pencil case, I study him equally hard. "If by romantic experience, you mean getting screwed over and left behind, sure. But, in a way, I'm thankful. I learned earlier rather than later in life that your version of romance doesn't exist."

Speaking these words makes the past I've tried so hard to forget rush to the surface, feel all the more real, and my chest twists tight. I never thought I'd have to admit this aloud someday, let alone to the person who caused the damage.

Jasper frowns. "Forget that person. They're long gone now."

I press my lips tightly together.

The next thing I know, Jasper reaches over the table to squeeze my cheeks together and smushes my lips into a fish face.

The courage I summoned prior zips out of my body. He's so close, I can smell mint gum on his breath. "*Whuat auh youh doang?*" He's *touching* me. My *face*.

"Look at me."

"*I auhm?*"

"Tell me you love me."

"Whuat?!"

Jasper finally lets go. Coughing erupts out of me like I'm a broken dam. If the librarian is finally shushing us, I can't hear at all.

"EROS Four. Craft for yourself—not your audience—for true connection," he recites over my choking. "But you've closed off your emotions about romance because you're scared. We must fix that."

My face burns as hot as lava. No, lava only reaches 1200 Celsius. I'm a bajillion-zillion. "N-no thanks."

"Then you may end our deal. No more room to yourself."

What if I strangled him? Then what?

Any feelings I once felt toward Jasper are history. Logically, saying I love him should be painless. But this is about pride, and I'd prefer to retain some after my time at Valentine so far. There must be a way to imagine Jasper is something—anything—else I love. What do I love?

Books. *Othello*. I'll pretend he's Shakespeare. I'm praising his work as a playwright.

Straightening in my chair, I fold my hands on my lap. "I..."

Jasper's lopsided dimple pops. He's *enjoying* this.

I hate you. I hate you.

I ball my hands into fists on my lap. I can do this. "I...I...love..."

"V.H.!"

Luis and two others, holding calculus textbooks. The three increase in size like phone service bars beside us, Luis standing at the shortest rung.

"H-hey ther—!" My voice spikes to a wonky pitch. What is *wrong* with me?

Luis claims the untaken seat by me. "Sorry I'm late. Had detention today."

"What? What'd you do?"

"Wore a T-shirt under my gift shop costume and forgot to put my dress shirt back on after. Residential retainers swarmed me like I was a bomb."

The guidelines sniping down someone so close to me shakes me. When the main person I talk to lately is Jasper, who doesn't need to follow them, how cutthroat they get over even little things was starting to slip my mind. "That sucks."

"Is it cool that I brought Emilio and Michael for STRIP?" Luis says. "I'm the only one who got a perfect score on last week's calc homework because of you."

Because of *me*.

A grin spreads along my face. "Congrats."

Jasper is too busy scrutinizing Luis up and down to offer a hello. His kindness must only extend to patrons who worship his every word. He points his journal's spine at an empty desk one row over and stands. "I'll wait there until we can finish our lesson."

I follow Jasper's journey to the next row with my eyes until Emilio and Michael distract me by talking among themselves.

"You good?" Luis whispers closer to my ear.

"Why wouldn't I be?" I say.

"Whenever you're around Jasper Grimes, you look a little anxious."

"He just gets on my nerves."

"I heard he's your roommate."

Does that mean people talk about us? What could they even be saying? "Unfortunately. What have you heard?"

"You haven't heard everything going around about you two?"

Brilliant. "No."

"It's breaking news that Jasper's living with someone. Last

year, he had the suite on the top floor that that one first year, Frank, has now. That's brought in speculation on who *you* are."

Nerves prickle in my chest. More spotlights. "I'm nobody, I swear."

"People are crafting all sorts of conspiracy theories. One's that you're a famous poet, too, especially since you replaced P.M. as our year's Scholar. Plus, your class schedules are mostly the same, right? From the outside, it looks like strings could've been pulled so you two stick together."

"Nope," I say, dead inside. "Just unlucky."

Luis shakes his head almost incredulously. "Why *is* the principal's nephew in a double?"

"There was a mix-up, apparently."

"Jasper didn't complain?"

"He thought having a roommate would be"—I toss up air quotes and frown—"fun."

"In what universe? Mine won't stop freaking out about spiders." Luis tugs on a curl so violently that I'm shocked it doesn't rip off.

"Yeah, I don't know. Jasper at least gave us *secret roommate knocks* yesterday, so maybe he'll stop barging through the door."

"I guess that's less obvious than a sock on the knob." Luis eyes me up and down. "He's not causing you serious problems, though, is he? He makes you work a lot for STRIP. You look, well, miserable."

Jasper *is* causing me problems, but not in the way Luis is likely imagining. Even if Luis did flag me as someone who would be interested in sending love letters on our side of campus, there's no way he'd guess Jasper's and my complicated history. I trust Luis the most here, but it's not like I'd tell him everything.

"Is he, V.H.?"

"No," I say quickly. "It's fine. I promise."

Michael waves to snag our attention. Similar to Luis, his good looks seem frustratingly natural, as if he just wakes up like this. But where Luis is all soft and smooth lines, his sleek crew cut and pointed face make him sharper in comparison. "Ready?"

Instead of answering, Luis laughs as if Michael told a joke deserving of a platinum medal.

This must be his not-so-hypothetical crush.

Holding back a grin, I walk the three through their inverse function questions. While we solve the first equation, my gaze drifts past Luis's shoulder, toward Jasper's desk. He's focused on the love letters in his journal like always. Never a textbook. Yet he has impossibly high grades for a second year. A perfect hundred.

How?

I inspect how his hand moves at a steady pace. Two years ago, he scribbled so fast that the ink would smear worse than nowadays. His thigh doesn't distractedly shake beneath the desk anymore. I'd have to clutch his knee during workshop to make him stop.

Jasper is different now. But he isn't different at all.

Luis passes me a sheet of paper. His completed equation. "Can you check this?"

I glance down at my barely finished one. *Focus, Charlie.* "Yeah."

Soon, the three are off with quick thanks.

Jasper returns to my desk. Instead of sitting across from me like last time, he claims Luis's chair, which is still pulled out. "Where were we?" he asks, assertively tossing down his journal.

I stay quiet, not particularly wanting him to remember, and glance around the library. After hearing how the student body is obsessed with us two, I feel invisible eyes on my back despite the vacant desks around us.

"Right," Jasper says. "My fourth EROS. Tell me you love me."

"Listen, I really don't want to keep saying that I lo—"

"You don't have to say that you love *me*. Just say *I love you*. To the wall. The desk. I only want to make you feel that vulnerability."

I grimace.

"I won't watch." As Jasper goes back to his journal, I pick out more changes in him. Unfortunately, he's always had a nice face to look at, but his jaw is sharper, and his brows really are bolder. The dress shirts he rolls to his elbows look eons better than our hideous camp uniforms—dweeby polo shirts, navy shorts, name tag lanyards, and socks rolled up to the knees.

But one thing about him might not have changed.

"I promised I wouldn't watch you," Jasper says, peeking up at me through the hair draped over his face, "yet now you're watching me."

I flick my gaze away, covering my lips with a propped hand. "I have a question."

"You're muffled."

"I have a question," I repeat louder. "Where do you keep going?"

"Can you please be more specific?"

"You're always late for lights-out. Are you using that special number pin on your collar to sneak into the sister academy at night and stuff?"

"I'm writing letters in my office."

"That's all?"

Jasper shrugs. A nonanswer.

I tilt my head at him. Jasper is obsessed with romance, yet I know the truth that he's secretly a heartbreaker. He should have at least five girlfriends.

"We non-tutors don't have any ulterior motives of hitting on sister students, if that's what you're implying," Jasper adds.

"So, you really only joined STRIP and stayed because of P.M.?"

Jasper's fountain pen goes still in his hand. "Excuse me?"

"Xavier mentioned it."

At first, his mouth only wobbles, yet he's usually such an open book that I'm trying to slam the cover shut. "I suppose I did enjoy his approach to STRIP's letters, and we learned from each other until he abandoned us. And I have always taken up any opportunity that allows me to write and improve my craft, so I've stayed. Does that answer please you?"

I peer at him. "What happened with you two?"

The moment my curiosity lets the question slip out of my mouth, regret hits hard. Asking about Jasper's life is the last thing I should do when a wall as towering as the cockblockade needs to stay between us. I shouldn't even *want* to know. I *don't*.

But it's too late. Jasper is already huffing so hard that his blond hair flutters around his face as he considers his response. "What is there to say? One day, he was STRIP's crux. The next, he was gone. He never warned us. Sure he's having a blast now, writing of his visits to France with his mother or the Philippines with his father. To leave us behind, though? A career can wait. I wish to make Valentine count."

The theory makes sense, but it doesn't align with how Xavier reacted when I asked; he *had* talked to P.M. before he left.

Still, a weight that hasn't left my chest in weeks lifts. The previous Excellence Scholar didn't necessarily fail. "So, when you joined STRIP, you weren't like Xavier."

Jasper frustratedly sets down his pen. "Von Hevringprinz, no,

I did not have a girlfriend like Xavier. I *have* not. Where are those *I love you*s?"

He's lying. He has to be.

"Not happening," I snap back.

Only once Jasper glances at the other tables do I realize how loudly I spoke and how many distant stares are finding us. Immediately, Luis's claim about the spreading rumors filters into my mind. How many times have I scolded Jasper in public like this before without realizing so many eyes were around? Maybe those rumors are partially my fault.

They aren't the only ones giving me looks. Jasper is, too, now. Although it's a much more intense one, almost probing, like he's recalling how many *not happening*s I also gave him back when we sat on the lakeside years ago and he insistently asked me to recite my poetry workshop assignments. The fact that I keep forgetting to watch how I talk to Jasper makes my heart rate spike higher than it has all day. He's getting too *familiar*.

No. I'm getting too *comfortable*.

We need to finish this deal. Quick.

"Then I hereby allow you a two-week extension for your nineteen letters," Jasper finally says. "One week to write, and one for you to discover how to stop being scared."

"I'm not *scared*." I try to say it quietly this time, but I'm barely successful.

Because if I can't even write a roses-are-red poem, how can I possibly follow his rules of seduction to get our room to myself? I flip through my notebook and stop at Jasper's third EROS.

Love does not have to make sense; neither do your words.

Maybe I can't do this alone, but there might be someone who can help.

Chapter 19
THE ART OF WAR
FRIDAY, SEPTEMBER 27

Outside of class and weekly STRIP deliveries to and from both campuses, Blaze A. Destroyer frequents the Dixon Writing Gazebo by Au Sable Forks Lake, and no one knows why. That's what Xavier claims when he invites me to sit with him during dinner and I ask where I can most easily hunt down Blaze.

According to Jasper, P.M. Laframboise sells thousands of copies despite barely anyone understanding what he means, let alone how he feels. Why can't I cover up my lack of feelings toward romance the same way? If anything can help me, it's Blaze's bizarre yet admittedly extravagant language skills.

But when I walk the path up to the Dixon Writing Gazebo, the place seems abandoned. The empty trellis gazebo is simply surrounded by diamond topiaries, the sounds of nighttime insects in the woods, and the setting sun reflected along the water.

The same lakeside where Jasper and I kissed.

A pang strikes my heart. We never sat on this side. Workshops were on the sister campus. But the air carries the same earthy undertones, and the waves roll over the same sand mostly made up of gravel. Jasper always whined that sitting on it was like getting a hot stone massage.

Then those three girls came to me on the last day of camp, and they showed me the letters he'd been sending them the whole time.

Forcing myself to shake the memory away, I step through the

gazebo entry entwined with vines. First Dixon Dining Hall, and now Dixon Gazebo, fit for a prince.

Unspoken Guideline 13: Be nice to Bingo A. Dixon when I finally meet him. Whoever his family is, they have a long history here—and a rich-as-hell one.

Rustling erupts behind me. I whip my head around, but the topiaries are motionless. No classmates on the shore.

"Hello?" I call out.

No response.

I warily approach the bushes.

A blur of reds and blacks torpedoes out of one, and I screech as I'm tackled onto the gazebo floorboards. A figure pins down my wrists and digs his knees into my thighs to keep me in place. His black-dyed hair is so floppy that I barely make out his childlike face, but the blazer tied around his neck like a cape is a dead giveaway.

"Blaze?" I mumble.

"Usurper! How dare thou speak my unceremonious title. Your lowly rank shall denote me as Chief Magistrate of the Brotherhood of Ancestral Darkness."

"Can I at least ask why you pounced me?"

"My ancestral ring forewarned me of your attendance." Blaze releases my hands to do his familiar, fluttering butterfly pose, showing off the ruby varsity ring that matches mine. The only difference between ours is how Blaze wears it on his thumb. His fingers must be too small.

"What are you doing?" I ask.

"'Tis the flames burning alongside the blood in my ring. Thus, I am cognizant of bloodlust from up to seventy kilometers."

So, not a butterfly. Flames. "I just wanted to ask you a question."

Blaze pulls out a slingshot and marble from his slacks pocket and aims the marble at my face. "Wherefore shall I, Blaze Alpha Destroyer (of Worlds), heed your qualms?"

This isn't working.

With the other twelve-year-olds I tutored in Queens, talking to them like an equal was key. Maybe the only way to speak with someone like him is to match him. "I desire your aid. I...must write to...womenfolk."

"Women—?" Blaze suddenly lets out a half cry, half bleat, and jumps off my body so speedily that his bangs scatter, revealing a pudgy face that could only belong to someone as young as him. His slingshot and marble clink to the floorboards. He points at my left hand—my varsity ring. "A Ring of Ancestral Darkness has passed down through your lineage too?"

"This isn't—" I stop. "Indeed. It was my mom's. Your family went here?"

"My kin gifted this gazebo. And the dining quarters."

"Wait, Dixon is your family?"

His eyes blow out. "No."

"You're Bingo A. Dixon. Our second year's Rank Three. Luis's roommate."

"I'm Blaze A. Destroyer (of Worlds)."

"Right," I say slowly. This whole time, I assumed he was a first year. He skipped even more grades than I thought.

Blaze sighs. "I have been detached from the Brotherhood for epochs, comrade. I do not even wish to be here. No one comprehends me. STRIP tries. After all, I did join those valiant warriors upon my arrival straightaway, for I was moved by their battle against Valentine's law. However, I fear they still fail to comprehend my own war against the arachnids."

It reveals more than Blaze says with his whirlwind of words. Like me, he seems to feel alone here. STRIP may even be a way for him to belong despite still being a kid. If that's the case, then for once, I can actually sympathize with someone wanting to join this ridiculous program. "You never wanted to go to school here?"

"I was never bestowed a choice. In Father's eyes, an education such as Valentine's is compulsory for Wall Street."

Wall Street. I suppose Blaze is Rank Three. "I get that. Kind of."

"You too are fighting for an occupation?"

I like tutoring. And I like books like Mom. But when Mom chased books, she tripped and came crashing down, even though I worked alongside her in the store when I could. Of course, without her asking. Mom would never ask for help.

"Maybe something smart?" I say, trying to think of a path as impressive as Robby's MIT or as lucrative as Blaze's Wall Street. But all I can think to say is, "Um. Math?"

I expect Blaze to laugh at me, but he just helps me to my feet. The moment my weight hits him, he falls back on top of me. Groaning, I rise up on my palms. Blaze's cape blazer is flipped over his head, spilling across my chest along with his seaweed hair.

He rolls off my body, then taps his ring against my own. "I will contribute to any mission under your command, comrade. But perhaps from here on the floor."

"Then, if you were to confess your feelings to someone, how would you say it?"

He considers before dramatically clearing his throat. "*Whilst lunation echoes along the lakefront, I contemplate your light. My moon, my moon, never wane from my sight.*"

Jesus. "Why don't you help with the letters again?"

"I am midmost fighting a war. Warriors have no time." Blaze grabs his slingshot and aims for the shore. "The day that the arachnids come from the west is nigh. I must keep watch here."

I grab my notebook off the bench and open to my unfinished one-on-one prompts. "I've agreed to help write letters for STRIP for a bit." Even though Jasper told me not to tell the other members, I'm too desperate to care. "If you give me ideas for these, and don't tell Jasper about it, I'll help you on the predestined day. How does that sound?"

Blaze agrees with a nod quicker than I expected. The moment I pass him my notebook and pencil, his little hands take off. No wonder he skipped two grades. He may be a worthy challenger for Jasper. Rank Three would be.

Jealousy creeps into the back of my mind as a current Rank Twenty-Eight. "How long have you been frie—acquainted with—Jasper, by the way?"

"My first year here, we encountered one another."

A question burns within me—one that has for a while. "Has he ever, you know, courted womenfolk here with his own letters?"

Everyone at Valentine has known Jasper longer than I have, so they must have an answer. If I want to shape these love letters to Jasper's liking once Blaze's handiwork is done, then having as much information on his love life as possible will only be a plus.

That's the only reason why I ask.

Blaze laughs so hard that it comes out like a squeal. "Jasper refuses to court anyone."

I sit there a moment, floored. "Why?"

Blaze just shrugs.

It's as Jasper claimed yesterday. Is he really not breaking hearts anymore?

And how do I find out the truth?

Chapter 20
THE BOOK OF DISQUIET
SATURDAY, SEPTEMBER 28

Of course the weekend is when my body naturally wakes up before the bell tower's obnoxious little song. Which is for the better. Midterms are approaching too quickly for comfort, and I need to study. But it's the principle of the matter.

Shoving on my glasses, I roll over to face Jasper's side. He stands at his dresser with his hands on his hips, half clothed in slacks and an unbuttoned dress shirt with his number-one enamel pin on the collar. He's studying the fragrance collection—eau de parfum, as he calls it—along the top. As if there's a choice to make. He always goes for the one called TEARS that torpedoes fresh lilac and orange flower petals up my nostrils.

Jasper's head tilts. Like he senses me watching. He turns.

I slam my eyes shut before he can catch me.

What the hell. Why was I watching?

I need to keep my head down. I need to keep my head down. I repeat this to myself so I don't forget it again. The more I watch Jasper, the more I instigate interactions between us. The closer he gets, the more dangerous it is for me.

Like now, as Jasper's footsteps approach the foot of my bed. The room falls so silent that I hear my pulse thrum in my neck. He just noticed a crack in my wooden bedpost. He dropped his tie, and he's glaring at it with hatred since he'd rather die than wear one.

Or he noticed something familiar about me.

My body locks up, dread crashing through me so hard that I feel like I'm drowning in it. I failed. I'm going home. I didn't get my single room in time.

But then Jasper's footsteps drift away, and a door closes.

I open my eyes again, mentally kicking myself for getting caught staring. For ever looking his way, even once.

Light shines from underneath the bathroom door, and I can hear him brushing his teeth.

My adrenaline shoots my body right out of bed. I can't keep my head down anymore; I have to know if he knows. I storm up to the door and knock once, so hard it makes my knuckles throb.

Jasper opens the door, eyes wide. His toothbrush hangs loosely in his hand. Toothpaste is splattered across the mirror like I startled him into spitting it out.

I follow the dripping spit-paste with my eyes. "Can...I join you?"

Jasper's surprise flips to a smile, and he quickly shuffles over to make space like he fears I'll change my mind. The way he acts whenever I approach him first. Like nothing has changed between us. He wets his toothbrush again and resumes brushing.

Did he figure it out?

As I grab my toothbrush from our shared wall holder, I realize we've never gotten ready together. Jasper is usually out the door before I'm out of bed.

Jasper spits out his toothpaste, into the sink this time. "Did I wake you?"

"N-no," I say, directing my stare to the sink.

"I'm glad. I try not to."

Is this why I usually sleep through his routine? "Thanks."

"You usually aren't up this early." His voice is as melodic and articulated as usual.

Same as always.

"I have lots of studying to do," I mutter, feeling like the most brainless Excellence Scholar to ever enter Valentine. Of course Jasper wasn't examining my face while I was sleeping. He was staring out the window. Or something. Right? After how much Ms. White harped on the scientific method in chemistry last week, she'd be ashamed of how Jasper makes me jump to conclusions. "I gotta keep up my grades to stay here."

Jasper looks right at me. His morning-person joy has been wiped away by a frown. "Von Hevringprinz, you were selected out of thousands to be our Excellence Scholar. Please, never think of leaving."

❤ ❤

"Jasper's love life?" Xavier asks, voice strained. He's fighting for his life with a jammed lever on the side of a workout machine, since I finally recovered enough from the cardio he had me doing to graduate to weights.

"Yeah," I say, wiping my forehead. We've just started our first weight training session with stretches, and I've broken a sweat. Somehow, Pragma Recreational Center always magically smells like a bouquet, even though each body in here has to be as sticky as mine. Must be the work of Saint Valentine's spirit. "What's going on there?"

"How come you're super interested?"

"Not *super* interested." But Blaze couldn't give me a firm answer last night, and without this information I'll never be able to write the love letters to Jasper's satisfaction. Xavier seems to know him best among the student population, so he's my last shot. "I should know since he's my love tutor, you know? His credentials. A résumé."

"You seem interested." Xavier manages to shove the lever down a few rungs, and it echoes through the abandoned room. Whatever he's changing seems related to the weights. He must need to make adjustments because I'm weak.

"I'm not." But as I say it, even I hear how ridiculous and whiny it sounds. I was already insecure enough working out with Xavier, but now I'm asking about another guy's love life when we're supposed to be acting like manly men. "Forget it."

"You sure?"

"Yeah, we got belldumbs to lift."

"Dumbbells. We'll start slower than that." Xavier stands, grabbing a curved bar hovering above the machine's seat. I swear I see his bicep pulse through his tracksuit. "This is a lat pull-down bar. It simulates pull-up motions on an easier scale, especially if you can't lift your whole body mass yet. As you get stronger, I'll readjust the lever I was messing with. Word?"

My zero strength *was* the reason for the adjustments. "W-word."

Xavier pulls a stopwatch out of his track pants pocket. "First, let's see where you're at. Pull down that bar as many times as you can in one minute."

I sit on the seat. At least no other students are here to witness my inevitable humiliation.

Shifting into position, I place one hand on the bar. My new

tracksuit might be a size M instead of Xavier's XL, and this equipment might be ten times my weight, but I'm as tall as Jasper at five eight. He could probably pull this bar a lot of times. I can match him. "Ready."

"Charlie?" Xavier makes a face. "You gotta use both hands."

"Oh." I place my other hand on the bar.

He doesn't stop staring. "Have you done a pull-up before?"

Should I have? Is this something boys innately know how to do out of the womb? Am I so unteachable that Xavier will walk away?

"Not really," I admit.

Instead, Xavier laughs deeply, in a manly way I wish I could, filling up the room. "I'll teach you the correct form."

He walks up behind me and readjusts my grip.

My body tenses. He's close.

"Face your hands away from yourself," Xavier instructs, and I try to pay attention over the blood pumping in my ears. "Your grip should be slightly wider than your shoulders."

"Okay."

After a few more adjustments, Xavier steps back, and my shoulders finally relax.

He lifts his stopwatch. "Go!"

I flex my biceps. The bar lowers, and my forehead nearly taps the bar. But then my arms give out, and the bar slaps back into place. I grunt.

"Try again!"

I follow Xavier's instructions. The bar gets closer. Closer. *Closer.* I finally feel a tap.

"One! Make it two!"

One turns into two; two turns into three in a row.

"Time!"

My arms crash down, burning like they went through a paper shredder.

"Three," Xavier calls. "Not bad, but we can improve."

So, I performed worse than he expected. The failure knocks me hard. "Do you actually think my grade rank will get better by finals?"

"Why wouldn't it? I'm the best trainer in Au Sable Forks." He grins.

A smile breaks across my face too. For someone so kind, the fact that Xavier has stayed single since his breakup last year is an eighth world wonder.

Would he say anything if he found out what I'm hiding?

"Did you know Jasper has a poetry book?" Xavier asks suddenly.

"Huh?"

"You had questions about his love life? That may help. You've checked it out?"

I keep forgetting Jasper handed me a signed copy when we moved in earlier this month. "No. How'd that book even happen?"

"I think Jasper already had a decent following online when he came to Valentine, but then P.M. helped him blow up over last year's winter break. His book came out a bit after. Sucks that Jasper isn't doing any new writing for his followers while he's here."

"He's leaving things inactive? Can't he update during breaks, like you said?"

Xavier bends down to perform more witchcraft on the machine weights. "I think he's chosen this hiatus on purpose to focus on Valentine." He smirks. "I don't know if you know how famous Jasper is—he's, like, over-a-million-followers famous nowadays. Power of Rank One for you."

Jasper's full name next to a *100* on the ranking board flashes through my brain.

"How?!"

Xavier startles so much that his grip slips, and weights slam together. "How what?"

Did I say that out loud? "I just don't get why he's Rank One."

"Tell me about it. I study every second and barely stay Rank Four in my year, yet the guy barely does for a second."

"Not even that. He's at a hundred numerical class average. That means he's never gotten a single point off an assignment?"

"Oh, Jasper can take one more core class than the rest of us because he's gotten out of the PE requirement. Even though Valentine readjusts our classes out of a hundred, he's inflated over that. They just don't show it, or there'd be revolts."

"Wha—?" So much rage boils inside me that I can't see straight for a second. "How'd he get exempt?"

I'm not sure why I bother asking. I already know the answer.

"Principal's nephew powers," we say at the same time.

I try to ignore my jealousy over how easy his life is, but I barely can. "If his aunt weren't the principal, you think he'd still hit top five?"

"To be real? I think so. It's like he has a photographic memory. Instructors could be being lenient on his essays, I guess, but most scores come from our multiple-choice tests. His always come back perfect. Not much subjectivity there, man."

I huff. Jasper's book smarts *are* why I fell for him at camp.

"Anyway," Xavier says, "Jasper has a few copies of his book lying around his office in the crypt. Maybe you'd get the answers you're looking for."

Chapter 21
THE BOOK THIEF
FRIDAY, OCTOBER 11

By a few copies in his office, Xavier meant *thirty-eight* copies.

Only Saint Valentine knows how many copies of *Love Is a Broken Party Clown* are also on our Mr. Grimes and Mr. von Hevringprinz bookcase back in our room. Jasper claimed we would meet here after STRIP Time for him to grade my love letters, but he hasn't shown up yet, and that's left me studying the bindings designed as red-and-white-striped circus tents. At least, until a pang snakes down my leg. I wince, but Xavier insists that pain means training *is* working.

I hope that methodology applies to these love letters I nearly ripped my hair out over to finish with Blaze's help. These last two weeks, my combined STRIP hours, gym training, and midterms workload kept me grinding until the witching hour, so much so that my chemistry quiz slipped my mind. I had to skip lunch with Luis to panic cram. Thankfully, Mr. Stern waited until today to introduce our project on Benjamin Franklin's neighbor—a man who apparently invented blackout poetry with newspapers. If I'd been given more poetry on top of my love letters, I'd have jumped off the Dixon Writing Gazebo.

While I wait for Jasper, I could sneak a peek at *Love Is a Broken Party Clown*.

My original mission was to uncover his love life in order to craft letters he'd undoubtedly appreciate, but with this week's workload, I forgot to read his poetry like Xavier suggested a couple of weeks ago. Really, there's no reason to dig anymore, since I've already finished my letters.

Yet I still glance both ways and grip one of the spines. No footsteps. Just the unsettling silence of the crypt. I snatch the copy from the shelf, a few horse trading cards tucked underneath it falling onto the floor. The clown's beady eyes on the cover stare at me judgmentally, like it knows I'm sticking my nose into something I shouldn't.

"Listen, this will help me predict the grade I'm about to get from Jasper," I insist to the clown. The clown doesn't respond.

So I flip to the first page.

> 1.
> *love is a broken party clown*
> *who has forgotten his lines*
> *after a thousand performances*
> *who honks a horn*
> *and no sound comes*
> *speechless*
>
> 2.
> *round and round*
> *the carousel of love*
> *we go*
> *spinning, spinning*
> *never catching up*
> *always chasing*
> *you*

My brow spikes. This isn't a Jasper encyclopedia like Xavier promised. This is barely poetry. Just weirdly constructed sentences. Yet he sold thousands of copies. I suppose this is what Luis meant when he called Jasper's writing *basic*.

And, without a doubt, it sounds nothing like what I wrote.

"What are you reading so passionately over there?"

I spin around on my heel. Jasper grins at the front of his office, holding two Laney's Bean Shack cups and wearing his leather JFG bag. I didn't hear the bookcase door open.

"Nothing," I say, tucking the book behind my back. "What's the *F* for?"

"Excuse me?"

"On your bag. Your journal. The JFG initials."

"Are you asking a fun fact about moi? I never thought the day would come."

"I just see it on your stuff all the time."

"Really? You're not trying to distract me from that book tucked behind you?"

My cheeks burn. "I—No."

"Firstly, it's Ferdinand. Jasper Ferdinand Grimes."

I thought my last name was rough. "Okay."

"Secondly." Jasper closes the distance between us, handing me one of his coffees. "You didn't sleep much."

We may be roommates, but I didn't think he cared enough to notice. Maybe this is a perk of him thinking I'm special, like Xavier said.

A small smile creeps up my face. "Thank you, Jasper. That's really nice of you."

Jasper's eyes widen a hair, shifting around my own.

A simple thank-you couldn't have triggered his memory. No way. But why else would he be staring? I hurry to readjust my blazer collar higher up my face. "What's wrong?"

That seemingly knocks Jasper out of his stupor. "Nothing!" He quickly gestures at the book in my grasp. "Thirdly, what do you think of my work?"

My stomach crumples into a ball. I lift the cover, focusing on the crying clown instead the humiliation confetti cannoning through me. "It's fine, I guess."

"Is that a compliment or a critique?"

I try to think of a kinder word than *basic*. "It's . . . straightforward. Different than I expected. You always read P.M. Laframboise's stuff, which is too deep to understand."

Jasper scoffs and tosses his bag on the floor. A puff of dust rises into the air. He grabs the duster from the cleaning bucket and knocks away a nearby cobweb. "That strawberry shortcake doesn't understand a lick about poetry."

"Why do you keep calling him a strawberry?"

"Apologies, Laframboise is French for strawberry. I forgot you wouldn't understand, not knowing such a romantic language."

"Doesn't *la framboise* mean raspberry?"

Jasper whips out a thin leather pamphlet from his plaid slacks' pocket. A French-to-English dictionary. He flips through the middle section until his face twists.

I raise my brow at him.

He slaps the dictionary shut. "To me, *straightforward* is a compliment. I'm expressing my feelings in a way an audience can relate to. Is that not the point of art?"

"Is that not what P.M. does?"

"Well, his poetry takes more effort to understand. Yet his emotions are still so visceral on the page. That's much more difficult to pull off. I suppose that's why he sells more copies than me." Jasper glances away.

Xavier mentioned their fallout was best not to be touched, but witnessing Jasper feel so strongly about someone else throws me. Apparently, he has a heart, but only toward others on his level. My time with him at camp just wasn't deserving enough. Mr. Talented P.M. is, though.

Maybe this coffee doesn't mean as much as I thought.

Swallowing the lump in my throat, I slip the copy of *Love Is a Broken Party Clown* back into the other thirty-seven on the shelf. Is relatability over art what gathers a million followers? *Is* this relatable?

The bookcase door opens again. A short white boy slips through the crack. Our first patron from the one-on-ones.

"Welcome back, Eli!" Jasper announces. He takes off the blazer cast over his shoulder and spreads it along the floor by the tome table. Then he sits and fans out my redone letters. "Please take a seat with us."

"What's he doing here?" I ask, joining Jasper at the table.

"He's grading your letter."

My heart races. Jasper reading my writing about romance is embarrassing enough. But a stranger? "You're my teacher."

"And soon, Eli will be your patron. If you please me but not them, what is the point?"

Eli approaches the table, brow deeply furrowed. "Sorry, but I thought you said you'd be writing our letters, Jasper?"

"I am, I am, I am," Jasper says. I guess lies come in threes. He makes room for Eli, who sits nearby on his knees. "But Charlie is my student. Would you mind reading the letter he wrote for your distant love?"

Jasper passes Eli the first page. Eli grins, leaning over the notebook like he expects my words to make his wildest romantic dreams come true.

I stay calm by recalling the facts. If Eli were scoring with a rubric, he'd write an A+ in every square. I used Blaze's words as a template *and* Jasper's EROS. I run through them again.

Use different handwriting for every letter. Check. I used different styles while combining my ideas with Blaze's on a separate page.

Write in an environment that will never sway your feelings. Check. No matter where I choose to write, my feelings can't be swayed when I don't believe in romance.

Craft for yourself—not your audience—for true connection. Check. I crafted these letters to save my ass and remain in STRIP to keep my deal alive. Not help my audience.

Love does not have to make sense; neither do your words. Check. At least, I think. Maybe I didn't go the simplistic route like Jasper, but P.M. is difficult to understand too.

When I look at Eli again, his smile has dropped. "This is a prank, right?"

"What do you mean?" Jasper asks.

"This sort of sucks."

My heart snaps into two.

"I heard a rumor that Charlie is another famous poet like you, Jasper, but that's not true, is it?" Eli goes on. "I can't understand a word. Would she even know I'm asking her to the mixer?" He points toward the bottom of the notebook. "What does *wherefore* mean? Where?"

"Why," I mutter.

Jasper gestures at the bookcase door. "Once more, you have my word that your letter will be written by me. Don't worry. We appreciate your honesty."

Eli's smile barely returns, like he's not sure if that should be believed. A percentage of his trust has been lost. He leaves the crypt.

Jasper pulls his broken fountain pen out of his chest pocket and points the nib at my face. "Do you believe Eli's review is correct?"

"Of course not," I say, swatting away the pen. "Read it yourself. How does Eli not know what *wherefore* means? He's fourteen. Hasn't he read Shakespeare's collection by now?"

Jasper silences me with a dismissive wave. As he pulls my notebook closer and flips through my other letters, I regret my answer.

A sharp *rip* pulls me out of my thoughts.

Jasper, crossing out my first letter in red ink so aggressively that the paper tears.

It takes my body a moment longer to catch up to my brain, to realize something is very, very wrong. I rush over to his side of the table. "What are you doing?!"

"I'm not approving these letters."

"Why?"

"I don't feel any love in them. Eli didn't either." Jasper flips to the next page. He crosses out my second love letter. My third. My fourth.

I'm too stunned to stop him. "What about your third EROS? Love doesn't have to make sense, and neither do your words?"

Jasper lifts his pen so suddenly that I flinch. His hand plummets back down, stabbing the notebook with the same destruction as a knife, leaving behind a hole and splatters of red ink. All my hard work, destroyed. "Even if I lack understanding, I should still feel your feelings. I feel nothing."

Nothing. After weeks. If this were a class, I'd have an F. My first F.

Defeat rattles through me as I stare at the destroyed notebook. The chances of Jasper thinking I'm special now are, without a doubt, zero. Just when I started to think maybe he—anyone— thought different.

"What does this mean, then?" I ask, my chest sinking. But I already know. No more deal. No more single room to myself.

"You'll still practice with me."

He's not calling it off? "But the mixer is already a month away," I say, confused. "I needed to start writing real letters with you, like, yesterday."

"We have time."

"What time? Aren't you wasting *more* time trying to teach me than if you'd tackle the letters yourself?"

Jasper twirls his pen along his knuckles instead of answering. Not believing in me. Like Mom. Like Ms. Nallos. Like everyone at Valentine.

"Is my effort that invisible?" My voice rises enough to be heard beyond the bookcase door, but I don't care, my chest tightening too painfully over what Jasper must think of me. Or rather, what he doesn't think of me at all.

At least Jasper finally looks at me. His eyes are wide. With surprise or fear, I can't tell.

"Don't you care how much STRIP stops me from studying? How much my grades are tanking?" I slap my palms against the table as I rise to my feet. The coffee he bought me—what I foolishly thought proved Jasper cared about more than just himself—rattles and tips, leaking onto the floor. I can barely perceive it. Too many afternoons we spent together flash through my mind. Every moment Jasper willingly sat so close, looking me in the eye like I so undoubtedly existed. Too many times he chased after me around campus, inviting me to eat lunch with him in Dix or study after classes. "Do you realize how thoughtless you are toward everyone around you?"

"Charlie—?"

"You don't. Because even after I got accepted into Valentine, became an Excellence Scholar out of thousands, and studied every waking second, you're Rank One."

"Charlie."

"You never try. Yet you're loved. You have no clue"—I squeeze my fist to stay in control, to stop my anger from turning into what the pressure behind my eyes threatens to—"*no* clue what it's like to be alone."

Jasper stands, too, but I storm out before he can use his own words as a weapon and get my hopes up, like years ago, just to leave me crushed.

Chapter 22
THE INVISIBLE MAN
FRIDAY, OCTOBER 11

At least no one pounces at me from the bushes when I do homework in the Dixon Writing Gazebo this time. Probably because it's only an hour until lights-out. Or Blaze is on delivery duty tonight, tiptoeing around the equestrian center for all the couples whose sole survival relies on STRIP.

Staying out late isn't enticing to me, especially when the temperature in Au Sable Forks is so low that I need my winter coat and the academy hasn't turned on the heat lamps in this gazebo yet. But I want nothing to do with Jasper.

Unfortunately, he lives in my bedroom.

Instead, I flip through Mr. Stern's blackout poetry assignment. The subject material fails to distract from thoughts of Jasper, but it is due tomorrow. The packet is scanned pages taken from "The Adventure of Wisteria Lodge," a Sherlock Holmes short story.

I pick a marker out of my case and pop open the top. At least the words are already here, waiting for me to find the right answer. Unlike Jasper's poetry, there should be a correct one, just like a multiple-choice test.

Maybe I can handle this.

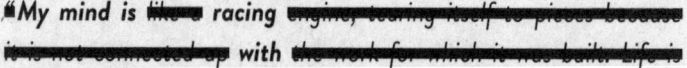

"My mind is ~~like a~~ racing ~~engine, tearing itself to pieces because it is not connected up~~ with ~~the work for which it was built. Life is~~

romance

whether I am ready

solemnly

pompous

But

"I have

Never in my life been in such a situation.

"May I ask you

be

date

I squint at the page. *My* date. There's no *my*.

Wait. Am I treating this like one of Jasper's love letters?

I smack my forehead with my notebook at the same time as laughter swells closer toward the cockblockade. An instructor leads four sister academy students through the gate, back toward their side. Each carries a cardboard box, and plastic cups stick out of one labeled MIXER. One of the students is familiar. Someone I've nearly forgotten to think about lately, being so entrenched in the never-ending unwanted surprises on this side of campus.

I jump up from the bench. "Delilah!"

The moment she flicks her head my way, a sense of relief I haven't felt in weeks washes over me. In the dark, I barely make out her reshuffling the box to wave back, and it's only then that I realize how much I don't expect her to. How much I wonder deep down, with her never responding to my letters, if I've done something wrong. All I can recall are memories of orientation when she briefly got annoyed, and how unresolved that feels now.

The instructor yells at her to stop waving, and the line continues through the gate.

Right. Because the academy won't even let me say hello. Seriously?

The two church bell towers chime in harmony. Ten minutes to lights-out.

Shoving my belongings into my bag, I head back to Philautia Residence Hall by myself, feeling even more isolated after seeing Delilah without getting to ask if she's receiving my letters. The air tickles my nose, the leaves of the woods rotting now with winter around the corner. Except for a few students exiting the library, the paths are deserted. For a moment, I get lost in that dream where I don't need a room to myself. Where I can make as many friends as Mom. Where I can live my days like any other boy here and not feel so on my own.

But once I'm in front of Room 503, reality comes roaring back. Time to face Jasper after leaving him behind for the second time in our lives. At least, to him, it's only the first.

I take a deep breath and knock once. *Grimes.*

"Come in," his voice calls.

I do cautiously. My eyes split open wide.

Jasper stands at the center of the Valentine crest rug, clutching a bottle of champagne against his stomach. His red dress shirt is tucked into his plaid slacks, and his blazer is buttoned, hugging his waist and shoulders in the right places. What's rarer is his blond hair left down, falling to his shoulders. He never even sleeps with his hair down.

He somehow looks even more attractive this way.

The thought knocks me back like a punch. I slam the door shut. So what if he's *objectively* attractive? He's not *subjectively* to me. "What are you doing with a *beverage*? Get rid of that!"

Jasper twists the champagne cork. It pops and soars. Foam trickles down his hand.

"What did I literally just say?" I shout.

"You can't even offer me a *honey, I'm home* first?"

"We're minors. We can't have that on campus. Where did you—?"

"It's sparkling apple juice."

"You—Oh."

"Yes," Jasper says. "Will you allow me to speak now?"

Pushing my glasses farther up my nose, I huff and scan Jasper's feet, surrounded by flower petals and cinnamon candles shaped in a heart. My notebook that I left in his office is nearby. So is a stack of pens and pencils. "Are you setting our room on fire?"

"I'm setting the mood for romance."

My heartbeat splutters. I try to stay very still and normal. "For me?"

The light of Jasper's buzzing bedside lamp suddenly hits his face at an angle that turns his cheeks rosier. Did he move? "For writing love letters together. Work! Non?"

"R-right." What else did I think? "Isn't a dull environment best?" I gesture at the pansy bouquet pattern on our walls. "I mean, even without the heart, we have that pink wallpaper."

"You mean *shabby chic* wallpaper?"

"It's baroque at most."

"If we're getting into specifics, it's French country," Jasper says, tossing a hand.

I frown. "Is there a point to this, Jasper?"

Jasper's mouth opens and closes before he hops over the fire hazard he's created, crushing petals in the process, and meets me at the door. "I have been thoughtless. You do have a lot of pressure on you. Thank you for being honest."

Now my whole body is what's on fire. Do I have a fever? Did I catch some illness from that freezing gazebo? "I yelled at you."

"You did."

"You're not mad at me?"

"It's an honor that you shared your feelings with me. You often don't with others."

"Oh." It's all I can say in the face of being read by somebody who shouldn't be able to. Who can't.

But it's true. While I have to monitor Mom's feelings over my grades, Delilah's over my own well-being, and every other students' here to ensure I've kept my head down enough, I never have to with Jasper. In a way, that part of being around him feels like freedom. Even if I'm simultaneously trapped in a room with him.

"However, you're misguided about one thing," Jasper says, playing with the bangs shaping his face. "People do not like me."

I'm not sure if I'm supposed to laugh. "Everyone loves you."

"My aunt is the principal. They have to. Isn't that why you've tried to tolerate me so for so long?"

My shoulders tense. "I. Well."

Jasper smiles, but it's bitter. "Same goes for the other top ranks. It's so sought after by everyone—rather, their parents, who practically threaten their own kids to kick us off."

I look toward the window and at the library beyond. "You help them with their love lives. They all thank you."

Jasper wanders to the windowsill. He grabs a chunk of the glass paperweight he shattered on the first day. "And some are friendly to get a date but would cheer if I got hit by a car. I'll never know who's who."

I stand there, unsure what to say.

"My advice," Jasper says when I don't respond, putting down the paperweight. "Whenever you do rank, do not trust anybody here either."

I'd already been telling myself that since I arrived. So why does my heart hurt so terribly, hearing the same from Jasper?

"Anyway, von Hevringprinz." Jasper closes the space between us and reaches toward me, only to pull back. His hand hangs awkwardly in the air like I shocked him. He's never had a problem with invading my personal space before.

"You good?"

"Y-yes," Jasper says, but on a strange trill. He tries again, taking my hand into his.

"What are you doing?" I ask with a waver in my voice.

Jasper guides me away from the doorway, deeper into the room, and I'm so thrown off that I let him. He sits in the candlelit heart, letting go, then pats the space beside him on the rug. As I sit, he pours me sparkling apple juice into a plastic cup stolen from Dix and hands it to me. "We're scrapping my EROS. What do you wish to write?"

"Me?"

"Whatever you'd like, write it now. No lesson. No rules. Five minutes."

"I don't know if this is better or worse."

Jasper leans his weight on a palm, his drink hovering by his lips. Waiting.

I aimlessly look around the room until I land on our bookcase. *Othello* catches my eye, then some classics, and then a box set of Sherlock Holmes. Getting back up and digging through my backpack by the door, I pull out my blackout poetry assignment.

"Care to share with the class?" Jasper says from the circle. The candlelight has his uniform glowing a brighter red than usual, and his lips even more.

I return beside him. "I was just—"

Jasper takes the packet out of my hand. "Let me see."

Nerves lurch up my throat as he reads. I pick at my nails as the minutes pass. Either he has the reading level of a first-grader as Rank One or he's analyzing the page multiple times.

Finally, Jasper lifts his head. He smiles as charmingly as the posters and cutouts on his walls, no matter how much I deny it.

"*May I ask you to be date?*"

"Couldn't find a *my*," I mumble.

"I see that."

"And the letters won't be personalized anymore if it's blackout poetry. But."

"I disagree." He twirls a finger toward our bookcase. "Inside any story over there, you'll find words that relate to our patrons' qualms. It's a compelling idea."

I squirm along the rug. "You can tell me if it's bad."

"Charlie. Blackout poems are some of the most difficult to craft. The fact that you got this close on your first try is"—he chuckles—"impressive. You're special, I hope you know."

Special.

Finally. The word comes from his lips.

People have told me that I'm special before. *A special student. A special candidate for our scholarship.* Yet my stomach won't stop flipping.

Why? Because an empty bedroom is closer in reach, knowing I might stand a chance at writing these letters?

But I wasn't even thinking about my room. This illness again?

No. This is something I've felt before.

Jasper clasps my forearm only briefly. I jolt. "Are you all right?"

"Yeah. Yeah, I'm fine." Except a phantom burn remains where he touched. This is a disease. The flu. I'm dying. I have to be.

This isn't anything else.

Jasper keeps studying my blackout poetry. "I once knew someone who had the same hesitations toward writing as you. Hated poetry, even."

The words suck out all the air from my lungs. I stare at him—at the way his voice is so distant and soft. Almost like he's remembering.

I force out a warbly laugh. "Really?"

"Really. You two had so little confidence, yet you eventually touched the stars."

I swipe the page out of his grasp and press it to my chest. "Well, thank you for being an incredible love tutor!"

That's when the regret hits. Because now Jasper's face is shifting, and the corners of his blue eyes are crinkling in a way I've never seen. I'm too terrified to move, to even scatter my bangs over my eyes or cover myself. Obviously, Rank One would assess this abnormal reaction. He remembered camp. Workshop. Our kiss. My first kiss.

It's over.

"Hey, Charlie." It's the first time Jasper has said only my first name, and I have no clue what that means, let alone what he's thinking that means. A fragile, almost pained look flashes across his face, but then he wipes it away with a head shake that comes off frustrated. With himself? "I think you're ready to help me with real love letters."

My body remains motionless, like if I shift a centimeter, he could still remember. "What comes next, then? There's only a little over a month left until the mixer."

"Correct." His voice is slightly more melodic now, back to his version of normal. "There are roughly eighty patrons left to be served. Take a third of those?" He points at our bookcase. "Rip out any pages from those books and use them."

"Once these letters are delivered, you'll still leave our room, right?"

Jasper hesitates. "I suppose that was our deal."

It *was* our deal. And it's more important than ever with how close Jasper keeps getting to the truth. Yet my heart illogically sinks at the thought.

I'm tired. That's why I'm dying.

Tomorrow, I won't feel a thing.

Chapter 23
AS I LAY DYING
SATURDAY, OCTOBER 12

Shakespeare once wrote "arise, fair sun, and kill the envious moon," but that is the worst ideology for a Saturday morning. I pull my blanket higher up my face to block out the light. The chatter coming from the Halo is too loud, and the scent of burnt leaves is too strong. The academy must take a blowtorch to every single sprig to keep up appearances for donors.

I have training with Xavier soon. I almost forgot.

Groaning, I tug off the blanket. The wall beside my bed isn't in front of my face where it should be. Same for the pillows. Instead, there's a sleeping Jasper.

I yelp and scramble to sit up. Not my bed. The rug is still littered with notebooks and burned tea-light candles, where I must've fallen asleep while writing letters. Ones that Jasper approved of, that made me feel so synced with him for once. I can't help but smile at how he lies on his side next to me, his blond hair frizzy and draped over a cheek. His blazer is wrinkled, barely on his body anymore.

I glance down at my fistful of blanket. No, sleeve. Jasper's sleeve.

Heat burns in the pit of my stomach and explodes into my head. I flick the sleeve away and touch my cheeks.

A fever. Definitely.

Health Services. Now.

◆ ▶

Welcome!
Health Services is closed on Saturdays!
In case of emergency, visit the checkout booth between
the two academies to contact our nurses in the off-campus
instructor quarters.

I throw up my hands. "THIS IS AN EMERGENCY."

"Charlie?"

Robby stands by the gift shop next door, not a wrinkle on his blazer or curl out of place above his drop fade. His number-two enamel pin is covered up by a plastic organizational binder against his chest, which I easily recognize since he always overfills it. Too many horse trading cards, maybe.

I hide my zipping panic by summoning a very calm, very normal smile. "Hi."

Robby inspects the Health Services door. "Are you ill?"

"Maybe. I'm supposed to meet up with Xavier, so I wanted to know if I'm contagious, but they're closed."

"You do look off," Robby says to me. "Do you suffer from anxiety stress? Sleeping problems? Dizziness? Any general worry over people, places, and things?"

He speaks almost like a real doctor, and one with an actually thoughtful bedside manner. When it comes to STRIP, Robby has always been the most professional and reliable. That must seep into every other part of his life too.

Jasper once mentioned that Robby wants to study biochemistry at MIT. Maybe he wants to become an MD.

I put my hands on Robby's shoulders, and he presses his binder tighter to his chest. "I just had a great idea. What if you did an appointment for me?"

"I-I'm not qualified."

"What about med school? Med school?" Did I just say that twice?

"I'm not planning to go to med school?"

"But you're on the biochem track."

"For veterinary school."

Right. The trading cards. "Because of the horses?"

Robby lights up. "I love all animals, but especially horses. They're friends. There aren't a lot of thoughts in their heads, but they're nice, and you can share snacks with them like carrots." His words quicken like I've asked what he's been waiting for someone—anyone—to. "And hay. And Fruit by the Foot."

I nod slowly, even though I felt like I was borderline tripping on cold medicine a moment ago. There's something about Robby's wholesomeness that washes a brief sense of calm over me. Maybe Robby is Rank Two because he's an MIT hopeful, but there's no doubt he must also be driven to hit the leaderboard for that unlimited equestrian center perk. "That's why you have so many cards?"

"Yeah." With careful movements, Robby opens his binder, revealing the many folders stuffed with his overflowing sparkly horse cards. "I've been a collector of Girth and Gallop trading cards since I was six. My parents couldn't afford to get me a real horse when I was growing up, but they had these for sale under the counter of the garden store my mom visited all the time, so I'd shove them in my pockets before I understood the concept of shoplifting. Half these cards derive from theft." He closes his eyes. "For shame."

It's a lot at once, but I'm still stuck on one part. "You couldn't afford a horse?"

"My family was sort of struggling until recently."

"Really?"

"Yeah, but my mom went back to school for years to become a nurse anesthetist, and then she started a fund to help me enroll in one of these academies. I'm really thankful for her."

"Wow," I say, stunned to relate to anyone else on campus in this way.

"And for STRIP, too, of course," Robby adds. "They let me talk about the Hackneys here all the time. For me, it's like a horse club. Plus friends."

In the distance, Blaze jogs toward us, the overcast sky behind him matching his ominous, destroying aura. His marker-stained dress shoes crunch against the path, and his backpack jostles against his back, the tip of a few letters sticking out.

"Cavalier Captain Robert, Charlie," he huffs as he approaches. The blazer tied around his neck flutters into his eyes, briefly revealing the number-three pin on his collar. He smacks the blazer away. "What a serendipitous coincidence to spot you yonder. I just now returned from the sister academy to acquire their correspondence."

"Charlie's ill," Robby tells him.

Blaze latches on to Robby's blazer sleeve. I can barely make out the alarmed look behind his seaweed bangs. "Charlie is a fellow warrior. He cannot fall ill. What if the fated day strikes?"

I'm still so desperate for an answer about my disease that I don't care about Robby's lack of professional doctor experience, let alone that I've been allowing him to see this much of me up close for several minutes. "You must know at least some medical basics, especially if you want to go into veterinary medicine. I bet you study this stuff in your free time for fun. You're second on our ranks."

Robby sighs, which means I'm right. He points beyond the five crisscrossing paths and marble fountain in the Halo, toward the outdoor picnic tables circling Dix. "Fine. Let's discuss there."

The three of us walk over, where another familiar face sits. Xavier, pounding down a bowl of rainbow marshmallow cereal with his lucky spoon.

Blaze shrieks and bolts over. He tosses himself over Xavier's shoulder, which is Blaze's whole width, and yanks out the spoon. "This lucky relic I bequeathed you is not for feasting. Only for warding off malevolence."

Xavier's mouth twists. "Can't it do both?"

Robby tosses his binder onto the tabletop. It's so heavy that Xavier's bowl of cereal leaps into the air. He sits beside Xavier. "Charlie needs help."

Xavier checks me up and down. "You do look whiter than usual."

"He's sick," Robby says.

I collapse on a seat across from them both. "I'm sick."

Blaze sits on my side of the picnic table, placing a tiny hand on my forehead. "Do you have a high temperature?"

More like a volcano in my brain. "Yes."

"Stomach pain?"

"Yes."

"Loss of appetite?"

I haven't considered eating since Jasper's sparkling apple juice last night. "Yes."

"I'll be blowed," Blaze mumbles, eyes spreading wide. "You have been poisoned."

"What?" Xavier and I say.

Blaze covers his face with his palms—as if his seaweed hair wasn't already doing enough of that—and whimpers like he's on the verge of tears. "By the arachnids."

"Oh," Xavier and I say.

Robby pulls lined paper and a pencil out of his binder and writes something down. "If you're overheating, then this may not be stress. When did your symptoms first show?"

"Last night," I answer.

"What were you doing?"

I hesitate, since Robby is the last remaining member who doesn't know the truth. "Writing love letters for STRIP."

His eyes go big, but he's quick to revert to a professional demeanor. "Where?"

"My room."

"You were alone?"

"I was with Jasper."

Blaze gasps beside me. "Jasper poisoned Charlie."

"No," Robby says without looking up. "Did you run into anyone else yesterday?"

I tilt my head. "I guess? We had classes. I ran into my friend at the sister academy from a distance. A group crossed over to plan for the mixer."

Robby's pencil abruptly stops moving. He neatly files the paper back into his binder. "This is an incurable sickness I've heard of many times in the STRIP Crypt."

My hope soars. "What is it?"

"Lovesickness."

The world slows to a stop.

I misheard him. "What did you say?"

"Praise the powers that be within the Ring of Ancestral

Darkness!" Blaze tugs on my blazer sleeve, shaking my whole body. "My comrade is no longer poisoned."

Robby grins. "Who from the sister academy caught your eye?"

"I—None of them," I squeak.

"Jasper can send a letter to her for you."

I try to answer. All that comes out is a wheeze.

A blurred Xavier clasps Robby's shoulder. I think. I can't see straight. "Give bro a break. He's so high on anxiety that shrooms wouldn't compete."

"Charlie would never take shrooms," Robby grumbles.

I shoot out of my seat and thrust a finger into Robby's face. "You're wrong."

Robby blinks in surprise. "You would?"

"No, I don't possibly have this disgusting disease you're talking about."

"You mean lovesickness—?"

I lean over the table to slap my palms against his mouth. "I said *no*."

"Say no all you'd like," Robby says, his voice stifled through my fingers. "Scientifically, the hormones involved in human attraction can't be turned off because you tell them to."

"If not one of the sister academy students," Blaze says beside me, "who else did you engage with yesterday?"

Only one.

Nausea devours me as I wander away. Voices call after me—something about where I'm going and if I've been hypnotized by arachnids—but I barely hear them.

I'm not sharing a room with Jasper for another second.

❤ ❤

"If you need Ms. Lyney, she won't be back until Monday," a middle-aged man in a red-and-black-plaid newsboy cap says from the office counter. Must be back-end weekend staff. The name tag on his blazer reads MR. ACOSTA on top and WE'RE LISTENING AND LEARNING. WE'RE VALENTINE! on the bottom.

Unspoken Guideline 14: Mr. Acosta wants me to slam my skull against the counter and split it in half, forever changing the trajectory of his life.

I stand there in defeat. The one day my body rejects itself, I need enough brainpower to explain my housing situation to another person in charge. The gnomes on the wall cackle and jiggle at my suffering.

"*Shut up*," I hiss at them.

Only when Mr. Acosta's buggy eyes bulge larger do I realize what I did. *Have* I taken shrooms?

"There was a mix-up with my residential hall room," I say. "I'm unsure if you could help me with this, but my roommate and I were supposed to have single rooms. There was a mix-up, so now we're in a double together."

"Oh, really?"

"Really." It leaves my lips desperately. Exasperatedly. I can't hold back any longer. "Ms. Lyney barely looked at my file before she dismissed it."

Mr. Acosta exhales like he doesn't get paid enough for this. But he does, according to the tuition I'll be demanded to pay if I don't reach the top five soon. "What's your name again?"

Optimism thrums inside me. "Charlie."

He types on the computer. "Last name?"

"Von Hevringprinz."

"German?"

"My name? Um. Yeah."

"Ah, your roommate is Principal Grimes's nephew," Mr. Acosta remarks.

Not *you're one of our Excellence Scholars.* Not *you're the transfer student.* I'm tied to Jasper with a rope. I need to burn it now. I'll do anything. Weep. Beg. Raise my voice at an authority figure for the first time in my life. "You know that?"

"It says so here. Strange. Mr. Grimes lived in Philautia's single suite last year. I believe I recall Nathalie—Principal Grimes—saying she converted her office space into a bedroom for him in the instructor quarters as well."

I stare back at him wildly. "She did what?"

This whole time, Jasper had another room. Of course the principal's nephew did. How did I never consider that?

Why didn't *Jasper*?

Fury burns in my chest. I clench a fist at my side, trying to hold it together. "Could Jasper move into his aunt's housing as a compromise, then?"

"I assume so. I'm surprised this was never suggested to you both as an option. Can you refresh my memory on what exactly Ms. Lyney told you?"

"Not much. My check was never sent in, so the academy randomly assigned me a room and roommate, and there's nothing else in my file?"

The longer Mr. Acosta's eyes scan the screen, the more his gaze narrows in confusion. "Not sure what Ms. Lyney saw, but there's indeed a file here."

"Wait, my check?"

"Not quite." He looks up. "According to our records, you and Jasper Grimes requested to be roommates."

Chapter 24
A MODEST PROPOSAL
SATURDAY, OCTOBER 12

I slam the door to Room 503 behind me with the force of a billion newtons.

Jasper shrieks where he sits on his bed and startles, tossing his book. The cover slaps the poster of him on the ceiling and then falls back to his lap. Yet another P.M. Laframboise collection. He's *this* obsessed with the guy? Come on. I bet even I can write better than that strawberry shortcake.

"What's gotten into you, Charlie," Jasper mumbles.

Gripping on to the baroque—French country—*whatever* wallpaper, I heave out breaths after marching up five flights, but not as many as I expect. Xavier's training is paying off. "I'm irritated. Wanna know why I'm irritated?"

"Why?" Jasper asks. His bedside lamp buzzes beside him, even though it's only afternoon, and the ambrosia design pattern of his quilt is spread smoothly over his legs. His hair is still left down and frizzy from last night. He looks sleepy. A bit cute.

What the FUCK, CHARLIE?

"You know how we were both supposed to have single rooms?" I say ten times shriller than I want to, thanks to my revolting thoughts.

Jasper nods, shoulders stiff.

"And we thought there was a mix-up?"

Another nod.

"There was more than a mix-up. There was a catastrophic, what-the-fuck, how-could-you-do-this mix-up."

"What was it?"

Tossing my workout bag, I make my way through our room, which Jasper must've cleaned. His optimal love-letter-writing environment has been wiped since last night. Thank Saint Valentine. "They insist we signed up to be roommates together. Isn't that ridiculous?"

"F-fascinating."

"How is this fascinating? Now we're stuck together because of some story they came up with out of nowhere."

"Yes." Jasper lifts a triumphant fist. "Lamentably so!"

"What's with you?"

"Nothing!"

"You're hiding something." Which reminds me. "Why didn't you tell me you have a private room in your aunt's instructor quarters? Why didn't you go there when I asked? No—on the *first* day of classes?"

Jasper makes an odd bleating noise. "Well. You see." He pauses.

"Seriously, Jasper?"

He just bites his lip.

I storm toward the bathroom. "Be that way."

"Wait—!" He hops off his bed and pulls my wrist back, spinning me around to face him. "Don't be upset with me."

I stare at our touching hands, my chest bursting with butterflies. Flu. Bubonic plague. "I'm not upset with you."

"I mean about what I'm preparing to say."

"Okay?"

"Over the summer, I may have helped my aunt with administrative stuff. And I may have noticed you requested a single despite your lack of a payment. Instead of flagging it, I roomed us together. Also, I synced our class schedules."

One million arrows to the heart.

Yet all I feel is numb. My body can't feel what my brain knows I should. I slip my hand out of Jasper's grasp. I step back. "Why did you do that?"

"Do you have any siblings? Cousins?"

"You're seriously trying to change the subject?"

"I'm not." He goes to his bed, pulls out a box beneath it, and lifts up a pocket-sized brown-leather notebook. It's different from his JFG one. I've never seen it.

"What is that?" I ask.

He returns, handing me the notebook. "I've been searching for someone I met a few years ago with your last name. It's a unique name, so I hoped you two were related."

I open the cover and flip through the pages. The daily entries date back to two years ago in smeared handwriting, starting from the June we met. I stop at the middle.

> round and round
> the carousel of love
> we go
> spinning, spinning
> never catching up
> always chasing
> you

Slowly, I look up at him. "These are from *Love Is a Broken Party Clown*."

"The first drafts. I'll be honest, these—" Jasper takes a sharp, almost nervous breath. "These are all about a long-lost love of mine."

He thinks I have a sibling.

Because he's looking for me. From two years ago.

More than that. I'm his *what*?

My body sways for the millionth time today. I shove the journal into his chest, gripping the doorframe instead to stabilize myself. "You trapped us in a room together, hoping I'd be able to connect you with some relative? Without knowing if I had one?"

Jasper's eyes flood with the same naivete I could only dream of having since he drained mine back at camp. "Does this mean you do? Please, will you tell me?"

Weeks of Jasper following me around. Weeks of him trying to get me to like him and steal my trust. Weeks of putting me through the stress of having a roommate. Of *him* being my roommate.

This fear. For *weeks*.

I've let him betray me again.

"I don't have any family like that," I spit out, my adrenaline spiking. It overtakes any and all logic that's been holding me back from letting out what itches on the tip of my tongue—what would make Jasper realize, once and for all, how he hurts me over and over while remaining untouched. "Because that person you're looking for is *me*."

Silence settles between us, the only sentence I promised to never speak at Valentine hanging in the air.

The synapses in Jasper's allegedly genius brain aren't getting there, his brow pinched. "What are you saying, Charlie?"

"Sorry that I'm so unrecognizable to you now compared to when we were at camp, but two years tends to change a person."

His face shifts. First, his eyes, racing as he searches my blazer, my slacks, and my now-sharper face. Then his mouth, which he covers with a trembling hand. He stares at the notebook in his grasp. "But—Wha—Hhh—?"

"Use your words," I grumble, crossing my arms. "You're supposed to be good at those."

"This is an academy for boys," Jasper says.

"Yes."

"So?"

"So, things change."

"Right." Jasper's gaze clouds as he looks toward the rug. "Things change."

"You said you were searching for your long-lost love," I say.

"I. Well." His face pales despite its usual constant pink glow.

My expression must look no better. If he believes I'm his long-lost love, then he's delusional. He spent that same summer writing love letters to *three* others.

"Why didn't you say who you were?" Jasper asks so quietly it's barely audible. "The whole time we've been in this room?"

Of course that's his first question. He could never understand. I pace the bedroom. "I don't know—why do you think I need a room to myself despite you messing that up for me?"

"You're a light sleeper?"

I groan. "Seriously, Jasper?! Are you really Rank One?"

Jasper winces. "You like privacy?"

"I *need* privacy. You know the academy's motto. It literally has *traditional* in it. You could tell someone. Your aunt. If you do, I could be—"

Jasper clutches my wrist, stopping me in place, his bracelet cold against my skin. "I won't do that."

AND THEY WERE ROOMMATES **179**

His typical showy self has vanished. All that remains is something so stern and sincere that it shocks me into silence.

I instinctively turn away, blocking my face, and find somewhere else to look. Anywhere else. The last time I trusted Jasper, I got burned, yet my shoulders are already lifting. Maybe I won't get kicked out. At least, not because of him.

It's an illogical thought. An impossible one. Especially when this news of him intentionally trapping us in a room contradicts our deal. Has Jasper been giving me this much homework in hopes I'd never finish and fail?

"Were you ever going to fulfill your end of the deal?" I ask him flatly. "Or did you plan to keep us trapped here together forever?"

Jasper hesitates.

I scoff.

"No, I always keep my word, Charlie, I swear. But I did admittedly want to buy a little time. If we were no longer going to be roommates, then I wanted you to see me as a friend first. But people kept getting in the way, like Luis Per—" He stops. "So we'd keep in touch about your famil—" He stops again. "*You.* I promise, I plan to get us separate rooms."

He's so desperate for me to believe him that he's tongue-tied.

Him. The famous poet.

"You never came to the beach like we promised," Jasper keeps going, gripping my dress shirt cuff tighter. My arm tenses. "On the last day of camp. Why?"

"Gee, let me think," I snap back, shooting daggers at his touch. "Maybe because I got busy with kayaking lessons. Or maybe because you pretended to care about me while chasing after three other people all summer."

Stuttering noises shoot out of his throat. "Who told you that?"

Another scoff rips out of me. Unbelievable. "Asking who told me isn't exactly what you should say in this situation."

"Right. You're right. You're right. I can explain—"

"You don't need to. On the last day of camp, those girls came up and showed me the letters you sent them." Recalling the memory surges more anger through me.

Jasper's brow furrows. "Love letters? I never sent any love letters."

He's *still* lying.

"Jasper, I saw them with my own eyes." I yank my wrist out of his grasp, and the fact that I didn't sooner has me kicking myself. Where is my *brain*?

"But I haven't even told you my side—"

"Stop talking, Jasper!"

Jasper Grimes falls silent for the first time in sixteen years. Everything about him shrinks despite his typical presence filling up a room with ease.

"You're moving into your aunt's quarters," I bark. "Today."

His eyes go wide. "But the mixer—"

"You think I care anymore? No more lessons. No more deal. We're done, Jasper."

Jasper's stunned gaze morphs into something emptier. He picks up his JFG bag, and his footsteps creak along the floor as he leaves.

Chapter 25
THE SECRET GARDEN
SUNDAY, OCTOBER 13

I need Delilah. An emergency contact phone call isn't enough. I need to see her, hug her—someone familiar after my fight with Jasper.

As I study in the library with Luis, I let him do the talking more than usual, even though I want to tell him all of this. But I can't. If I expose myself like I did last night, then the risk of everyone finding out grows.

Besides, I hardly have the energy. I couldn't sleep despite the silence of Jasper's absence now that he left for the instructor quarters. How could I after he revealed I used to be his *long-lost love?*

Jasper doesn't know what love is. His ego is just tied up over me never meeting him at the beach and getting away. That's all.

I barely make it to dinner hour. When Luis and I step out of the library, I spot Blaze across the Halo. The very tip of what I know to be rubber-banded letters poke out from his front backpack pocket.

An idea strikes me.

It's reckless. Nothing an Excellence Scholar should request. But I still give Luis a quick goodbye and rush over to tug on Blaze's blazer-cape. "Blaze."

His eyes light up beneath his seaweed bangs. "Comrade, what ho?"

"You're delivering letters, right? I want to come to talk to my friend. I've been sending her letters, but I don't think she's getting them."

His gaze drops to my lapel, void of a top five enamel pin.

"I'm an Excellence Scholar," I say before he questions how I'll get into the equestrian center. "And a new kid. Say I never got a tour and want to see what my perks will be once I rank."

Blaze's mouth twists. He's still hesitant. "I have never once failed at STRIP's deliveries finding their rightful recipient. Are you unwavering in this belief?"

"Yes," I say as levelly as I can, even though I want to drop to my knees. "Please."

I must fail at the whole "level" thing because Blaze's demeanor shifts to pity. He nods and leads me toward the cockblockade. Instead of approaching the usual gate, he makes a left and continues down until we reach a different side gate. Beyond it is a barnlike structure with white paneled walls and a Valentine-red roof. A second checkout booth rises before it, where a middle-aged employee sits.

By the time I catch up, Blaze is in the middle of saying, "He requests a viewing of the equestrian premises to preview his future ranking privileges—"

"Just go through, Blaze," the employee interrupts. He presses a button inside, and the gate opens, its hinges shrieking. "Both of you."

I blink, stunned.

Unspoken Guideline 15: Top five's rapport really does beat all guidelines.

The moment Blaze and I walk through the gate, we're standing in an enclosed white-picket paddock surrounded by well-kept pink-and-red flower beds, where eight brown horses that double my height meander. No employees or students.

"Where is everyone?" I ask.

"Stable hands unofficially depart prematurely on weekends," Blaze says, tapping numerically labeled buttons on a panel by the locked door. "We hold the code."

There's a click, and then Blaze twists the handle. I follow him through a hall of empty stall gates and bales of hay, then into a back storage room packed with multicolored treat buckets and enrichment toys shaped like fidget spinners. By the only exit door stands a girl with light-brown skin, wearing a plaid skirt and thigh-highs. She's digging through a tarp bag.

"London," Blaze whispers.

London turns around so rapidly that her straight, dark hair swishes into her face. The number-three pin on her dress shirt collar matches Blaze's. She reaches for Blaze's backpack, takes out the rubber-banded love letters, and shoves them into hers set on the ground. In return, she hands him a fresh stack from the sister academy students.

I silently watch the exchange. Even though this room is tucked away, I imagined way more secret-agent-level dexterity here. "Hey, do you know Delilah Miller?"

London doesn't look up from the backpack. "Kind of."

"Could you tell her to come around here? Now? She's not top five, but if she could just pass the sidewalk here or something, I can step out for a sec—"

"Is this for STRIP?"

"He can be trusted," Blaze says simply.

She hesitates before nodding. She sets off with the letters and heads out the back emergency door leading to the enclosed paddock of horses.

So, we sit cross-legged on the back-room floor and wait, picking at stray hay. Blaze glances my way every few seconds, radiating nervous energy even though he's done deliveries plenty of times before. Maybe my own nerves are contagious.

Eventually, the ten-minute warning bell rings.

"Milady may hath been captured on her passage to seeth thee," Blaze says through a frown.

I'm sure she wasn't caught. Odds are she just wasn't in her room when London went to find her.

But a gut feeling that something is off persists. I rise and offer Blaze a hand. His eyes swell as he accepts it, but not without knocking his head against a helmet hung on the wall. "Maybe we should get out of here," I say uneasily.

Blaze leads the way out of the equestrian center. We pass the horses in the paddock that barely pay us any mind, then the gate. My shoulder knocks into a rake, and it falls and clanks against the handle. I jump, looking over my shoulder.

"Comrade?" Blaze calls. He's already by the cockblockade.

"Nothing." I hurry to catch up with him before the crash gains the attention of anyone it shouldn't.

"Would you like to speak with me instead?" Blaze asks once I catch up, voice quiet. "Instead of milady?"

Blaze, who's in STRIP? At Valentine, period?

"How dare I be so forward?" Blaze says as if my slight pause alone turned him self-conscious. "However, you heed of my war. And although I fail to possess such a real tie, I envisage you as someone as trustworthy as an elder brother—" His pudgy eyes widen more. "I mean, brother of ancestral darkness."

I try not to laugh as we head through the cockblockade again.

AND THEY WERE ROOMMATES

In Queens, there were middle school girls who were indifferent toward me during my tutoring lessons until goodbyes, when tears would suddenly launch out of their eyes. I never thought I'd find that here, let alone from another boy. But then I remind myself, Blaze *is* only twelve.

"Jasper and I fought," I say honestly.

"Are you not both eternally quarreling?" Blaze asks.

"What? You've seen us?"

"Such is never a laborious effort. You both excel at commotion."

My body tenses at the profound weight of being perceived. My conversations with Jasper always feel so isolated, like the rest of the world doesn't exist, that I always forget people can see them, let alone think about or draw conclusions from them. Luis said before that there are rumors about why we're roommates. But are there more?

"This was worse," I mutter. "I think I'll be quitting STRIP."

Blaze glares at the crescent moon above us. "Jasper, that *crook*."

The fact that he takes my side without needing any explanation warms my heart again. But the words *quitting STRIP* still hang heavy in the air between us as we walk back to Philautia Residence Hall.

Strangely, the possibility of leaving STRIP hurts as much as leaving Delilah behind on the other side of the gate.

Chapter 26
SOMETHING WICKED THIS WAY COMES
MONDAY, OCTOBER 14

"Happy Monday, students and instructors! This is Principal Grimes." Her voice comes from a ceiling speaker. It's excited and quick, cutting through the seven a.m. haze, like she drank one too many coffees with her balanced breakfast.

A few people in my homeroom groan, including Robby farther down my row, who'd much rather focus on his paperback of *Seabiscuit*.

As Principal Grimes explains how cable-knit sweaters are allowed over dress shirts now that November is near, Ms. Wu walks over with paperwork. She places a sheet on my desk.

CHARLIE VON HEVRINGPRINZ | ID: V183019
PROGRESS REPORT
Physical Education: 89.5/100
Advanced Chemistry: 98.5/100
Advanced English Literature: 99/100
Advanced Calculus: 92/100
Advanced World History: 99.5/100
First-Year Civics: 100/100

I shoot out of my chair. "YES!"
Stares drift my way from every angle.

Mumbling an apology, I slink back down, but my stomach keeps leaping. Mom must've gotten emailed this progress report and seen my B in PE. Not C. Training with Xavier already has me closer to the top five.

"Lastly, a notice," Principal Grimes says. "Access to the sister academy is paused indefinitely, including special clearances and top-ranked student benefits."

My head lifts. The homeroom is a sea of horrified looks.

"This does not mean the winter mixer is canceled. However, there was an incident with students sneaking into the equestrian center after hours, and—" Principal Grimes sighs. "The horses have been let free. If you see any in the woods, please notify an instructor."

Whispers pop up around the room.

I barely hear them, my thoughts swarmed by memories of my trip with Blaze to the equestrian center. The paddock gate. We walked through that.

"Until we know who caused this, we've placed twenty-four-seven security guards at our checkout booths to ensure top safety for students. Have a wonderful day."

Five minutes later, homeroom is over, and I'm out the door on a burst of nerves. There's no way we're connected to this. Blaze had everything under control.

"V.H.!" someone shouts across the swarm during passing time. Zain, a typical midthirties rank who I tutored in chem last week. Apparently, Luis's nickname for me is catching on. The moment he reaches me, he traps me in a hug tight enough to seize control of my body. "You SAVED my LIFE."

"You're ending mine," I wheeze through my crushed lungs.

"Oh," Zain says, letting go and stepping back. "I got a

ninety-eight on that chem quiz, thanks to our tutoring sesh. I love you, man."

"Same," another voice says behind Zain. Jack, a typical high-twenties rank who joined the tutoring last week, too, stepping better into view. "I scored a ninety-five."

A smile travels up my face. "You guys deserve it."

"You gonna be stuck in the library later?" Zain asks.

Maybe they want more tutoring. "I'm...not sure. What's up?"

"We wondered if you wanted to tap into our Frisbee match. If you're down, meet us at Dix after dinner hour?" With that, he takes off with Jack.

I follow them with my eyes as they walk away, a bit stunned. I'm supposed to keep my head down, yet all I can think is about is how much I'd rather play Frisbee than study in the library all night. How much I want to take that risk and spend time with some new friends.

"Charlie," Xavier says over my shoulder. I jump and spin around. He's rushing toward me. "You hear those announcements?"

"Yeah," I say.

Xavier groans. "We're holding an emergency meeting after classes."

A piece of me wants to come to the STRIP Crypt to know what's going on, but I know I shouldn't. Not when I'm done with Jasper and the love letters. "Hey, Xavier, actually—"

"Oh, my bad. We were gonna train after class, weren't we?"

"Ah, no, it's fine."

"After the STRIP meeting?" He playfully knocks my shoulder. Just a few seconds of discussing his passion for ripping apart his muscles revives him. "You *are* ready to train again, yeah? Or do you still feel off from"—his voice lowers—"lovesickness?"

"No—!" I lift my calculus textbook in front of my face, then glance around to check that Jasper isn't staring directly at me. "I mean, yeah. Yep. I'm good now."

"Cool. Your stats should hit testing day requirements soon." He grins.

"You think?" I bring the book down, but I still can't return a grin. If I walk away from STRIP at a time like this, will Xavier stop training me? What will happen to my PE grade?

Will I have to say goodbye to everyone?

Maybe I have to go. Just this once. To find a way to leave STRIP without hurting everyone.

Xavier fist-bumps me. "See you at the meeting."

◆ ◆

"Blaze let out the horses."

We all blink up at Robby. He stands on a tome table in the STRIP Crypt, his overfilled organizational binder wrapped tightly in his arms.

Blaze pauses drawing a foreboding symbol on his shoes. "What?" squeaks from his pale lips. Usually, his hypothermia look would be a cause for concern, but I'm 90 percent sure his new-found twelve-year-old hobby is dabbling in effects makeup. He clears his throat and lowers his pitch. "What ho?"

From his binder, Robby pulls out a brown horse trading card. "The academy has Hackneys. Those are the worst horses you could've accidentally let out. They're the best breed for carriage driving, harness events, and long-distance sprints. They just keep running." Robby worriedly looks down at the card in his hand. "I know they're okay, there's plenty for them to eat and take shelter under, but I'm not sure how we'll get them back."

"You hold no evidence this was my blunder," Blaze shouts back.

"I do, but first—" Robby points to where I stand on the very left side of the crypt, then Jasper on the very right. "We *are* starting the meeting, right?"

I don't dare look at Jasper. He arrived before me, so, naturally, I stood as far away as possible.

Xavier and Blaze shift unnerved looks between us. The tension is palpable.

"Yes," Jasper finally says, his tone strangely coarser than usual. Still, I don't look. "Carry on, Robby."

Before starting, Robby readjusts his dress shirt collar flipped upward despite him usually being put together. The stress of being a Rank Two and STRIP's admin personnel is catching up. "Blaze delivered letters yesterday evening. The announcement was made this morning. No one, to my knowledge, was there in between those two time stamps. So, he must've left the equestrian center unlocked."

"The doors always automatically lock," I say unsurely. "There's a code."

"The *building* doors lock," Robby says. "Not the gate to the horses."

The rake I knocked over. That hit the gate when we left.

Is this *my* fault?

"Even if this wasn't Blaze, he's on their suspect list now," Xavier says.

"Maybe all of us," Robby says. "We're the only ones who have such an easy way of entering their campus." He points to the gold number-two pin on his blazer. "All we do is show this. They never write down our names. But that also works in our favor. Blaze, if they ask you anything, deny it, okay?"

Blaze salutes.

My heart sinks deeper as I debate coming out with the truth. *It was me. Not Blaze.*

But Blaze is twelve. And one of their own members, through and through. Forgivable. If this is my fault—an Excellence Scholar who's expected to excel in all areas—there's no way STRIP would react with the same forgiveness. Maybe that would be for the better. When I first arrived, I did promise myself not to talk to anybody too much.

But everything has changed. Xavier helps me with training. I've gotten to know other students at tutoring and one-on-ones well enough to be invited to Frisbee matches. Before this meeting, I thought I was prepared to lose STRIP. Only now, as I'm faced with the fate of this hundred-year-old organization resting in my hands, do I realize I shouldn't leave.

Not yet. Not until I fix things.

Xavier sighs so miserably that everyone looks his way. "The mixer is only a month away, but we can't risk sending any more letters from this point on, right?" His misery turns to a weak laugh. "Even if we wanted to, I guess we can't since we've lost contact with the top five girls now. Jasper, how many mixer letters have been sent?"

"None," Jasper announces from his corner. "Blaze's last delivery was our usual couple correspondence."

"What?"

"I have been *working* on the mixer letters. But I prefer those specifically be delivered all at once so no one feels left out. I was waiting to pass them to Blaze."

"If worse comes to worst," I say, "can't people just ask each other out at the mixer without our help?"

"Didn't you hear what I said?" Jasper says.

I still don't look over. I pick at my nails. "Hear what?"

"Losing our connection to the sister side isn't only about the mixer. It's about what comes after. Before. Between. Couples need to stay together all year-round. We're their glue."

I scoff under my breath.

"Our biggest issue isn't any of this," Robby announces from the tome table he stands on. "It's getting shut down by the student body."

"What?" I say in sync with Xavier.

"Haven't you heard everyone in the halls? They know we use the equestrian center. These letters weren't confiscated, but now it's been put into everyone's minds what *would* happen if they were. They'd get in trouble for communicating with the sister academy too."

I did hear a lot of grumbling during homeroom, but nothing specific with so much happening at once. Was that all about us?

"Everyone would turn on us," Robby goes on. "They might tell the academy STRIP's true intentions. We already ride a nuanced likability line with them as top ranks."

I bite the inside of my cheek. Would they try to get us expelled?

"I know," Jasper says, and my thoughts are in such a jumble that I accidentally turn to face him. His dress shirt isn't tucked, and the sleeves aren't neatly rolled for once, dropping past his wrists. Even from a distance, his dark circles are noticeable against the pink tinge to his skin. Did he sleep in the barn with the horses instead of his aunt's instructor quarters? "It's simple, really. We'll still plan to deliver the mixer letters. If we pull this off despite the twenty-four-seven guards, we'll regain everyone's trust."

Xavier tilts his head, considering.

Frustration sizzles in my chest. I could've thought of that too.

Robby struggles to climb down from the tome table while holding his binder. "Great in theory, but how? Our enamel pins don't allow us through anymore."

Jasper just rubs his neck, getting out a knot.

"My emergency contact is over there," I say a bit too quickly. I want to get these words out before Jasper comes back to life to prove I'm helping too. "My best friend."

"Really?" Xavier asks.

"Yeah, she's a third year."

So much hope surges through Xavier that he kisses his lucky spoon. "Call her. We can toss the letters over the cockblockade for her to pick up. Once we know if she's down, we'll meet a week before the mixer to strategize?"

A few more nods come around the room, and then Xavier dismisses the meeting.

"Are you holding STRIP Time this week, Charlie?" Robby says, trying and failing to stuff his massive binder in his backpack. "I wouldn't blame you if you canceled. I personally fear no one will show up. They might all be reluctant to associate with us already."

"He's gotta keep holding tutoring regardless, though, right?" Xavier asks. "The shutdown timing may look sus to librarians."

It's not like I want any more targets on me. "I'll keep tutoring."

Xavier pats my back. "I wouldn't be surprised if people showed despite everything. Your tutoring's gotten super popular. Way more than when P.M. was in charge."

An unsure laugh leaves me. "I'm just a face."

"You're more than that, man. No one here could ever tutor as well as you."

My chest warms. Even if this weren't my fault, would I have found it in myself to actually quit STRIP and leave the other members behind? Looking around, this crypt almost feels like home within a campus I'm struggling to trust.

Clattering comes from the other side of the room, where Jasper's grip on his bag has slipped, books and pens spilling across the floor. He stares emptily.

"You okay?" I ask instinctively, and instantly regret it.

Jasper nods in silence.

"I told you to take the bed, bro," Xavier grumbles, collecting his books for him.

"What?" I say.

Jasper's posture snaps straight. "Nothing."

Xavier glances between us. "Yeah, nothing. Charlie, I'll wait for you outside to go to Pragma." He leaves with Blaze and Robby.

Instead of following, Jasper starts toward his office beyond the brocade curtain.

"You slept in Xavier's room?" I call toward his back.

Jasper stops in his tracks. "Whyever do you say that?"

If Jasper thinks I can't figure out that exchange, then he looks down on me more than I already thought. "*Jasper.*"

Jasper turns, journal tucked beneath an arm, the ocean-blue gemstone clasp sparkling in the antique lamp lights. He sighs. "My room in my aunt's quarters is gone."

"What, like, bibbidi-bobbidi-boo?"

"She reverted it into an office earlier this year. I asked about my suite from last year too, but it's permanently occupied by that first year with a senator for a father. So, yes, I slept in Xavier's room. Well, the floor."

"You can't sleep on the floor of your aunt's office?"

"We don't particularly speak much," Jasper says. "So I'm not sure how to broach the subject of sleeping on her floor. And she is technically still my principal, and..." He massages the back of his neck, faltering.

I grip my forehead. "Okay, you can't keep sleeping on Xavier's floor. I'll feel bad."

Jasper's tired eyes open wide. "For me?"

"For *Xavier*."

His shoulders shrink, and I don't feel bad for him. I *don't*. "He could've declined my request, so I'd refrain." He studies me. "I didn't expect you'd come to the meeting. You told me you were done."

I rub the back of my head. "I'm under fire here too. I'll keep helping STRIP for now."

"We should finish these hundred letters together as soon as possible, then." Jasper nudges his head toward his office. "You can use the fairy-tale books back here for your blackout poetry."

Working together? Now of all times?

"Yeah, no," I say. "I'll talk to my friend and help with the redelivery, but that's it."

Jasper's mouth hangs open slightly, like he's deciding how to say whatever comes next. "I admit, I no longer have enough time to finish the letters on my own."

"Wait, seriously?"

"I have an estimated seventy left. I need you, Charlie."

The words make my stomach flip in a way it shouldn't. I cover it up with the biggest sigh I can manage. "Fine. Whatever. But we'll write separately."

Jasper barely nods. "Very well."

Chapter 27
OUR MUTUAL FRIEND
WEDNESDAY, OCTOBER 16

"Family emergency?" Ms. Lyney repeats behind the office counter. Her fuzzy sweater shouts VALENTINE NAM AMOR TRADITIONALIS EDUCATIONIS at the top of its lungs.

"Yes." My voice comes out half robot, half butler. I can't control it when the number of lies I've told since coming to Valentine has stacked up like Tetris blocks.

"How could you have possibly heard about a family emergency without first hearing from your said family emergency contact?"

Fair question.

"Um." My gaze shifts toward a few gnomes staring back with their beady, foreboding eyes. "I'd rather not talk about something so personal."

She picks up the phone. "Shall I call your mother and ask?"

I reach forward so quickly that Ms. Lyney jumps, and I internally smack myself for being so obvious. This might be my only chance to convince Delilah to help STRIP. As my eyes land on the gnomes again, an impressively poor strategy hits me, but it's all I've got. "M-my mom got cast on *Gnome in Love* over summer vacation."

Ms. Lyney gasps. Like she believes me.

Will this work? "This season, the final three gnomes meet her family for the last episode. I only just realized that my family friend and I never communicated our winter break schedule with the production team. I need to ask for hers." I pause. "And then call the production team, too, to let them know. It's a whole disaster. I want to say more, but the NDA—"

Ms. Lyney holds up a finger. "Promise an autograph."

Mom was right. Breaking the rules spirals. It spirals. "Sure!"

I go sit in the lobby and wait for Delilah to be called down to the sister academy's office. After thirty minutes of brainstorming how to dig myself out of this lie after break—season got canceled? Mom got fired?—Ms. Lyney hands me the phone. I rush into the copy room and explain everything.

"So," Delilah says over the line, "the first real conversation I get to have with you after nearly two months is about STRIP? After all your letters were also about STRIP?"

"You *did* get my letters?"

An awkward pause passes over the line. "Sort of."

There must be a reason why she ignored me—maybe it's about the brief irritation she showed at orientation—but an illogical betrayal creeps up my chest regardless. "You didn't send any back? Wait, why didn't you show up to the equestrian center when I was there with STRIP?"

"There's STRIP again."

"What?"

"Nothing. STRIP is just all you talk about lately."

Is it? I hadn't even noticed. "What else do you want to know, then?" The moment the question comes out, I bite my lip. Answering any other questions about my time here may end in Delilah setting more things on fire with sparklers. "Because I promise, I'm doing fine."

"Good." That's all she says.

Another pause, just as painfully awkward.

"Is something wrong?" I finally ask her.

She sighs and then everything tumbles out. "Well, I'm awesomely twenty-two in the ranks. If this keeps up, I can't run for the student council board and fight for actual change here because you have to rank in the top fifteen to even be eligible."

"Oh," I say. "That really sucks. You're still helping student council with the mixer, right? I saw you carrying boxes."

"Only because it's part of my duties as a basic member. Look, I am sorry for ignoring London's ask to come talk to you that night. It's not that I don't want to hear about you either, but I just really don't like STRIP."

My brow pinches. Delilah should support anyone who breaks the guidelines. Not hate them. "Did they do something to you?"

She huffs so loudly that the line blows out. "One of them."

"Who?"

"Xavier. My ex."

Xavier once mentioned that he supported STRIP to keep in contact with a girlfriend he had. But there's was no way that person was—

"He was so needy," Delilah drones. "Followed me like a puppy. And he always carried around some spoon."

Never mind. "You really dated Xavier? That's, like, huge. You don't like people."

"I know. Something dark happened within me."

"Why didn't you say anything?" I ask, the betrayal within me only twisting deeper. "We talked all throughout winter break. Summer too."

"Well, you were going through a lot over the last year."

Unease settles in my chest over what Delilah is implying.

"That's nice of you. Really. But I don't want you to sacrifice sharing news about yourself because of that. Can't we both tell each other about our problems?"

"To be fair, I would've told you if you asked."

The accusation throws me until I filter through my memory bank for times I've asked how she's doing lately and draw a blank. This insulated campus really has become my whole world. So much so that I've forgotten who my world was before.

But she was clearly upset at orientation too. Maybe this has been going on even longer. I've been focused on monitoring Delilah's feelings over my own well-being since the summer I told her I was a boy. Have I simultaneously failed to realize she's monitoring her own since then too? "I'm so sorry," I say. "I should've asked. I really should've."

Delilah sighs into the speaker. "It's whatever. I almost said something but decided not to since I assumed it'd be temporary. Once we were both living at Valentine, I thought I could start being real with you again since you'd be done with all of that."

"Done with all of what?"

"Boy stuff."

"Boy stuff," I repeat, confused.

"Figuring it all out, I mean. You're staying on the campus you always wanted to be as a boy, right? Your life should be easier now. But all your letters just list more problems."

I nod patiently, even if offense digs its way into my chest. "Dealing with all these problems is still a million times better than dealing with how I felt before the world saw me as a boy, for what it's worth. I am way happier now. But also, I didn't necessarily go through with this to make my life easier. Maybe that's a misconception people have."

"Yeah. I don't think I got that."

"I still want to hear about your problems regardless. We're best friends. I'm so sorry for making you feel like that wasn't the case."

Delilah fakes a gag. "You're getting too real."

"Just this once. Promise we won't hold ourselves back from one another?"

"Fine," she grumbles under her breath. From anyone else, it would be rude, but it's exactly what I want to hear when she's usually too fired up to admit to real emotions. "Cross my heart and hope to kill. Or whatever."

"Hope to die."

"Close enough."

I'm still not sure if this fixes us. All I want to do is hug her and hash this out in person. Maybe we can't fully be fixed until then.

"If we're really doing this, then I have a question for you," Delilah asks. "Why do *you* care about STRIP so much? You sound like you care about their love letters. A lot."

"About the letters?" I almost laugh. "No. But—They might get in trouble, Delilah, and I think it's my fault. I can't bail now. Xavier's been helping me train for PE too."

"You two are actual friends?"

Are we? "I don't know. Maybe."

Ms. Lyney pops her head through the door. She holds up a finger. One minute.

"Just this once," Delilah says.

"You'll help?"

"For you." She pauses. "And to break some rules."

Chapter 28
PRIDE AND PREJUDICE
FRIDAY, NOVEMBER 1

Sitting in the library like every other day these last two weeks, I tap my marker against my forty-eighth blackout poetry love letter. By some miracle, despite STRIP's waning reputation, a few of my regulars showed up for STRIP Time. After helping Zain, Xuan, and Jack with English literature essays, my brain is fried, but I have two more letters to finish by tonight.

Tonight we risk our sister academy delivery.

I smear my marker across the page as thoughts of Jasper percolate in my mind. Now that he's taken residence on Xavier's floor, I only see him in the halls or during class, where he stares out the window, never paying attention yet somehow staying Rank One. When I'm in Dix with Luis or Xavier and Robby, he walks right by. After our fight, he should have plenty of fuel to tell his aunt who I am, but I haven't heard a word from her. Yet.

Peace from Jasper is what I wanted.

Now that I have it, something feels missing.

My watch strikes five just as I finish my fiftieth blackout poem. The most colossal sigh of my life heaves out of me. I deserve a medal. A crown. I quickly pack up my bag and head to the stacks for STRIP's next delivery strategy meeting.

When I pull on the thin *Cupid and Psyche* booklet to open the crypt, a mixture of cable-knit sweaters and plaid blazers stands on the left side. Everyone huddles around a tome table where fairy tales and mythologies rise on the walls. Robby points at a sheet of paper spread before them, but the rest have their backs to me.

Xavier glances over his shoulder. "Just in time!"

Jasper does the same, but he stays silent. Not like I expected anything else after two weeks of separation, but still. Nothing? He can't even ask if I finished my mixer letters without his help?

Trying to exude my best don't-care energy, I approach and inspect the paper—a campus map marked up with black ink.

"Thanks again for asking your friend," Xavier says. "Who is she, by the way?"

The incredibly awkward realization that I never told them who she is, let alone how well Xavier knows her, hits hard.

He's Xavier, the big and strong. He can take it. "Delilah Miller."

"*What?*" Xavier's whole body jerks, and his foot catches on a book. He slips and falls, landing flat on his ass.

Or not.

I glance at everyone else's collection of winces and frowns.

"What happened between you two?" I ask, although I'm unsure if I should.

Xavier readjusts his dark bangs so they split evenly across his forehead again. Robby helps him back to his feet. "The distance made me clingy, I guess," he mutters. "Especially when Delilah's so independent."

"Even with the cockblockade in the way?"

"I used STRIP to constantly keep in touch with her. That didn't scream independent. If I'd understood her, I would've let her live without me sometimes."

Even if romance is illogical, Xavier seems like he learned from it. Unlike another person I know. I'm almost impressed.

"I'm glad she agreed to help us anyway," Robby says. "We're currently planning the delivery route. As of now, we'll stuff the letters into two garbage bags and toss them over the checkout booth for Delilah to grab."

I snort.

Everyone else blinks. Like that wasn't a joke.

These are seriously the smartest guys on campus. "Right in front of the new security?"

"The cockblockade is too tall," Xavier answers, pointing where the wall splits the academies on the campus map. His arm looks even more ripped in his tight knit sweater and next to Robby's lanky arm. "It's thirty feet. But the gate? Only twelve."

"There're no cameras," Robby adds, "but it's easier to be seen by instructors outside rather than in the seclusion of the equestrian center, which is why we've never done it this way. Unfortunately, we have no other choice now. We'll need to distract the guard by splitting into teams. I'm on lookout with Xavier. As for tossing the bags, that's on you and Jasper."

"What?" Jasper and I say.

I expect to see my irritated expression on Jasper too, especially when we've worked hard at avoiding each other. Instead, though, he looks more uptight than anything else, his shoulders tense in his half-buttoned dress shirt.

Before I can process the reaction, Robby says, "Blaze is the vital piece. Our distraction."

Blaze shoves his Ring of Ancestral Darkness in Robby's face, then breaks into the butterfly gesture that he believes is a flame. "Only the Chief Magistrate of the Brotherhood of Ancestral Darkness could ever defeat—"

"Here's a map." Over Blaze's shoulder, Robby hands me a

smaller pamphlet version on the table. "You're right that I don't trust Blaze. He needs to be watched."

"I'm talking!" Blaze shouts between us.

Robby clasps me and Jasper on the shoulders like he isn't there. "That's your other job, got it? Watch him. Especially with the way he'll have to distract this guard."

"Which will be?" I ask uneasily.

Robby grimaces in a way that makes my heart drop.

⁂

Thirty minutes before lights-out, the five of us make a break for the cockblockade.

By the time we reach the path that leads up to the checkout booth, the sun is already setting beyond the surrounding woods. We crouch behind a shrub by a lamppost, observing the alleged security guard inside, doing some sort of crossword puzzle on the desk.

"On three," Robby whispers, his breath visible in the cold air. "Ready?"

Jasper and I trade a look. Tonight, we need to be partners no matter our feelings.

"One—" Robby starts.

Blaze lunges for the booth, his sneakers kicking up dust from the sheer speed. Once he's almost there, he trips, falls, and face-plants on the ground. Grabbing his ankle, he wails to the treetops.

Robby worriedly reaches forward, but Xavier lowers his hand. Maybe Blaze's execution was more extreme than planned, but this is what we wanted.

The guard scuttles outside. In the dull lamppost light, I barely make out her windbreaker that shouts SECURITY on the back. Same for her slightly confused but mostly concerned expression. No walkie-talkie on her hip. Just as we hoped with Valentine's disdain for technology. "What are you doing out here?"

Blaze screeches again. "My ankle is ... *fragmented*."

"You need Health Services. Can you walk?"

Blaze rises on a shaking arm. "No..." He collapses again.

The guard pulls Blaze up by the waist, and they head toward the center of campus. Robby and Xavier split off to keep watch. Jasper and I snatch our bags of letters and race toward the cockblockade gate, but mine slips and hits the ground. A slew of letters falls out.

Jasper stops, his laugh as bubbly as always.

I shove my fists against my hips. "Focus, please?"

He kneels to help me fix the mess, but he's still laughing under his breath. We shove a stack of letters back in at the same time, our fingers grazing, and my heart leaps.

"You all right?" Jasper asks, his words turning to fog between us.

It's because we haven't interacted in weeks. That's all. "Yeah."

The worried crease in Jasper's brow doesn't leave. He's wearing a beige Valentine-branded sweater over his red dress shirt tonight—his number-one enamel pin still shimmering for all to see on the popped-out collar—and the lack of visible chest and collarbones strangely has me staring. Typically, he looks the way the Sexiest Poet of the Year should, but with this sweater up to his neck, he looks more charming and sweet.

My throat goes dry.

A whistle cuts through the night.

Our eyes open wide. The signal that the coast is no longer clear. Already?

I look both ways, but there's nowhere to hide. No trees or buildings.

Jasper drops his bag of letters, then tugs my own out of my grasp. He scoops up my arm and drags us toward the booth.

"What are you—?!" is all I manage to say before we're standing in front of the sliding door. He throws us inside, slamming it shut behind us. As I stumble to regain my balance, I scan the glass walls boxing us inside like a fish tank.

I face Jasper perfectly parallel, crossing my arms. He's so winded that he's leaned a palm against the door. "Hey."

Jasper just keeps huffing and puffing.

"*Hey*," I repeat. "Do I need to sound angrier to get your attention?"

"No offense, Charlie, but you tend to always be angry at me. I don't exactly know when I'm supposed to be paying attention."

My mouth whips back open, but I swallow whatever heated words were coming next. I refuse to prove his point. "You don't see a problem with this hiding spot you've chosen?"

"What do you mean?"

"We're surrounded by *glass*."

"I know, I know. I'm thinking." Jasper's gaze lands on a back cabinet that's as tall as our hips. He goes to open it. The inside is empty except for scattered paperwork at the bottom.

We squish ourselves into the cramped space, Jasper clunking his head in the process. Our legs twist into pretzels, small enough that I can shut us in.

Everything goes dark.

Our synced breaths fill the quiet as we sit shoulder to shoulder. Jasper's flowery fragrance and the cedar cabinet twinges my nose, and his hand presses up against mine. For once, he's burning hot. He's that scared?

Footsteps come from outside. Crunching gravel. Jangling keys on a belt.

My heartbeat pounds so hard that I'm positive Jasper can feel it in my wrist. The guard realized Blaze's foot wasn't broken. Or worse. She spotted us.

The booth door slides open with a squeak.

"Where are you?" the security guard mumbles.

I squeeze my eyes shut. We're caught. Expelled.

Rummaging noises come from the desk, like a junk drawer being opened. The booth door slides open again, and more footsteps wander into the distance.

Furrowing my brow, I shift on my knees to peek out of the cabinet.

Jasper grabs my shoulder. "What are you doing?"

"Making sure she's gone." I crawl out and readjust my glasses to check through the glass. Farther down the path is the guard's backlit figure. She offers a flashlight toward Blaze, who's leaning against a tree trunk with a limp stance.

That's all she wanted.

Sighing, I fall back into the cabinet beside Jasper, our shoulders knocking again. He's pulled his legs into his chest, staring at his knees like he's becoming more scared by the second. "You're this nervous about getting caught?" I ask. "She was only grabbing a flashlight. No need to be so tense."

"That's not why I'm tense." Jasper looks right at me, and his soft, unsure tone speeds up my heart rate more. "I know you told me to leave you alone. I've been trying to respect that. But I also made it clear that I still want to explain my side of things from camp."

"Wait, what?"

"Can I? Please?"

"Now?"

"Perchance."

Panic seeps through me. Even in the dim lighting, I feel too on display as we stare at each other. The last few weeks, no matter how much my logic screamed at me not to, I couldn't stop thinking about Jasper. But to talk now of all times? "Maybe when we're not breaking the number one guideline here. We need to toss the letters." I start to climb back out of the cabinet.

"It was my fault," Jasper calls. He stays put.

Glaring, I whip my head back around. Guess his question of whether he *could* start explaining was hypothetical. "Yeah, Jasper, I think that's been obvious since the start."

"But I didn't realize anyone at camp thought we were together. Let alone that you did."

"You kissed me."

"Actually, you kissed me. And that threw me off guard."

My cheeks burn. *Did* I?

I flick my face away. I'd rather die than have Jasper witness me turn red. "Okay. Well. How could that have thrown you off? We'd been spending so much time together after our workshop. You flirted with me every chance you got. You called me beautiful, and you always sat so close to me, and—"

"I do that with everyone, Charlie!" Jasper says, tossing his hands.

The words stun me. I scoff and leave the booth.

He calls my name, but I don't turn around. The rage inside me is too hot. *I do that with everyone.* Unbelievable. I keep going until I'm at the gate. Our bags of letters are still where we dropped them. Thankfully, the guard didn't notice. When will she be back?

I pick up a bag. "Hurry up."

"That came out worse than intended." Jasper's not picking up his bag. "Yes, I acted overly romantic toward others without realizing any of it was being taken seriously. That's a problem. But after summer was over, you were all I could think about. None of them."

I ignore him.

"We never met at the beach on the last day of camp," he goes on, "so I didn't have your number, and I couldn't find your social media. That's why I posted my poetry online. I hoped, someday, you'd come across my name."

Clenching my jaw, I lift my bag over my head and align my aim with the bushes off to the side. "I deleted most of my pictures after that summer."

"That's it?"

"Yeah, Jasper, what do you want me to say?"

He finally picks up his bag, but he's not tossing it. "I was just a poet back then, okay? I had an overemotional personality."

I narrow my eyes at him.

"Okay, fine, I *have* an overemotional personality," he says. "I didn't even think those letters I sent to those other girls *were* love letters. I thought we were practicing poetry together. At a Shakespeare camp! Right? So, I apologize, Charlie. Truly. But now I've learned."

I chuck the bag over the gate as hard as I can. "I'm glad that I could be your love tutor, Jasper, even though I didn't sign up for it."

"But I—"

A groan releases from my deepest depths. I snatch the bag in his hands to toss it myself. Mom's varsity ring catches on it and locks with his bracelet, trapping us in place. I try to free myself. Nothing budges. I pull again, again, *again*.

"If you wanted to handcuff me, you could've just asked," Jasper mutters.

Heat flares through my face. "Shut *up*." Summoning my strength, I whip our conjoined arms up in one quick motion and fling the bag high into the air. Our ring and bracelet pull taut, snagging on something, and Jasper's bracelet snaps in half. Crunching leaves come from beyond the gate as the bag lands, finalizing the mission.

We stumble away from each other, sticking out our arms to steady ourselves.

Jasper blinks at me. With only the moonlight and the distant lamppost light, his blue irises look so magically shimmery. I didn't notice until now. "How'd we do that?"

"I don't know."

"I hope it landed okay."

I scan the path again for any figures in the distance. "We need to go."

Jasper steps forward. "Will you forgive me?"

"What? No, Jasper. What are you talking about?"

"What more can I apologize for? Tell me what I can do to fix this."

"Nothing."

"Then why won't you forgive—?"

"Because I never want to forgive you!" The words erupt so loudly that my voice echoes through the night. I'm so past my limit that I don't care if the guard hears. Anyone.

Jasper's face goes slack.

An undeniable regret swirls inside me. The words I had to say to make him shut up hang heavy in the air, but they're not how I feel.

Because now, logically, there's a chance I did throw Jasper off with a kiss, and he didn't realize we were anything more. That, logically, he then *did* grow feelings after that summer. And that, logically, he hasn't been with anyone else since.

I don't know what to do about that.

So, with nothing left to say, I head back through the campus, leaving Jasper behind. Xavier and Robby run into me on the path. They toss me high fives.

"Where's Jasper?" Xavier asks. "He didn't get caught after our whistle signal, did he?"

"No, he's"—I readjust my glasses—"on his way. He's fine. We're both fine."

"Nice. And with six minutes to spare until lights-out."

Robby smiles. "Then tonight's a winning success."

Chapter 29
THE AGE OF INNOCENCE
SATURDAY, NOVEMBER 2

I have no clue why Luis and four others from his physics class have dragged me into one of Valentine's campus gazebos—the Aguilar Piano Gazebo—during STRIP Time, but at least they're keeping my mind off Jasper.

After last night's delivery, I went straight to bed. Now that it's the weekend, I won't have to worry about seeing him in class for two more days. At first, distance sounds good. I need a chance to think. But my memory of telling Jasper I'll never forgive him keeps replaying, forcing me to see him in my mind's eye regardless.

An icy wind blows from Au Sable Forks Lake. I lift my scarf up my face, shoving aside the guilt hanging over me. "Wait, did you just say eggs?"

Squatting on the grass, Luis opens his backpack full of raw eggs wrapped in a plaid blazer. Everyone else came dressed for the outdoors, but Luis took things to the next level: a puffy parka falling to his boots, fuzzy pink earmuffs, and matching fuzzy gloves. I've locked in my final answer that Luis is popular, but for a special reason—he says and wears whatever he wants, and that translates into a confidence that pulls people in. I wish I knew how to do that. "Thirteen eggs, bro."

"From Dix?"

"Yup. Asked a chef. We tossed eggs in physics yesterday, and all of us sucked."

"*Dropped* them," Michael corrects him, nudging Luis with his shoe.

A single touch from Michael's foot turns Luis's face red. Definitely his crush.

"The force equals mass times acceleration thing," Emilio says. "We have to keep a raw egg from cracking when dropped from 'ever-increasing elevations.' Ms. Andrew offered us plastic bags and stuff, but I couldn't even figure out round one. Which was, like, two feet."

"I think I know this," I say, sparking back alive. "David Donoghue threw an egg out of a helicopter and onto a golf course in the UK from seven hundred feet. That was considered an egg drop toss."

"How'd you know that?" Luis asks.

"It just came to me."

"Jesus, you're smart."

My chest warms, but not fully from the compliment. More knowing that I'll be able to help them. I grab an egg from Luis's backpack. "Think about—"

Luis points toward the gazebo roof. "Not here. Up there. If I can make a raw egg survive that, I can handle anything."

"My feet stay on the ground," Jackson says, shaking his head.

"Agreed," Michael says.

I clasp Luis's arm. "I'll go with Luis. The rest of you, split into pairs and see what you come up with. Hint: Think about your plastic bags."

While the others wander deeper into the trees, Luis and I climb the gazebo, which isn't as hard as expected when the vine trellises work as ladders. Soon enough, I'm sitting on the roof, looking out at everything that makes me never want to leave Valentine despite its flaws—the marble cupid fountain and tight-knit academic buildings to my right, the lake to my left, and the woods that stretch for miles.

"These are the only materials we got," Luis says, sitting beside me. He sets out the plastic bag, string, scissors, and a raw egg, then slings an arm over my shoulder.

"Mhm. What can be made with a plastic bag and string?"

"Another bag."

"No. What can get trapped inside that bag?"

"Air?"

"Yes. When considering force equaling mass times acceleration, what do you need to do to the acceleration, specifically, while the egg falls?"

That's all I have to say before Luis connects the dots. He lifts his arm off me to cut four pieces of yarn. He feeds them through the bag, then stands, holding the egg attached to his makeshift parachute over the roof. "This better work."

I rise to my feet too. "It'll work—"

My left shoe hooks in Luis's backpack strap, and then my balance is shaking, and my body is tilting, and I'm slipping off the roof on a yelp.

Luis snatches my arm and yanks me back, pulling me against his chest. "Bro, you're not an egg!"

My heart hammers as I clutch harder to Luis's coat. "It's not like I meant to be!"

Clunking comes from our feet. Twelve eggs, rolling out of Luis's backpack and off the gazebo.

Then cracking.

"AUGUH—?!"

Furrowing my brow, I peek over the roof. The shattered eggs

aren't on the grass, nor the gazebo steps, but on a blond head of hair and a cross-body bag with a JFG emblem.

Just when I thought my heart couldn't race faster. "Jasper?"

Jasper outstretches his coat sleeves drenched in translucent goop. His fingers are taut and curled, and his mouth wriggles in revulsion. "What is on me right now."

"What are you doing out here?"

He rakes a hand through his soaked bangs. "Eggs?"

"They look good on you," Luis says.

I elbow Luis, and he winces. "I'm coming down."

According to the theory of relativity, venturing back down the gazebo vine trellis should take as long as it did going up, yet the trip feels endless as my countless thoughts fight for attention. What *is* Jasper doing here? How am I supposed to look him in the eye after refusing to forgive him last night? He must be angrier at me than the eggs.

My feet hit the grass. I snatch his gooey hand and lead him toward the lake, our dress shoes clumsily sinking into the sand. Once we reach the shore, I unwrap my scarf and dip it in the water. "Use this."

"N-no, it'll get dirty."

Did he stutter? *Jasper* stuttered?

Maybe he was chattering. His thin Valentine-branded excuse for a peacoat can't be fighting off the cold when he's definitely only wearing a dress shirt underneath. "What are you going to use, then? Your coat caked with more egg?"

"Perhaps."

I roll my eyes. "Come on, Jasper."

He huffs and closes his eyes. "Thank you."

I step closer, and his body stiffens way too much to just be from the cold. Like *I'm* making *him* nervous.

His nerves spread to me as the sound of waves fills the uncomfortable silence. I wipe his forehead, and his face contorts from the near-freezing water. Inspecting him this closely, all I can think about is the dejected face I saw after he'd apologized for not realizing how I felt. How, eventually, he realized how *he* felt. How he's been sleeping on Xavier's floor since.

I bite the inside of my cheek. "I'm sorry."

Jasper's eyes flutter back open, blue and shining.

"About what I said last night," I say.

"What...specifically?" His voice is breathier, dazed, like he's in disbelief. Does our past mean *this* much to him? "You said a lot."

I hesitate. I hate that I do. I'm in high school—an Excellence Scholar—and still don't know how to express how I feel? "Specifically, about never wanting to forgive you."

"What did you want to say?"

"That I think I need time. I believed you left me behind on purpose for so long. And if I'm being honest, that summer shaped a lot of who I am today. So."

A pained expression crosses his face. "Like how you feel about romance."

"I guess."

"Right."

The vulnerability becomes too much, and the need to puff up my shoulders and stop anything more from leaking out of my mouth consumes me. "Romance is a scam whether or not that summer happened. But. You know."

"Of course." It's obvious Jasper is holding back a grin, but I prefer that over how he looked before. "I'll be honest with you too. About why I came over here."

"Yeah, why were you at the piano gazebo? You play the piano?"

"No, I was just walking by. I saw you slip off that roof, so I rushed over. But I suppose I saw you and Luis before that."

"You were watching us?"

"You guys seemed alone, and together, and close, and I thought you two were, perhaps—" He shakes his head, stuffing his hands in his peacoat and staring at the sand.

"What?" My logic kicks in. "Oh."

"Which is fine."

"We weren't. He likes someone else, I think." But Jasper shouldn't care.

Jasper smiles. "I see."

It's not like I'm his long-lost love anymore. That's impossible. I'm not who I used to be.

My brain sparks with confusion as I bend over to wash the raw egg out of my blazer, then move on to his rosy cheeks. The curve of his chin. "Sorry for the cold. And the eggs."

"It's all right. I probably needed to be humbled after last night."

My laugh morphs into a humiliating snort. I cover my face, which reminds me that I should've probably been standing farther away. Jasper has been able to pick apart the intricacies of my face this whole time. How didn't I realize?

Jasper's upper lip hitches. "Do you find me that much of a comedian?"

"No. Please don't get a bigger head."

Jasper laughs. He leans forward. Closes the distance.

My body stills as his hand lifts toward my face. His thumb

drags across my forehead. "Sorry," he mutters. "I got some egg on you."

My face flares so hot, it's dizzying.

He doesn't like me anymore. I don't like *him* anymore. Yet I thought he was doing something else. Something he never, ever will again.

So why didn't I move?

Why do I feel so strangely empty now that he's no longer touching me?

"No problemo!" I take a jerky step back, then forward again to hand him my scarf, and trip on my own foot. My palm slaps his chest. "Ah—sorry!"

"Don't be, Charlie," he says, holding my forearm. Smiling.

It makes my head spin. Forces me to feel every conflicting emotion of the incurable sickness that I thought was cured.

I walk away as fast as I can, but a nagging voice in my head tells me to wait, to do Xavier a favor and tell Jasper to get off his floor.

"Oh, and Charlie?!" Jasper calls.

I spin around. "Yes?"

"My aunt changed her office back into my room. No need to worry. We're officially no longer roommates."

Chapter 30
A ROOM OF ONE'S OWN
SATURDAY, NOVEMBER 2

Jasper's cinnamon candle collection on the windowsill assaults my nose the moment I step into Room 503.

I thought Jasper would have come to grab his things now that he has his aunt's bedroom back. The patchwork ambrosia flower quilt he took when he was staying with Xavier is still missing, but the eleven throw pillows on his bed are untouched. As are his old-fashioned suitcases, which still poke out from underneath. And the candles. All the candles are still here.

The door closes behind me.

It's quiet.

That's a good thing. Only ten days until finals.

As I head toward my desk to start my daily eight-hour study session, the scents of Jasper's candles keep distracting me. To spare my nose, I could throw them out. At the very least, I could suffocate them in one of his suitcases.

Instead, I walk over and pick up a piece of the broken heart-shaped paperweight beside them. The one Jasper shattered upon seeing me the first day. Holding it up to the lamppost lights beyond the window, I sigh at the cracks. I could've helped him glue it together.

From the corner of the room, Jasper watches me.

I flinch, only to realize he's made of cardboard, and Mardi Gras beads dangle from his neck. Not Jasper. The humiliation that I've been caught still runs deep, though, making me rush to set the paperweight down and retreat to my desk. I start with my packet of every chemistry vocab term we learned so far this year. I have to memorize each one.

Opening the packet, I start at the top.

Covalent bond: formed when atoms share electrons; typically between two nonmetals.

No buzzing bedside lamp.

Covalent bond: formed when atoms share electrons; typically between two nonmetals.

No page flips.

No rustling pillows.

Covalent bond: formed when atoms share electrons; typically between two nonmetals.

I blink at the page. How many times did I read that?

I look to Jasper's side again. I get up, turn on his lamp, and go back to work.

Chapter 31
CRIME AND PUNISHMENT
MONDAY, NOVEMBER 4

ATTENTION
Due to safety guidelines, permission to access the sister academy is not allowed until further notice. Any correspondence—verbal, written, or otherwise—is discontinued. Disregarding these regulations will result in suspension and, in continued cases, expulsion.

My grip on my backpack strap tightens as I keep rereading the sign taped to the Philautia Residence Hall door. The academy is just getting around to posting these signs now. This has nothing to do with our delivery last Friday.

Yeah.

But when I walk to Dix, the same sign is taped on the window. Then by the grade rank announcements board and flyer posts. On the recreational center doors. Even on the front of Mr. Stern's desk in English literature.

Robby, Jasper, and I exchange nonverbal cues to talk after class.

"As you all know," Mr. Stern says as the lesson comes to an end, "finals are next Monday and Tuesday. But I'm still expected to hold class on Wednesday. Why? Because Valentine has simply always done things this way." Sarcasm coats his tone in a way I don't expect. "So, I'm bringing in a fun guest speaker. Don't fake an illness at Health Services to get out of class, all right?"

The bell rings, and we all start toward the hall.

"Mr. V!"

Halfway out the door, I turn around. Mr. Stern flags me down. At least, I think. I'm distracted by his cheetah-print suit.

Jasper stops beside me, a distressed crease between his brows. His thought process is clearly the same as mine. *Is this about our latest delivery?* He nudges his head toward the hall, then carries on with Robby, leaving me to fend for myself.

As I walk back into the classroom, Mr. Stern leans sideways to drag a chair toward him, which must be a challenge to do in such tight pants. I sit and fold my hands in my lap. The ATTENTION sign on his desk yells at me again.

I sweat more. "Yes?"

"You're acting like you're in trouble."

"Am I in trouble?"

Mr. Stern smiles brightly enough for his eyes to squint behind his glasses. From his briefcase set on the floor, he pulls out a stack of paperwork. On top is my character analysis essay about Salinger's "A Perfect Day for Bananafish." "The opposite. As usual, I enjoyed your latest work. Could I share this with the English board as an example for this unit? Your angle on Seymour is better than what we came up with ourselves."

Me.

Even though Rank One is in this class, he picked me.

"You seem surprised," Mr. Stern says when I don't respond.

"I'm just low on the ranks right now," I say. "Others in here are higher."

"Good thing those ranks don't mark true intelligence. Some of the finest storytellers and writers are the least book smart of all. Either way, you *are* smart, Mr. V."

"But I'm an Excellence Scholar. I need to remain in the top five."

He studies me. "I've overheard many students of mine discussing how well you tutor them. How much they admire you."

"Really?"

"Their grades have also improved significantly. You're not only one of the best students I've had, I think you're the best Excellence Scholar we've had. Whether or not you rank in the top five, I believe you're meant to be at Valentine."

Meant to be at Valentine.

The compliment makes my head spin, especially when someone like P.M. walked these halls. But Mr. Stern's words don't change reality. If I don't rank in a little over a week, I'm gone.

"Thank you," I say anyway.

"I just hope Valentine Academy is giving back to you as well. Is it?"

"I'm sorry?"

Mr. Stern leans back in his chair, his cheetah-print blazer shifting around his shoulders. "You're taking advantage of the facilities? The research labs? Meeting with other instructors after hours? You can't just give and give, and not gain anything."

"Um. Sort of."

"What are you gaining, then?"

This suddenly feels like a quiz. "The Student Teaching Remediation Interdisciplinary Program keeps me busy—especially with having to study so much in between—so not as much as I'd admittedly like? But I love the writing gazebo by the lake. And the library. Oh!" I toss up my hands. "I want to try to read every book back in those stacks before I graduate. They're endless. It's like a forest."

"We have the best collection in the nation."

"I believe it. My middle school never had anything even

slightly comparable. Or my online school, obviously. Everything at Valentine is so incredible."

"I'm glad to hear you'll enjoy these next few years." He smiles.

I smile back, even with the threat of losing my scholarship looming over me. I have to keep at PE, the ranks, and everything else standing in my way. I have to stay.

"All right, Mr. V, you're free to go," Mr. Stern says.

"Okay." I rise out of my chair.

"Oh, Mr. V?"

"Yes?"

"I've noticed a change to your writing compared to your original Excellence Scholar essay. More exploration of the human condition, I suppose. Emotions. Keep leaning into that."

I rub the nape of my neck. Of course *he* gets brought up one way or another. "That's probably because of Jasper. He's been teaching me a bit about that."

"My two best students are close, it seems."

I raise a defensive hand. "We're just in STRIP together. And roommates."

Then I remember. Not anymore.

That's for the better. Because I like Jasper. I can't deny that anymore. Sharing one room with the only person I've ever felt that way toward, and who won't ever feel the same, would be torture. Besides, I don't suddenly trust Jasper to *never* tell his aunt what I'm hiding. My brain knows better. Things can change.

Still, a pang remains in my chest. With one last wave, I head out the classroom door. As I turn the corner, I slam into something hard.

Jasper's shoulder. He grins. "Talking about me?"

My face shoots with heat. "You were eavesdropping?"

"I gave you a head signal that I would wait for you." He starts down the hallway. "Robby's waiting around the library already. He said he would hunt down Blaze."

I clench my hand at my side as if that'll squeeze out all my embarrassment, then follow Jasper through the academic center and into the Halo.

"Jasper! Charlie!"

Robby and Blaze sit along the library steps, and we join them.

"I'm guessing we all found the timing of those signs *not* great," Robby says, squeezing his binder like a stress ball.

"You believe someone saw us that night?" Jasper asks.

"Xavier and I stood guard on either side of that booth to keep watch. No one was around that close to lights-out."

"I lament my involvement," Blaze says in a dark, deep voice, biting his nails. "My cries attracted the third awakening of the Battle of Arachnid Doom."

"I don't think it was you, Blaze," Robby says. "Maybe the trash bags looked suspicious even from a distance, and someone saw."

I look toward the church bell tower and sister academy beyond. "Well, if our side didn't get caught, then the other side did."

Jasper faces me. "Call Delilah. Now."

Chapter 32
PROMISE
MONDAY, NOVEMBER 4

Ms. Lyney leaps out of her chair, her red hair bow flopping against the peak of her head. "Everything okay with your mom?"

I summon my best puppy dog face by the office door, debating the quickest way to dial Delilah. This visit is vital, but it's cutting into my daily eight-hour study session for finals, and I already have to stay up an extra hour at least to make up for it. "Actually, no. I really need to contact Delilah again about scheduling time off for—you know. The finale of—Um."

"Gnome in Love."

"Gnome in Love. Yes." My attention drifts toward the counter, where a flyer advertises the winter mixer in an orange-and-purple font, bordered by ghost clip art. It's Halloween in November–themed, apparently.

Mr. Stern pops out of the back room. He points at a shelf of gnomes. "Ms. Lyney, isn't that your favorite reality show?"

Ms. Lyney swivels to face him. "Why, yes, it is."

He shakes his head, but a teasing smile peeks through. "Fabricated love. A disgrace to our storytelling ancestors."

"It's not *fabricated.* It's about a young woman meeting a room of men dressed as gnomes to see which she falls for."

"You can't simply shove two people in a room and expect them to fall in love."

I raise my hand. "Am I allowed to speak with my friend now?"

Only ten minutes pass before I'm handed a phone. Once I'm in the back room, Mr. Stern is gone, and I can tuck myself into a corner.

"That was fast," I say.

"I was already in the office," Delilah whispers over the line. "I got caught."

My blood runs cold.

"No way," I mutter. "How did they spot you?"

"One of the bags was ripped. Probably some animal. I was kneeling there longer than I should've to clean up the mess. A residential retainer saw."

Ripped. Is that what happened when Jasper and I tossed that last bag over together? His bracelet and my ring tore it apart? How many times can I completely mess everything up?

"I'm sorry, Charlie." The exhaustion in Delilah's voice only makes my heart sink deeper. "The mixer is a flop now."

"Who cares about the mixer?" I say too sharply, the guilt already consuming me whole, but I try to calm down so she doesn't feel bad for me too. With the awkwardness that's been clinging to our friendship lately, another issue is the last thing we need. "Are you okay?"

"I talked to the vice principal. I told them I wrote the letters and was just trying to send Xavier a bunch of ooey-gooey junk. They bought it."

"Really? So you're not getting kicked out?"

"A week of detention for now. They didn't want to touch those letters with a ten-foot pole, so they thankfully threw them out before they read them."

This should be a relief, but I only feel more defeat. Technically,

I got exactly what I set out to get. A room to myself. But now STRIP is losing everything they care about.

Jasper is. Our last few months together were for nothing. Every tutoring session. Every argument. Every sleepless night.

All our letters, dumped in the trash.

We're back at the start.

❤ ❤

"THOSE DIRTY ARACHNIDS," Blaze shouts, standing atop the fountain ledge in the Halo.

Robby yanks Blaze down and slaps a palm against his mouth. Now that it's November, the water has been sucked out of the basin, and the ugly cupid statue at the center has stopped shooting a steady stream from his bow and arrow.

Beside the two, Jasper's and Xavier's eyes are wide, too shocked to speak.

I shove my hands into my coat pockets as I stand before them, unsure what else to say after conveying the bad news from Delilah and the letters beyond a wall we can't cross. A poster pole next to us advertises the Halloween in November mixer date, cruelly reminding us of its impending arrival in ten days.

"What's Delilah's punishment?" Xavier asks, his deep bro-voice in its frailest state yet. Even his muscles look deflated in his knit sweater.

"Detention," I say, the shame from our call still eating away at me.

"Milady needed your lucky spoon," Blaze says, patting Xavier's chest.

Xavier covers his face in his palms. "I'm the ex from hell."

I take in the dejected faces I've caused. If only I'd never screwed up the equestrian center gate and ruined STRIP's safe delivery method. If *only* I'd never fought with Jasper and torn the bags. An Excellence Scholar is expected to be perfect, yet all I am is the opposite.

I have to fix this for them.

"How convenient; you're all in one place," an abrasive voice shouts our way. Foot Cody, walking alongside the quiet, shy Eli and five others I vaguely remember from past one-on-ones. Witnessing such social-food-chain opposites hanging out together spikes my nerves.

There's only one reason why they would approach us like this. They figured out what happened to the letters.

How? This fast?

"How can we be of service, patrons?" Jaspers says, rising off the fountain ledge. There's a rare cautiousness to his voice. He came to the same conclusion.

Cody smirks. Unlike everyone else, he only wears a flimsy dress shirt despite today's temperature being the coldest so far all season, probably in an attempt to prove something. "You can stop calling us your patrons. Especially now that you've screwed us over."

"You have no evidence this was our blunder—" Blaze shouts—a seemingly default monologue of his—but that's all he gets out before Robby covers his mouth again.

"It was, though," Eli says, wringing his gloved hands. "Our residential retainer heard about someone at the sister academy getting caught with tons of letters. The academies can read them now, right? Our names?"

"Incorrect, Eli," Jasper responds, smiling. There's no dimple. "You're safe."

"How do you know?"

"The student who picked up your letters took the blame. Isn't she kind? She says the sister academy never read your letters as well."

"We're just supposed to believe you?" Eli says. "We've been compromising so much after you obviously lied about these letters only being written by you." He flashes a cold look my way. "It's obvious Charlie is helping you."

Jasper's mouth opens as he looks to the rest of the STRIP members, but he finds no rebuttal. He remains silent.

Cody sneers way too happily. "Bro's right. What's stopping us from visiting your aunt right now and telling her about STRIP's true business?"

Unspoken Guideline 16: Jasper was right. Classmates simultaneously want to befriend the top five and want them gone—and even the shyest and meanest will team up to make that happen.

There must be some way to convince them to hold off from ratting out STRIP and everything it brings into an otherwise stressful academic environment.

"So, you don't want to keep your dates to the mixer?" I ask the crowd, an idea coming to me. I walk toward the poster pole, gesturing at the mixer advertisement drowning in cheesy Halloween-themed clip art.

Eli crosses his arms. "Of course we do."

"Then I'll make this up to you. I'll rewrite and redeliver your letters."

A shocked, choking noise launches out of Jasper.

Everyone else stares, perplexed. I can't blame them. This promise might be impossible. But I refuse to let the other members to get kicked out because of me.

"The mixer is next week," Eli says. "Besides, the deal was Jasper would write them. Not you."

"Well, I know, but." I falter.

"Then *I* will rewrite the letters," Jasper interjects. He's nervously pressing out the wrinkles in his blazer as he looks at me. "And Charlie will help me redeliver them."

A small bit of warmth finds its way into my heart.

"How *will* you redeliver them?" Eli asks.

"At the mixer itself," I say.

"How is that safe? Nearly every instructor will be chaperoning. What if they spot the letters and figure out we were all behind your guys' last failed attempt? They could figure out everything that's been going on for over a *hundred* years."

Technically, this is still dangerous. The administration could connect us back to Delilah if we're caught. But I was hoping they'd overlook that at the promise of a new and shiny attack method. "We have a plan." The lie feels filthy on my tongue, but I have to. We need this one last chance. "Hopefully, this is a good enough offer. Otherwise, everyone's tradition—and only way—of communicating with the sister academy will vanish forever, right? If we fail, report us."

Eli's mouth twists. "Until the mixer."

As the crowd leaves, Jasper faces the rest of us. "Apologies, everyone, for not disclosing Charlie's involvement with the love letters. I wished for this to remain as hidden as possible from our patrons."

"I already knew," Xavier says.

"For I, too, did," Blaze says.

Robby points a thumb at Blaze. "Blaze told me yesterday."

Jasper's brow spikes high. Slowly, his focus drifts my way.

"Sorry," I say through a wince. "It kept accidentally coming up."

"You really think you can rewrite hundreds of letters from scratch?" Robby asks Jasper.

"During finals?" Xavier adds, equally skeptical.

"No," Jasper says, "which is why Charlie will still help me write."

I trade confused looks with everyone. "But they don't want my letters."

"They *think* they don't want your letters," Jasper says. "I, however, know you are more than capable. And you wish to help. Therefore, you will."

I *do* want to help, especially when Jasper is calling me a talent. But knowing him, those could just be flowery words he doesn't mean, and ones I shouldn't trust. Besides, today alone, I've lost multiple hours of finals study time to STRIP. To get back on track, I'll have to pull an all-nighter. If love letters get added back to my schedule, I'll never sleep again if I want to rank. Would *that* even be enough?

"Even with two people, I'm not sure if we'll finish in time," Robby mutters.

"The reason we took so long last time is because Jasper had to teach me first," I say, but I'm not sure if I'm trying to convince them or myself more. "We can do this. The two of us will just have to... spend a lot of time together." I look to Jasper.

He nods, but his stare is vacant. Uneasy. Why? Does he think we can't do this?

The bell tower chimes twelve times. The lunch bell.

After goodbyes, Robby, Xavier, and Blaze wander toward Dix.

Jasper stays at the fountain, pulling me aside by the coat cuff. "I apologize, Charlie. For all of this. That's why I feel especially bad asking something else of you."

"What is it?" I say, nerves prickling in my chest.

"I told you that I planned to move back in with my aunt, but I fear she'll notice what we're up to. She may see my journal. The letters."

"You can't write in the crypt after classes?"

"We're on a time crunch. I'll need to work through the nights, and my aunt will notice if I stay out past curfew. Won't you need to work the same?"

"I guess," I say, not following the logic, but I'm too overwhelmed with the weight of what I've promised to think any more. "You're back to Xavier's, then?"

Jasper's blue eyes bounce around the maple trees in the Halo. "Being closer to you over the next ten days could help us complete these on time."

He's asking to be roommates again.

"Oh," I say.

"I know how much of an ask it is to return to the room." Jasper's cadence is quicker now. "But our futures at Valentine depend upon this, do they not? I won't be a distraction, I promise."

My smile comes out more like a grimace. Because only months ago I would've done anything for a private room. Especially during the week before finals.

But since Jasper moved out, all I've been distracted by is the *lack* of him there. No more page turns. No more buzzing lamps. No more eleven pillows shuffling through the night. Every noise I once loathed is all I want to hear.

"I can survive until the mixer." My heart makes me say it, and I've never wanted to dig a hole out of my chest more. There's no way I can survive rooming with the one person who could never return my feelings. "But promise you'll leave the moment we're done."

Jasper's mouth twitches in a way I can't read. "I promise."

Chapter 33
THE THREE MUSKETEERS
WEDNESDAY, NOVEMBER 6

"*Charlie!*" Xavier lunges for the machine bar slipping out of my fingers, and I jolt. He snatches and slaps the bar back into place above my head with a clang. "Where were you, man? You just kept going and going after your reps."

Did I?

I sit up from the machine, glancing around the workout room. All I remember is thinking about all the study guides I have to finish after this. "Sorry. Zoned out."

"Last month, you couldn't get through one power lift without passing out, so good work. But overdoing it can strain your muscles. We don't want that one week before testing day."

As if I could forget.

"COMRADES," echoes from the workout room doors.

I look over. Robby waves at us in a tracksuit uniform. Blaze poses behind him, fluttering his hands like a butterfly. They weave through the rows of machines toward our side.

Before I can ask why, Xavier says, "I mentioned we'd be here today. They said they might join."

Blaze shows another innovative pose—a finger gun. The Ring of Ancestral Darkness on his thumb sparkles not from magic but from the fluorescent lights. "It is but my curse to push my body to its breaking point."

"Hope we're not intruding," Robby says, adjusting his tracksuit collar.

"Not at all," I say, but my pulse speeds at the lie. With Xavier comparing us three side by side, I'll look weaker than I already am.

We follow Xavier's lead toward three pull-up bars. Robby and Blaze take the first and third, leaving only the second available. Great. Xavier will *literally* compare us side by side.

Xavier raises his stopwatch. "One minute. As many pull-ups as you can."

I place my feet firmly on the floor. This will be a tough match against Robby and Blaze—maybe an impossible one—but I have to give this my all. I can't let Xavier down.

"Go!"

Flexing our muscles, we all pull ourselves up.

Instantly, Blaze drops to the floor.

I freeze halfway up the bar, staring at his tangled limbs.

"I will not be defeated by those eight-legs," Blaze mumbles face down, lifting the Ancestral Ring of Darkness on his thumb.

Xavier wiggles his stopwatch. "Keep going!"

To my left, Robby pulls himself up again. He's going fast. Too fast.

I focus on channeling the correct amount of power. Xavier taught me how to conserve. By the time I hit three, Robby's arms are shaking, and his forehead is drenched in sweat.

"Stop!"

I jump down. Blaze is still wheezing on the floor. Robby also doesn't look good with how much he's wiping his wet face with his shirt. I only feel warm.

Xavier points at Robby and Blaze, then the dumbbell shelves

by the long mirror. "Collect your breath over there. I'll start you guys with something easier."

Robby helps Blaze off the floor. They wander off in their downfall.

Xavier high-fives me. "Knew you'd crush them."

I *did* crush them. "I'm surprised."

"Why? You've been training for months."

I want to be thrilled. But. "I thought they'd also reach three easily."

"Robby's been struggling to pull an A in his PE class. And Blaze rarely shows up to his, but he's a Dixon. His family owns half the buildings on this campus. Must be why Ms. Nallos conveniently keeps him at an A-plus."

All this time, I thought everyone else was stronger, and I had to work out every hour of every day to catch up.

"Something up, man?" Xavier asks. He must've noticed my inner spiral.

Ever since we started training, Xavier has never asked why I've been obsessed with my PE grade. I've appreciated that. But we know each other better now. Delilah even called us friends. "I never asked," I say, disappointed in myself for not doing it sooner. "Why do you train so much?"

"Always have, I guess. In middle school, I was the lacrosse team captain."

"Why'd you go to Valentine if there are no sports?"

Xavier bends over to grab his sports drink on the floor. It feels like a distraction. "My dad's an ambassador for the UN. Needed to move to the UAE for the next four years. I could go with or enroll in a boarding school. This is the only one in New York that my parents 'approved' of."

"You had to stay here?"

"Nah, but I can take a train into the city to see my old team this way. I'm doing that during winter break. Miss them mad bad."

"That's cool."

"Yeah. Don't really hear from the parents anymore. But sometimes you gotta choose." He shakes his drink, watches the off-orange liquid swirl inside.

Even if Mom is sometimes disorganized and a bundle of nerves, at least she would never do this. Suddenly, her never mailing my single room fee check doesn't sound as bad as it did a month ago. "Sorry."

"It's cool. I've talked to Ms. Nallos about getting a team going here. She's down, at least. Just wish I could make it coed, but the guidelines are too uptight to let that happen. The fact that everyone has to be split up is so cringe. I mean, what year is it?"

So, Xavier also chafes against the guidelines. The first time I met him, all I could see was how tall and strong and *giant* he was. I assumed he was like the other students who encapsulated the definition of tradition and could never relate to someone like me.

If even he feels this way, do others?

"You wanna join the team?" Xavier adds, showing a playful smirk. "I know you're only here for your PE grade, but you got potential beyond that."

It's a compliment I never thought I'd get from anyone, let alone another guy.

And it pushes me enough to want to take a risk. "To be honest, I haven't been training just to improve my grade," I say. "I want to keep up with the other guys. I'm sort of scared about the academy finding out who I used to be."

"Who you used to be?"

My logic tells me to turn back, but I don't. "I had a different name before surgery. And hormones."

Xavier nods gradually.

I'm not sure how to read it. "If the admin finds out, then they could make me leave campus and you all behind, you know—?"

"No."

"No?"

Xavier's expression is taut. "Don't get me wrong, I get being concerned. I hope they wouldn't do that, man. But if they do, I swear, I'll punch them in the throat."

"Oh."

"The rest of STRIP would do the same. We'll aim straight for the board of trustees."

My chest warms. STRIP *would* have my back. Lately, there's no denying that. But everyone else at this academy?

Even Jasper?

A bitter ache strikes me—I can't believe that even now, despite everything, there's a part of me that wonders if I could trust him. "Thanks."

Xavier points at Blaze and Robby digging through a bucket full of latex resistance bands. Blaze straps one around his head and stretches it too far, and it slaps into his eyes. "Go help those losers. They need an expert like you."

Chapter 34
AND THEN THERE WERE NONE
WEDNESDAY, NOVEMBER 6

No one shows up to STRIP Time.

I work on a calculus study guide at my desk, hoping someone—anyone—needs help during the last week before final exams. Even though the last thing I need is an interruption from studying. As more time passes, the reality becomes undeniable, and an overwhelming sadness weighs down my chest. Robby was right. After we screwed up the love letters, no one will risk associating with STRIP. And without any patrons to serve, this hundred-year tradition will truly cease to exist.

The first day of being STRIP's face flutters back into my memory, when I sat here alone among packed, busy tables. That same loneliness creeps through me now.

Through the evening, I tap my graphing calculator over and over again until one question stops me in my tracks. A digital 47.22 glows back at me—not an option on the multiple choice. I try again. 47.22.

What if this were the test next Monday?

The bell tower strikes ten times.

I glance around the surrounding empty desks, then at my watch. Ten minutes to ten. One study guide is taking me *four* hours.

Embarrassment crashes through me as I file the STRIP Time sign into my bag, then head back to Philautia Residence Hall.

Cold air bites at my face, and I wrap my coat tighter, slightly wishing Jasper hadn't kept my scarf but mostly relieved he'll at least stay warm tonight. After training with Xavier this morning, I never got a chance to shower before homeroom. Now the sheen of sweat I didn't mind twelve hours ago has clogged every pore, and my shirt crinkles uncomfortably against my skin. Despite having gained the perfect PE body, maybe it'll be my brain that fails me next week. Maybe I won't rank.

Maybe I should get a head start on packing.

It's an incriminating ten minutes past lights-out by the time I reach Room 503. I knock once. *Grimes.* Nothing. Not here. Jasper said he'd be moving back in, but maybe he decided to stay in his aunt's instructor quarters after all.

My chest aches, even though it makes no sense. He *can't* be my roommate.

Before the door even shuts behind me, I'm ripping my sweater and dress shirt over my head and tossing them at my dresser. As I go for my pants, a page flip comes from the other side of the room. Jasper, still in uniform minus his hair tied back in a scrunchie, working at his desk.

He's in here.

He's in here?

"You're in here?!" flings out of my mouth.

Jasper turns around in his chair. His eyes lock on the last place I'd ever want them to.

A shirt. I need a shirt. Now.

I sprint to my dresser and snatch my sweater again to cover the scars. "You didn't say anything!"

Too many emotions pass across Jasper's face for me to understand them. Whatever they are, they make his eyes and mouth twitch. It takes three more seconds for him to shield his eyes with his palms. "What was I supposed to say?!"

"*Come in.* Our signal!"

"Only when you knock once."

"I *did* knock."

Jasper lowers his hands. "Did you? Apologies."

In a panic, I chuck my sweater in his direction. "Don't look!"

The soft fabric sails over his head and knocks into the glass fragrance bottles set on his dresser instead, instigating a domino effect of clinks and clangs. Two bottles fall onto the floor.

At least Jasper isn't looking at me anymore. Instead, he's looking at his toppled-over bottles.

I should apologize for my not-so-ceremonious outburst, and part of me wants to, but he's seen me. Truly seen me. Who I am is all the more real to him. This could change everything.

My irrationality seizes control of my body and convinces me to snatch a pajama set from my dresser, run for the bathroom, and slam the door shut. I stand there, back glued to the door as breaths heave out of me. Not the first time. Almost definitely not the last.

At least, until my reflection catches my eye in the mirror. My collarbone sticks out more, and my arms have a bit more mass. With the slight definition to my chest, my scars are almost hidden too. Not fully, but also not a focus. This can't be the same reflection I had when classes started, but two months of training couldn't have possibly done this much either.

Maybe this is the same reflection. Maybe I looked like this all along, but I couldn't see it.

I walk closer to the mirror. I don't usually look. It's subconscious. My face, rarely. The rest, never. If Jasper wasn't staring at my scars, then what was he looking at?

Did I yell for no reason? Was his stare all in my head?

No, he was staring. Hard.

I don't want to go back in that room—I can't even imagine how uncomfortable it will be—but there are study guides to complete and practice exams to take. By the time I shower and come back in my pajamas, Jasper sits, his back leaned against his headboard. His ambrosia flower quilt is back from Xavier's, pulled to his waist, and his various fragrance bottles have returned to their perfectly lined up position on his desk. He's working on the mixer letters, journal on his lap and number-one pin on his pajama shirt collar—because of course it is.

I wait for him to say something, but he keeps working away, silently.

Trying to ignore the embarrassment washing over me, I sit in my own bed and grab my journal to join him. Behind it is my English literature guide. Six potential essay prompts are listed for the timed final, but only one will be chosen. I haven't done any. I pick it up, flipping through the empty pages. I promised STRIP I could manage the letters and finals.

Maybe I can't.

"Work on it," Jasper says from his bed.

I startle. "What?"

"Your guide. You're smart, so you'll finish it quickly. Then join me for letters."

The proposition makes me feel equally relieved and like a failure.

I flip to the first question.

1. The driving rhythm of "The Raven," created by Poe, has a signature hypnotic sound and creepy atmosphere. What literary techniques does Poe utilize to achieve this? Be sure to consider the careful use of rhyme and meter.

My chest shrivels at the poetry question right off the bat. Sucking on the end of my pencil, I pull out my printed copy of "The Raven" from my English folder and study the verses.

Jasper could help.

I glance toward him. Although I just chucked clothes at him, I doubt he'll want to come anywhere near me. "Jasper?"

He looks up from his notebook. His gaze shifts toward the pencil tip resting against my bottom lip, then my eyes again.

"Can you help me?" I ask.

Jasper slips off the bed with his journal and approaches mine, and his unexpected willingness throws my emotions in a jumble. As he hovers at my side, he traces the prompt with a finger, moving back and forth at a leisurely pace, his pajama sleeve grazing me.

I focus hard on the page. "I'm not good with poetry."

"You've gotten better."

"Not with questions like this. How could different rhythms create different emotions?"

Jasper sits beside me on the bed. His leg brushes mine, and he jerks. "Sorry."

"It's fine," I mutter.

He must be this jumpy because I yelled. The need to apologize claws at me more, but I'm not bursting at the seams to bring up my bare chest either.

Jasper points at my copy of "The Raven" on my thigh, his flowery scents whirling around me. "What stands out to you about this ABCBBB rhythm?"

"B is repeated way more?"

Jasper's smile brightens. He really loves this stuff. "And how are these B rhymes similar?"

"*Lenore? Door? Nevermore?*"

"Mhm."

This can't be right. "*Oo* sounds spooky? Like, *oo*, ghost?"

"Yes!"

"Seriously?"

Jasper scratches his temple. "Technically, most lines use trochaic octameter: sixteen syllables, following a pattern of stressed and unstressed. But the B schemes are catalectic and drop the last unstressed syllable." His passion grows with his gestures. "Plus, repeating the bird's refrain of *nevermore* insistently reminds the reader of the grief he's facing. Haunting effect. Mr. Stern is an emotions guy over technical, though. *Oo, ghost* should suffice."

Jasper's poetry may cater to social media's bias for normie content, but he might know more than even Mr. Stern. Maybe to make *basic* stand out among millions of other poets, he needs to. I can't deny how impressive that is.

I jot *oo, ghost* so I don't forget. "Thanks. I couldn't have answered this without you."

Usually, Jasper would milk this, but he simply rises off the bed. "I won't keep bothering you. Unless you have more questions?"

He still thinks he bothers me.

My heart sinks. I suppose I am still demanding that he move out. Constantly. "You're not bothering me," I say, turning back to the study guide. The next question isn't about Poe. Robert Frost. Two roads diverged in the same cursed, poetic wood. "I might still need you."

Jasper's forehead wrinkles in surprise. "Tap me when you want help." He sits again, twirling his broken fountain pen between two nimble fingers, oozing red ink on his skin.

"How long have you—?" What am I *doing*?

Jasper's head lifts, his blond bangs swaying over his eyes. Waiting.

"Never mind," I say. "Well, no. I was going to ask how long you've had that pen since it's broken. It must be old."

"My aunt gave it to me." He holds out the pen, but he doesn't lean closer to show me the details, even though I wish he would. The 89 engraving along the barrel gleams in my bedside lamp light. "It was a gift after I published my poetry collection."

"That's nice of her."

"Yes, we're not close, but she's supportive of my work. She understands how Valentine can restrict it. Really, I'm glad she understands this place. How lonely it can be."

Once, I accused Jasper of not knowing what that's like. But despite how charming and talented he is, he doesn't have many he can rely on or relate to at Valentine either. I've had that proven time and time again, especially as STRIP threatens to fall apart.

"Your mother went here, correct?" Jasper asks.

"Did I tell you that at camp?"

"Yes." Jasper sets his journal to the side. "I also remember that your favorite food is breadsticks because that's all you ever ate. And, well, it's odd."

My face heats. "You can't talk. Yours is blueberries."

"You remember mine too," he says, his upper lip quirking, but it vanishes quickly. He even clears his throat. "Any questions yet? And don't feel bad. You're not a distraction. I'm ahead on my set of letters."

Of course he is.

The shame settles deep, especially as I catch another glimpse of his glimmering number-one pin that I've dreamed so many times could be mine. "To be honest, I don't know how long this guide will take me."

"No probl—"

"Or the four others in my backpack. With the final rank announcements coming up, every grade I get needs to be perfect, so I'm a little overwhelmed—"

"Charlie, it's—"

"—or they'll take away my scholarship. Then it won't matter that I hid that I'm transgender because they'll kick me out for my bad grades, or if our entire class tells the academy about STRIP, then they'll kick me out for that, and then Mom will be crushed. No matter what, everyone will regret putting faith in me as an Excellence Scholar. They'll think someone like P.M. should still be here, so I probably should be packing instead of talking to you."

Jasper stares.

Only then do I realize how much came out of me and how long it must've been building up. Why did it have to explode onto Jasper of all people?

I wish I could crawl under these covers and be *nevermore*. "Forget I said anything."

His brows remain crossed. "Cancel STRIP Time this week."

"What? No way."

"Barely anyone shows up anymore, anyway."

A pang strikes me. "We need STRIP to keep looking unsuspicious. I can do it all."

Jasper's hand twitches and lifts off his knee, but then it sinks back down. "Just because you *can* do it all doesn't mean you *should*, Charlie."

I stare at his unmoving hand, overcome with crushing disappointment that it didn't move farther. Every day, this incurable illness gets worse.

"Charlie?"

"Y-yeah," I say, jumping. "Hi."

"Hi. Did you hear me? It's all right to take a break."

My exhaustion tempts me to, but I can't listen to Jasper and blow everything.

"Although I don't know why I'm wasting my breath," Jasper adds with a sigh. "Right now, you're thinking about how you'd never listen to a word of advice I give you."

"How did you—?" I stop.

But it's too late, yet another smile tugging at his lips as he returns to his journal. Like he thinks he knows me better than anyone.

Jasper *is* the only one I've ever shared a bedroom with. The only one I've spent a summer with outside Mom or Delilah. The only one I've kissed. Does he know me better than anyone?

Can I trust Jasper?

"Jasper?" I say toward my lap.

"Yes, Charlie?"

"I meant my surgery scars. Earlier, when I said not to look."

"I know. I figured it out."

Still not an apology. I *need* to. I lift my head. Look at him. "I'm sorry I yelled. And threw clothes at you. And I'm sorry I knocked over your bottles. I know you like them a certain way."

"It's all right." Jasper smiles at his journal.

My heart pounds at how kind it looks. Understanding, even. I still waver before speaking again. "I told Xavier."

His pen stops moving. "Xavier won't tell anyone. But I know you're even unsure about me, so I don't expect you to believe me—"

"I want to believe you." The words come out before I fully comprehend I'm saying them, and for a second, I regret it for how open and raw I feel in the aftermath. But that's also how I know what I said is the truth.

Jasper blinks back at me. "I hope you can someday."

Chapter 35
THE SUN ALSO RISES
THURSDAY, NOVEMBER 7

When the bell tower curses campus with seven bongs, my face is planted in a book of blackout poetry. I grunt as I sit up in my desk chair, trying to piece together my memory from the night before. After Jasper helped me with my literature guide, I moved over here to work on mixer letters. I finished four.

Only thirty more.

I glance around the room. No Jasper. But there's proof of his morning routine in the way pieces of his uniform are newly strewn around his desk and bed.

Something slips off my shoulder. I look down.

A patchwork quilt, dotted with ambrosia flowers.

Chapter 36
BREAKFAST OF CHAMPIONS
MONDAY, NOVEMBER 11

"**D**ON'T DIE ON ME, V.H.!"

I jolt upright and grip my surroundings. My face is wet. Beneath me is my bowl of Cheerios on the table.

A paper napkin thrusts into my view.

Luis, his mouth wriggling like a worm in disgust at my milk face. "Bro, did you zonk out in your cereal?"

I take the napkin and rub my nose, then the rest of my drenched face. It's more of a challenge than I expect. My limbs are limp noodles, and my brain is on fire from this headache. "What were you saying? Your cat?"

Instead of answering, Luis plucks a soggy Cheerio off my cheek and flicks it on the Dix floor. "How much did you zonk last night?"

This last week has been a blur of training and studying and letter writing with Jasper, and now it's already finals for Hours 1 through 3 on my schedule. Has my head hit the pillow once?

"I don't"—I yawn—"remember."

"So you didn't zonk."

"I didn't say that."

"Have you taken a break lately? At all?"

"A lot's on the line," I say, thinking about the impending last grade rank until the end of classes.

And right after is the mixer. With the intensity of exams,

STRIP hasn't even started discussing the delivery plan for the letters.

"We need to be perfect this week," I go on.

Luis picks up his fork and stress-twirls his curls like spaghetti. Fear clouds his gaze. "Yeah, my massive calc exam is today."

I stare at the fork. "You ready?"

"Dunno. Crossing my fingers that your tutoring saved me. At least I closed my eyes last night." Luis's gaze refocuses on my face. "Unlike you. Your dark circles have dark circles. I'm worried."

I attempt to eat some Cheerios, but my stomach curdles. "I'm fine."

Luis is spinning the fork through his hair faster now. "Don't you have PE for first hour? Your fitness exam is in, like, a half hour."

"Don't worry, I can handle it."

◆ ▶

My arms won't move.

I tug myself up on the pull-up bar again. *Again.* Nothing.

"Forty-five seconds," Ms. Nallos calls, her gaze flipping between me and the stopwatch set on her clipboard. I can feel the line of students in the Pragma Recreational Center trailing behind her, watching.

Panic courses through me. I got three pull-ups easily last week while with Xavier.

"Fifteen seconds!"

No way am I failing this fitness exam. I *can't*. I flex my arms so hard that they burn, and I bite back a wince. I fight through the pain until my chin taps the bar.

My arms give out.

"Time!"

My sneakers hit the floor. Every bit of me throbs. One pull-up. After all that training.

For nothing.

"Next," Ms. Nallos calls, signaling the next student in line to take my spot, her cheery polka dot braids bopping along her shoulders in the face of my defeat.

Before she can reset her stopwatch, my desperation makes me approach her. There must be something I can do. Anything.

Think. "Ms. Nallos, can I have a redo after class? Please?"

"No need," Ms. Nallos says, dismissing me.

"I swear, I can get to three. I've trained—"

"You passed."

"I can prove—I'm sorry?"

"I've seen you and Xavier train through these windows for weeks." She points toward the doors, where the workout room resides deeper in the center. "In my opinion, that deserves a grade change."

Hope flutters inside me, but I can't possibly be understanding correctly. "To what?"

"You'll see in the next progress report handouts."

"But can I know now?"

She glances around the track. "Let's go with an A. Please keep this to yourself, Charlie."

I do mental math in my head. "We've been scored ten times so far, and I averaged at a C-minus in October, so I should only be at a B at most. And the rules about PE—"

"You've worked *hard*. Turn off that brain of yours and walk some laps." Ms. Nallos focuses back on the next tester.

As I head for the indoor track, I can barely think straight, too many emotions shooting through me. An *A*. Others are already done testing and walking, too, including Xavier and his buzz-cut crew. At least his friends have stuck by his side during STRIP's downfall.

I join them. "Hey."

"What'd you get, man?!" Xavier shouts in my face.

Buzz-Cut One glances my way. Xuan. Then the other. Zach, I think. He goes in for a bro handshake—a basic slide into the standard grip that I've started to learn means *I have no clue who you are, but you seem chill*.

I don't have to think too hard about how my hand moves as I return it. "I passed." My voice comes out distant. I'm too in shock.

Xavier picks me up off the floor and squeezes me so hard that I almost snap. "Hallelujah!"

By the time my feet hit the floor again, my equilibrium is dead. I stumble to the left. "But I only got one pull-up. Ms. Nallos gave me the credit anyway because you and I have been training so hard together. So, thank you."

"Really? Dang. You're welcome. But." Xavier's forehead crinkles as he leans into my face. I don't move back. "No offense, but you look like shit."

"I'm fine. I just pulled an all-nighter."

"Before *this* test?"

"I have to study for all our other tests."

The excitement Xavier showed before has been completely erased by worry now. He digs into his pocket and pulls out a protein bar. "I brought this for you just in case." He throws it my way.

My brain doesn't process in time, and it slaps my temple. I jerk.

Xavier winces at the protein bar now on the floor. "Really thought you'd catch that. You look like you haven't been eating. Stuff that in your mouth."

I pick up the bar and follow orders, wondering if that means I've lost weight. It's not like I've had time to look in a mirror.

Xavier slaps my back encouragingly. "C'mon, you'll make the ranks on Wednesday. You've worked too hard not to."

I smile back, trying to believe this for once too. But I have no clue if I should.

Chapter 37
THE STRANGER
WEDNESDAY, NOVEMBER 13

The rest of finals went by in what felt like a hazy, metaphysical state of panic. The English literature final essay topic was, thankfully, *oo ghost*. Chemistry, world history, and first-year civics, I turned in early. Calculus, though, I finished right as *time* was called. Then I finally took a breath.

Now Wednesday classes are already beginning—the day instructors scramble to entertain us after the trauma we've faced before the mixer and winter break. Ms. Nallos lets us play any sport we want, and I spend the time anxiously walking the track, my legs dragging like they're 100 percent uranium—the heaviest element in nature and question eleven on the chemistry final. Did I answer that right?

After this and one hour of English literature, the grade rank board will update to finish off the semester. Everyone and their parents will know where they land. Delilah will know if she's hit high enough to run for the student council board. I'll finally know if I stay or go.

Soon enough, I'm in English, and Mr. Stern is kicking open the door, the hem of his deeply memorable leopard-print blazer flapping behind him. "Testing's over! How're you feeling?"

The ceiling chandelier hums. A cough comes from the back.

Mr. Stern sets his briefcase on his desk. "I hope you can wake up for our guest speaker today. A few of you may recall him as a past student here."

Someone who looks around my age follows Mr. Stern into the classroom.

Straight, dark hair that's half pulled back, half left down, falling to his chin and shaping his soft cheekbones. A light brown turtleneck sweater and navy cardigan combo that complements his brown eyes and tan skin—the spitting image of a poet.

There are plenty of past students this could be. But when I glance at Jasper one seat to my left, his face is pale, like he's seeing a ghost of his past come back that he thought was nevermore. In a way, I suppose he is.

Pierre-Marie Laframboise drifts toward the desk. He's almost as tall as Mr. Stern—not exactly a strawberry shortcake. When he smiles, it's calm instead of arrogant like I expected. "Hello." His voice is so quiet, I can barely hear him.

His name comes from every corner of the classroom. Shouted. Whispered. Adored. Except for directly to my left.

I stay silent too. I'm too stunned, sitting before the previous Excellence Scholar. I reach for my pencil and notebook to take notes and gather anything I can about him. In a way, he's my competition.

"This is P.M., if he even needs an intro," Mr. Stern says with a laugh, and it doesn't make me jealous. Nope. "Who already has a prosperous literary career at your age. I wish I could say his success comes from my guidance, but his fan base started right before Valentine."

Beside me, Jasper aggressively kicks his feet up on the table, making a spectacle out of himself as he looks out the window.

P.M.'s attention briefly drifts toward Jasper in the front row. If he shows any change to his professional expression, I don't catch it. "Mr. Stern is too kind. Valentine helped me. More importantly, it gave me life experience. If you don't have that, then what is there to write about?" His accent is only slightly noticeable. It doesn't sound fully French or Tagalog but a subtle blend.

"Our next unit will focus more on attempting to write the genres we're studying," Mr. Stern says, "so he'll discuss his own creative work process."

P.M. starts scribbling on the whiteboard. Cursive, of course. "I actually wish to start my lesson by showcasing something I learned from a person in this very room."

Then he writes rules I've seen before. Studied before.

He only spends five minutes discussing how one should choose an environment that won't sway your feelings. What he does spend time on, however, is how emotions do not have to make sense, so neither do your words, and then provides examples. He wraps up the lesson with how you should always craft for yourself.

I don't have notes to take when they already exist in my notebook. Eventually, he moves to how these rules have morphed into his own unique set over time, and that craft advice flourishes when you add your subjective tastes. I barely listen, instead debating how talented this previous Excellence Scholar is compared to me—to all of Valentine—and how Jasper would truly feel about him if he were honest.

"Questions?" Mr. Stern says from the side of the room as the lesson ends.

P.M. watches the class with another smile.

Jasper raises his hand, feet still kicked up on the desk.

P.M.'s face just barely tenses into something uneasy. I would only be able to tell from my place in the front row. "Yes?"

"Have you decided to come teach us because you believe you're better than us?"

My mouth hangs open, and I swat Jasper on the arm.

Whispers come from around the room.

"Another question, please," Mr. Stern says, his tone firm for once.

Suddenly, I feel like I'm in calc class instead because P.M. is treating me like an X he's trying to solve. He squints at my shoes, then my hands, and up to my face. I'm not sure why. If anything, that should be my job. He turns to Jasper. "It's okay. Didn't I say Valentine gave me valuable life experience?"

"And once you were done using us for that, you ditched us, right?"

"Jasper," Mr. Stern says. Hearing him refer to a student by their first name shoots even my own spine straight. Mr. Stern only ever uses last names. "Step into the hall."

Jasper huffs like he's simply been told to put his feet down. He picks up his bag and disappears through the door. Mr. Stern whispers something in P.M.'s ear—*watch the class*, probably—and follows Jasper into the hall. The door shuts.

P.M. clears his throat. "More questions?"

When the bell rings, nearly half the class swarms P.M. instead of leaving for their next one. Even Robby, who's as thrilled to see him as everybody else. Between Robby's behavior and Xavier's previous neutral intel, Jasper and P.M.'s fallout must not have affected other STRIP members. That's hard to believe, considering Jasper's claims—that P.M. abandoned them all.

I don't move at first, instead trading looks between the commotion and the door, where Jasper must still be getting talked to. Or he's been sent to the office.

Eventually, I walk up to Robby's side amid the crowd swarming P.M. According to Jasper, P.M. should be bragging about the places he's visited and the followers he's gained. Instead, everyone else does the talking, spitting back and forth their hypotheses about the starring man himself as he stays quiet at the center, shoulders scrunched in a way that negates all intimidation, even at his six-foot height. Every once in a while, his attention shifts around the classroom—the old ceiling chandelier, our Edgar Allan Poe projects lining the back wall, the desks—like he's trying to drink in Valentine before he leaves. Like he cares.

"Are you close with Jasper?" P.M.'s voice comes from nearby.

When I look at who he's talking to, his gaze is locked on me. He's stepped closer, farther from the other conversations.

My eyes blow out. "What?"

"You sit beside him."

"I mean, I'm in STRIP. I write letters with him."

His head tilts in a way that's difficult to interpret. "Oh?"

"They're roommates," Robby says, joining the conversation. He's giving me a strange look. Am I sweating as much as I feel like I am? "And Charlie's the new Excellence Scholar."

P.M. smiles so genuinely that it stuns me. Up close, he really does echo Jasper with the slender fingers, narrow shoulders, and straight hair that wisps around the face. Must be a requirement to be a poet. But where Jasper's whirlwind of a personality distracts from his delicate features, P.M.'s shyness enhances it. "Has Jasper spoken of his resentment toward me?"

Are *all* poets also this forward?

"Um," I say slowly. "Just that you left without any warning."

"I see. I have faith you don't harbor the same emotions toward me. Leaving was for the better; I promise you that with my heart."

AND THEY WERE ROOMMATES

"What do you mean—?"

"Charlie." Robby leans toward me. "The combo of his poetry collection and influencer stuff has made him rich."

P.M. laughs lightly. "Not rich. But the Excellence Scholarship deserved to go to someone new who"—his stare lingers on me—"needed more help than I did."

"That's mad selfless," someone mutters from across the circle.

If there are other eavesdroppers, I don't hear them. According to this story, I do owe P.M. for that. But something still feels off. "You could've stayed."

"Well, I did always plan to visit," P.M. says. "If you're roommates, then you must know how Jasper is. A bit dramatic."

Dramatic.

Because P.M. left Valentine without asking how anyone would feel. Because one day, he was there, and the next, he was gone. Because this wasn't the first time Jasper watched someone slip through his fingers when, in his eyes, I'd done the same to him.

"It wasn't because he's dramatic," I say, and the rush of my own complicated guilt sharpens every word. "It's because he cares."

P.M.'s and Robby's brows lift in unison.

Voices surge through the closed window so loudly that it interrupts our conversations. Red-and-black-clothed bodies, swarming the ranking board.

Robby taps my shoulder. "Ready to go look?"

Chapter 38
HIS LAST BOW
WEDNESDAY, NOVEMBER 13

SECOND-YEAR LISTINGS
1. Jasper Grimes (100/100)
2. Robert Walker (99.92)
3. Bingo A. Dixon (99.73)
4. Nicolas Burton (99.08)
5. Kamari Barrera (98.99)
6. Charlie von Hevringprinz (98.90)

My knees give out, and I collapse in front of the board. A startled yelp comes from somewhere. Someone tries to grab my arm. Robby, maybe.

Sixth.

I'm leaving Valentine.

"Charlie?"

P.M. is kneeling on the pavement beside me, his brow tense in a way that doesn't suit his soft face. He holds out a hand. "Let me help you up."

I don't take it. "What am I supposed to do?" A crack cuts through my words, but I barely notice. No sleep. Constant studying. Xavier's training.

For nothing.

"Sorry," I say, lifting my glasses to scrub my face. "I don't even know you."

"But I know it's unfair. I faced this too."

"You never ranked?"

P.M. takes my hand to pull me up himself, and I'm so disoriented that I let him. He won't meet my eyes, though, like he regrets revealing what he just said. "I left before I could find out. But I knew I wouldn't."

"So, that's why you left?"

He sighs deeply. "I suppose there were many circumstances at play, and they all merged in an unfortunate way." He looks to the top of the list as a way to deflect, indicating he won't share more than that. "Six is still impressive, Charlie."

"Thanks," I force myself to say.

Because P.M.'s words should help. I fought longer than him and got closer than he ever believed he could. But six doesn't keep me at Valentine, and now I can only think about how the one person I want to talk to isn't here.

I flick my head to the left, where the Gothic turrets of the library rise into the overcast sky. Yesterday, Jasper and I agreed to pull an all-nighter tonight to finish the mixer letters by tomorrow, starting at the library and then moving to our room. It's possible he's being reprimanded in the office after his class outburst, but as the principal's nephew, also doubtful.

I make my way to the library and my usual STRIP Time desk. It's empty. With finals being over, the other nearby desks are too. No Jasper.

"Charlie, I need you more than anything."

My stomach flips. I whirl around on my heels.

Luis stands before me, holding a stapled packet far away as if it's poisonous. His curls are the frizziest I've ever seen, proving he's been tugging them for hours. "Bro. It's my score. Calc final. Help."

Why did I think that was *him*? In what world? "What'd you get?"

"You think I'm looking? I need you to tell me how bad it is."

"You know the ranks are up now, right? You can go see where you fell."

"We worked on calc together, V.H. This is history."

I try to push aside my own problems eating away at me. Luis has relied on me for too long for me not to.

The moment I take the packet, Luis covers his already squinted eyes. Although the exam isn't mine, my heart skips a beat. At our first tutoring session, Luis's parents demanded that he get an A. For that, he'd need to score at least a 95. I slowly check the paper.

On top, circled in black ink, is a 97.

Luis peeks through his hand. "How bad?"

I hand the paper back, a smile creeping up my face.

He deflects, chopping the air with a hand. "I can't look!"

"You can!"

"Not!"

"But you got a 97!"

Luis takes the paper and stares in shock.

I can't help but keep grinning at the reaction I've seen plenty of times, even before I started STRIP, back in Queens. The one that constantly makes me think I could do this for the rest of my life. "Looks like your hard work paid off."

Luis slings an arm over my shoulder, pulling me in so snugly that I nearly choke. "*Our* work paid off. The whole student population has been saved because of you."

A sudden heaviness travels up my legs and builds pressure behind my eyes, weighing me down with more exhaustion.

What did Luis say?

Right. "I wouldn't say that," I respond uncertainly, fighting it off with a few blinks. "People don't come to my tutoring anymore."

"They'll come back. Who could resist you? Oh, guess who has a date to the mixer?"

Well, not me. "You?"

"Yep. Michael asked *me*. You know, I used to hate this mixer since my friends would ditch me for their dates every year, but now it's my era to ditch. My orange bow tie is gonna kill this year's pumpkin-Halloween-whatever theme. Anyway, can you believe it?"

I really can't, considering the campus we're standing on. Even more so, how happy I am for Luis's love life. Once again, how tired am I? "You deserve it."

Someone at our side clears their throat.

Jasper, playing with his repaired silver bracelet instead of making eye contact. In his cross-body bag, the knit scarf I gave him peeks out of the top, like it's actually become part of his daily list of things to pack. Once I leave Valentine, I suppose that'll be all he has left of me. "I apologize for the interruption. STRIP is holding a meeting now, but I can—"

The rest is lost to me. The heaviness from before takes over my body, and the world narrows into white.

Pressure hits the small of my back, sparking me alive again.

I blink up at Jasper's face, hovering above my own. His hand still presses against me, holding me upright. "Charlie? Charlie."

"What?"

"You were passing out."

"Oh."

"Oh? That's all you have to say?" Jasper's a mesh of high

staccato notes, and his blue eyes race around my face. "You slept last night after I went to bed, didn't you?"

"I'm *fine*," I say more aggressively than I should. I straighten myself to no longer need his support. Luis is gone. Was I passed out for more than a few seconds? "Why are you late? Did you get in trouble?"

Jasper clenches his jaw. He sets his cross-body bag on the table, turning his back to me and whipping out his journal so hard that he could be slapping cockroaches with it.

Okay.

As I unzip my own backpack, I recall everything that happened right before I fainted. No more STRIP for me. No more Mr. Stern. No more Dix. No more Valentine. No more trying to fix this awkwardness between me and Delilah—I'll be so far from her that I might even lose her as my best friend for good. Next term, a new STRIP face will be needed. I should've warned them, should've already packed, should've *never* thought otherwise.

"I didn't rank," I mutter.

Jasper stops moving, but he doesn't turn around to face me. That's probably for the better. I'd rather not see the pity on his face.

"I'm sorry," I add, staring at the textbooks in my backpack that I'll no longer need. "You'll need a new face. But I can still help with the mixer."

"Our writing plans are canceled today," Jasper says with such a strangely charged rasp to his tone that I stiffen. When he finally turns, there's no pity like I expect. Only an expression so tense that a vein pops on his forehead.

He's angry? At me? Because of what I said?

I stare back at him, thrown. "But we only have one day left till the mixer."

"I'll take care of your ten remaining letters."

"You have to write twenty more yourself, though! That's impossible—"

"*Charlie*," Jasper says strictly. Coldly. It makes me realize how much admiration he used to exude when saying my name, now that it's gone. "Go back to our room. Now."

Chapter 39
WAR AND PEACE
WEDNESDAY, NOVEMBER 13

Charlie von Hevringprinz, your mother called the office eleven times regarding final grades, which were emailed to all parents this afternoon. Please visit at your earliest convenience.

—Maverick, the Residential Retainers Commission

I rip the note off my door and ball it in my fist.

I don't go to the office and return Mom's call. I don't pack up my uniforms. The moment I unlock the knob, I chuck the balled note at Jasper's cardboard cutout as hard as I can, flop into bed without even changing out of my uniform, and go to sleep.

By the time I wake up again, my watch reads two in the morning. I blink around the room, where Jasper's bedside lamp shines into my eyes. He sits at his desk, flipping through his notebook. He wears a headband that shoves his blond bangs up every which way, like he's ready to put on cucumbers and a relaxing face mask. Totally calm.

Like we never fought.

My rage jerks my body awake. I swing my legs over my bed and stare him down. "What is *wrong* with you?"

Jasper yelps and flings his fountain pen, which soars across the room. He spins in his chair, his rolled sleeves slipping down his forearms. "Sleep."

"How do you expect me to sleep after you practically freaked out and barred me from helping you finish the letters while you stay up all night?"

"I beg your pardon?"

"Fine. Play clueless." I head into the bathroom. I need to wash my face and brush my teeth and get this worst day of my life off me. "Don't care that I'm leaving Valentine."

Jasper doesn't respond. Of course he doesn't. I spread toothpaste along my toothbrush and shove it into my mouth. Unbelievable.

From the other room, Jasper's chair squeaks. "That was the last letter, Charlie."

"*Whu-ay?*" I call back.

"They're finished. The letters. It's not a burden." There's a pause. "In the library, I was angry because I saw the ranks. Not because of you."

My brow furrows. I spit out my toothpaste and walk back into the room. Jasper stands at the center, fist clenched at his side. A less stubborn piece of me tells me to drop it, to let go of this fight and celebrate that Jasper somehow finished rewriting the mixer letters. That we did it, even though we doubted we could.

"*You're* angry?" I repeat instead. "You're Rank One."

"Yes. Because this academy has taken P.M. from me, and now it's trying to take you. Because there are loopholes in our system that should not *exist*. Although my grades are flawless, I would prefer to leave my excused PE credit out of it. This isn't fair to—" His gaze steadies on me. "I'm going to make sure you stay. I give you my word."

The words render me speechless. Jasper does have principal's nephew powers. But can he really promise something as seemingly impossible as keeping me at Valentine?

"Why would you do this for me?" I finally mutter.

"Because I've seen you," Jasper says. "And when you push yourself so much that you pass out in the library, you probably think you're only hurting yourself—or maybe you don't even realize how much you are. But do you know who else you are hurting?"

I scoff. "No one?"

"No, Charlie. Everyone around you. I admit, I never understood how unfair this all was until recently, and that was"—his fist clenches tighter—"so, *so* ignorant of me. But quite frankly, you're hurting me too."

"You?"

"I care about *you!*" His voice cracks. "Is that not obvious by now?"

My heart stutters. By caring, he means as a roommate. A friend.

But that crack in his voice didn't make it seem that way.

"I'm sorry," I say, and I mean it. "But I can't just stop trying to handle everything. That's my one job."

"Says who? Because I can't imagine it's you. Is it what you want?"

I consider Mom, Grandma, and Grandpa, who were so disappointed in her and her store, and Valentine as a whole—but no one has ever said this out loud. Either way, as I stand here in my exhaustion, I know the answer to Jasper's question. It's not what I want.

The words stay lodged in my throat.

"You have to tell me what you're thinking," Jasper says, his blue eyes hardening from the other side of the room. "I may be a genius, but I'm not a mind reader."

"I know that," I grumble.

"Do you? Because every time I do try to read your mind, you

get mad at me because I'm always getting it wrong. So, please. The spotlight is yours."

What *am* I thinking?

I'm thinking about how Jasper is trying to help me, even though he's supposed to be a self-obsessed poet with posters of himself on the ceiling. How he's the most obnoxious person I've ever met but one of the most inspiring minds I've ever known.

I'm thinking about Jasper. Always. And that's *wrong*.

I grip my forehead. "I don't know what I'm thinking."

A groan leaves Jasper. He crosses the room and stops in front of me, his bangs shoved up by his headband flopping dramatically around his forehead. "With all due respect, I don't know what I'm thinking about you either."

My chest lurches. I lean backward. "Jasper?"

"I had many expectations for my second year at Valentine. Win the Critical Junior Poet's Award. Model for *Poetic Fortune Digest's* Sexiest Poet of the Year. Remain Rank One. But being attracted to my roommate at an all-boys academy was not one of them."

All my breath drains out of me.

I try to find the logical map for him meaning *friend* again. There are too many roadblocks this time. "That's what you're thinking?"

Jasper's cheeks tinge pinker than they already are. "I don't know. I just said I don't know what I'm thinking."

"You said you're attracted to me."

"I suppose I did say that."

"Okay."

We stare at each other.

Jasper starts to pace our bedroom and tosses up his arms. "I mean, of course I said that. Yes. I've been searching for you all these years because I fell for you. Those feelings don't simply poof"—he does some jazz hands—"away!"

I cautiously follow his pacing with my eyes. My face must be as red as his with how scorching it feels. "That doesn't mean you're attracted to me now."

"How could I not be?!" His voice hits a high note I've never heard from him.

I readjust my glasses. "You're panicking."

"I am not. I'm always composed."

"Jasper."

"It all began when I brought that dreadful bookcase in our room. Why ever did I engrave our names like that? Have you noticed it looks like a wedding invitation?"

"Wait. Then? That was before you even knew who I was."

"That's why I was having a CRISIS," Jasper shouts, breaching into hissing basilisk territory, and his eyes blow wide. "I thought I was falling for the love of my life's BROTHER. I was about to set myself on FIRE."

"Jasper."

"And I have been trying so hard to be very, very normal since, but I cannot. Why, Saint Valentine, did I put us in a bedroom together?" He slams himself against my bedpost, sinking toward the floor like a dead body.

Before he falls too far, I walk over, tug him up by the collar, and press my lips to his.

I just want him to shut up, to *listen* to me. His lips are warm despite the rest of his body always being freezing, and it's so strangely intoxicating that I almost let him keep kissing me.

Except he's not kissing me. *I'm* kissing *him*.

Like two years ago.

Abruptly, I pull back. Do I *ever* learn from my mistakes? "Sorry. I'm—I should've asked. But. Do you at least know what you're thinking now?"

Jasper doesn't look horrified, even though I expect him to run away, slamming through the wall so forcefully that only the outline of his body remains. Instead, he peruses up and down my body in a way that makes my heart simultaneously plummet and explode.

Then my own shirt collar is tugged, and I'm being lightly shoved against the bedpost. Jasper cups my jaw and kisses me with the passion of someone starved for weeks. For two years. Every second thought I've had about Jasper melts out of my head, his touch lancing electricity through my core. This is nothing like our first kiss years ago. It's more. It's too much.

A muffled sound leaves me as I place my hands on his chest. "Jasper—"

His hand travels from my jaw to my hips, shoving our bodies closer. He's barely unruffled, only a few hairs escaped from his stubby ponytail, yet my lips are already swollen and my uniform is a wreck. "Please, Charlie, can you stop arguing with me just this once?"

My body screams at me to finally listen to him.

I try to regain my balance on the bedpost, but my legs are too close to giving out. "Somewhere else."

Jasper is merciful enough to oblige, but I barely catch my breath before his arm is wrapped around my waist and he's pushing me into our bookshelf, pinning an arm over my head. Fluttering pages fall to the carpet. Shakespeare, Jasper's poetry—that's all I catch before his lips are on mine again.

"This isn't much better," I manage on a gasp.

"Never liked poetry much," he says. "Poets are snobs."

"*You* are a poet."

He pulls back with a soft, low laugh. His blue eyes search my face, the same way they do when I read my writing aloud. The look that constantly floods my head with so much heat, I can't think straight.

"What are you doing?" I cover myself with a palm, but he gently brings it down.

"Why do you always hide your face?" Jasper says. "I like your face."

"Wh-what?"

"I said, I like your face. It's my favorite part about you."

I thrust my hand over *his* mouth instead. "I *heard* you."

"Why don't you want me to keep saying that?" he asks, muffled through my fingers.

"Because, well, you're really close—and—I'm insecure about it." My hand falls gradually off his mouth after admitting the truth I've never said aloud.

"But you have no reason to be insecure."

"Thanks," I drone. "No longer insecure."

"I'm serious," Jasper says. "I'm not sure what you see when you look in the mirror, Charlie, but I have a hypothesis that it isn't what others see."

I've tried to tell myself this for years but could never believe it. For some reason, right now, it feels like a piece of me is starting to.

My lips are back on his in seconds. We tumble into his side of the room until we fall on his bed. I finally yank off his ridiculous headband and thread my hands through his hair, and he does the same to my curls. Our teeth clink, and my glasses slide up my face. I pull away for air, and he gives me the chance. He's listening. I'm listening too. What I've wanted all along.

Good. All I need is to get this—him—out of my system. And he just needs to be quiet. That's all this is.

But what if it's not?

"Wait" heaves out of me.

Jasper stops. "What's wrong?"

"Does this—Does this mean you want to be together?"

His chest rises and falls as he takes me in. At first, I think I've worked him into a panic again, but his lopsided dimple pops. "Is it not obvious?"

It is. But if what Jasper says is true, that he'll figure out a way to keep me at Valentine—us together, at a place like this, the spotlight would be huge. To students. Instructors. His aunt.

All that attention. On me.

Dread rolls through me, and my heart squeezes tight.

My gaze drifts away from Jasper, but he leads my chin back with his pointer finger. "Hey," he says. "I do. Want us to be together." His smile softens, almost shy now. "And if you'll allow it, I would be honored to take you to the mixer. As your date."

I imagine us walking hand in hand into the mixer tomorrow. All those eyes following us. Slowly, I nod.

His face falls gradually, emptily. "You don't want to."

It's not a question. The words fall out from under him.

I stare back into his pained eyes. My hands itch to pull him closer. My heart tells me to let go of my fears and say *yes*.

But my brain won't let me this time.

Chapter 40
THE WINTER OF OUR DISCONTENT
THURSDAY, NOVEMBER 14

Xavier thumps my back so hard that I lurch like a pinball flipper. His crisp black suit was definitely tailored to account for his biceps, but his bow tie threatens to snap off his thick neck any second. "Stop messing with your cuffs."

"Okay," I say as we walk through the crowds of other black suits heading to the mixer early, only to move on to my tie and collar. Apparently, sister academy students are walked over in single-file lines by instructors right before. Because if they weren't, we would all run off into the woods and crash mouths.

Even though I haven't spotted any girls yet, my eyes wander in search of Delilah. She must be coming tonight. I have to see her. I have to know she's all right.

"Stop!" Robby says to my left, swatting my hands off my suit cuffs. His own suit, of course, is as put together as a celebrity's. "You look good."

Xavier and Robby seem adamant. I should believe them. A few months ago, the last place I would've guessed I'd wear my pack-in-case-of-emergency suit to for the first time was a hormone-ridden mixer, let alone one I wrote love letters for. Worse, Mom wouldn't let me buy a normal black one. *What about a shiny navy? It's a classic!*

Unspoken Guideline 17: Everyone owns a black suit, *Mom.*

Who I still haven't called back. Getting yelled at is the last thing I need right now.

"You sure it's okay?" I ask Xavier and Robby.

"Yeah, it's chic or whatever," Xavier says. "Like Mr. Stern."

Never mind.

"Thanks," I say through a yawn. Breaking news: It's impossible to fall asleep after making out with your roommate. We went to our separate beds in silence. He eventually left at a prompt seven a.m. like usual. Now that the letters are done, he hasn't told me yet if he's moving back to his aunt's quarters. Maybe the answer should be obvious.

Last night, he promised he'd stop me from being sent home, but there's no way he will now. Not after everything I said or, rather, didn't say.

Tonight is my last night at Valentine. I have to make it count.

Xavier and Robby halt on the path. I follow their gaze.

Horses. At least fifteen strapped in orange-and-black harnesses to fit the mixer's Halloween in November theme, circling the stone steps of the ballroom, which partially hangs over Au Sable Forks Lake like a stilt house. Between the marble statues of Saint Valentine on either side and the Gothic architecture pulling me back two centuries, I expect classical music to fill the air, but all I hear is "Monster Mash."

"They found 'em," Xavier mutters.

My guilt over accidentally releasing the horses finally lightens. "I'm glad they're okay—"

Robby screams, cutting me off, and makes a break for the ballroom.

Xavier yanks him back by the collar. "Self-control."

"Xavier's right." Jasper's voice comes from our left. "We have deliveries to make."

I turn, and my eyes spread wide.

Jasper's suit isn't black. Not navy. It's bright white, like the pristine-quality paper in his journal. Same for the vest, bow tie, and handkerchief folded in his breast coat pocket. His blond hair is worn down—a rarity. Tonight, he looks better than any poster or cardboard cutout version of himself. He makes eye contact with everyone except me.

It stings, even though I'm the one who caused this. His cross-body bag, which must hold the letters, is slung over a shoulder like he's off to class. "Apologies for running late. Blaze and I were discussing a potential plan."

Blaze steps out from behind Jasper's back, wiggling his butterfly pose. He's so small that I didn't even notice him there. Instead of a suit, he wears a tracksuit uniform.

"First things first," Jasper announces. "Is Ms. Delilah around?"

"She got in trouble because of us, dipshit," Xavier practically growls, crossing his arms, his suit-coat sleeves stretching taut. "There's no way she'd want to get involved with us again."

A hand thwacks Xavier upside the head. He yelps.

"Wrong, as usual," a familiar high voice says behind him.

Delilah.

Just hearing her voice has my spirits soaring. The moment she steps around Xavier, I pull her in for a hug, tucking her head beneath my chin. "You're still in the clear?"

"Do you know me?" she says, squeezing me back.

I take in her sleek black gown that makes her blond hair and blue eyes—which are both a shade darker than Jasper's—pop. Then the three-inch stilettos that could puncture my eyeballs. Threatening, but still beautiful. "How's everything else? Student council?"

She tosses a peace sign, but her expression retains its usual deadness. "Your girl ranked high enough to run for student council vice president after break."

"Seriously?" I squeeze her again, and it feels just like that time we hugged and shared goodbyes at the end of camp all those years ago. Like we're those same best friends. But we're older now. There have been so many changes. Even our friendship has changed from long-distance to real-life.

Maybe, with all these changes, we actually need to forget who we used to be. Instead, we need to work more on learning who we are now.

"What about you?" Delilah says through a grin. Like she expects good news.

My heart sinks as I pull away, knowing what I have to say next. That I'm leaving her behind alongside STRIP. "I ranked sixth. Not fifth."

Delilah's brow line soars. "What?"

"But it's all right."

"No, it's not. That's basically the top fucking five. Can't they secretly shove some extra credit in your face?"

That fact that Delilah is willing to hear out yet another problem of mine pulls a bit of warmth to my chest, even when the conversation is as miserable as this one. "I doubt it, but—"

Jasper interrupts us with an awkward wave. That's when I notice London and another girl from the sister academy standing beside Delilah. His eyes are only on the girls. "Apologies for the interruption, ladies, but may we ask for one last favor?"

Delilah scowls, shooting me a firm look that's giving *we'll continue this conversation when we're alone*. "The fuck is this guy?"

He extends a hand for a shake before I can answer. "Jasper Grimes, miss."

She glances at me. Jasper. Me again. "Is this—?"

"Principal Grimes's nephew," I cut in. "You must've heard of him."

Delilah makes a face like she tastes Clorox. Even if I never told her more than Jasper's first name back at camp, with him standing beside me now, there's no way she isn't putting two and two together that the principal's nephew has been the culprit all along.

"Where are the rest of the top five?" Jasper asks. "Sophia? Mary?"

London, the antithesis of Delilah tonight in her hot-pink minidress, frowns at the question. "They're too scared to help us anymore."

Silence falls among the circle.

I turn to Delilah. "You're okay with helping us again?"

Delilah clicks her tongue. "I finish what I start. And Valentine's rules are pissing me off."

So, Jasper stands before us all and addresses everyone but me. My guilt distracts me from paying attention. Knowing Jasper, he'd treat me like Foot Cody if he hated me. He would have no problem with looking directly at me, insulting me with the most pretentious vocabulary, and smiling in a way that doesn't reach his eyes. What else would cause this?

My chest aches as I consider the only other possibility. Can he not bear to look at me because it hurts too much?

I know he likes me. He told me. But this much?

"The mixer is three hours," Jasper is in the middle of explaining once I lock back in. "A hundred letters need to be delivered—preferably in the first two hours. Blaze will pass them out since he's the quickest and smallest." His face hardens. "Remember, not a single instructor can spot these letters. They're the most intelligent educators in the nation. They'll surely connect them to Delilah's bag of letters if so."

"Blaze will need to deliver fifty per hour, then," Robby says. "Nearly one per minute."

"Can't Blaze sit his ass down somewhere and have people come up?" Xavier asks.

"That could pool a crowd, Xav," Robby says.

"How is that better than Blaze running around like a headless chicken? If an instructor spots one letter, we're done."

"I've prepared for that," Jasper says, rummaging through his bag more. He pulls out a white sheet and tosses it over Blaze's head. From a hole ripped on the side, Blaze's hand juts out and waves. Two more frayed holes barely reveal his eyes.

Everyone stares at Blaze the Ghost.

Next, Jasper pulls out a pumpkin trick-or-treat bucket and slides the handle up Blaze's arm. "We have twenty minutes until this mixer starts. We're going to spend that time rolling the letters into candy foil I found in my aunt's kitchen and writing every recipient's name on them. Then we'll put them in this bucket."

"You *do* know that we can see this ghost, right?" Xavier asks.

"That's fine. Because Delilah, our lovely student council member, asked Blaze to pass out candy around the ballroom."

"I did?" Delilah asks.

Jasper winks. "That's the story you tell."

"If any faculty walk up and ask for candy?" Robby asks unsurely.

Jasper yanks peppermints out of his pocket and tosses them at Blaze's sheeted head. Blaze grunts. "He has spares."

"And I always come prepared to cause a distraction," Delilah says, patting the chain of a handbag slung over her shoulder. What she means by that is an enigma—possibly those sparklers she accidentally set oak trees on fire with at summer camp, or even homemade poison.

"Ladies," Jasper says, turning to the three, "you're the only ones who can match sister academy student names to faces. Direct Blaze in the right ways, please?"

"Simple enough," London says. The other two nod.

"Anything to make everyone trust us again," Xavier says. "I don't want STRIP to die. Or to get kicked out either, but, you know."

The words resonate deep within me, reminding me just how much this is all my fault. The knocked-over gate; the ripped bag. Maybe I have to leave Valentine, but if everyone else suffers the same fate, I'd never forgive myself. And they'd never forgive me.

Lately, I'm losing so much. I can't lose them too.

Tonight, I'll fix this once and for all.

"We'll fight until the end," Jasper says to everyone except me. "Ready?"

Chapter 41
DADDY-LONG-LEGS
THURSDAY, NOVEMBER 14

The ballroom is full of spiders.

Plastic spider rings are piled on every cocktail table, surrounding taper candles burning in centerpiece sconces. Tablecloths are patterned with cartoon spiders. Polyester webs are stretched across the ceiling. Even a massive spider sculpture made of plastic cups hangs from the ceiling by two strings like a marionette.

We go still in the doorway.

Blaze slams into my back. He starts to readjust his ghost sheet to see through the eyeholes. "Wherefore did we stop walking—?"

"NO," Xavier shouts, and Robby lunges to cover Blaze's eyes.

I lean closer to Delilah's ear. "Don't let Blaze see the spiders."

Delilah nods despite her confusion.

The ballroom's décor can't compete with the strange behavior of our classmates. They huddle on either side, boys on one and girls on the other, pointedly—and irritably—avoiding eye contact. It feels dramatic until I remember the brother academy never received responses to their letters, and the sister academy believes they were never invited. On the best night of the year, everyone feels rejected.

Even more, failed by STRIP.

Without the support of the student body standing before us, this hundred-year tradition ceases to exist. Just like that. It's happening right before our eyes.

We have to save this tonight.

Xavier frowns. "They don't know what to do after relying on us for so long, huh?"

"Both sides must be angry and confused," Robby surmises like I did, surveying the ballroom. "Xavier, you'll distract Ms. Nallos on the left. P.M. has a few occupied too."

"He's here?" Jasper looks every which way for him.

I do too. He's easy to spot, even among the crowd of instructors laughing with him. His suit may be black, but the slim stripe pattern and light pink tie are almost as bold as Jasper's suit.

"Jasper should talk to his aunt," Robby says. "She's already herded tons of other instructors. Charlie and I will cover Mr. Stern—"

We turn to look at him; he's standing at one of the cocktail tables bordering the walls. He hands a stuffed gnome to Ms. Lyney, whose face matches her red gown in color. *William Stern* is etched on the gnome's belly.

Robby pinches the bridge of his nose. "Never mind. They're gone. We'll stand guard in the back to monitor any suspicious activity."

Everyone splits off.

As Robby and I claim a table by the plastic cup spider and speakers to keep an eye on the operation, the bass of "Thriller" booms. I watch Delilah and London from a distance as they whisper a direction to Blaze. He zooms off and rams into three other girls, then hands one a wrapped candy letter. Once she opens it, her eyes light up. She searches the ballroom for her date.

Maybe this *will* work.

"How're you holding up?" Robby says loudly enough to be heard over the electric guitar and synthesizers. He's picking out pumpkin and triangular candy corns from a bowl and dividing them on the table.

"We have the easier task tonight," I say, popping a few of the candy corns in my mouth. "So, not too nervous."

"I mean still being roommates with Jasper. Isn't he what started your incurable illness?"

"Wha—" I choke on my candy corn and spit it out on the table.

Robby stares at the orange-and-yellow goop. "Not trying to pry. I just wanted to check up on you. As a friend."

In a desperate attempt to stay totally calm and cool, I join Robby in dividing up candy corn. "D-did someone say that? Who said that?"

"No one."

"Then how did you know—? Er." Butcher me.

"It's always something new with you two. Burning hatred, total obsession, utter indifference. Anyone with a brain can see something's up. Unfortunately for you, as top ranks, we have those."

"We?"

"Xavier and me."

The embarrassment hits hard. "I'm still surprised you figured it out. I thought Jasper was straight."

Robby giggles and peeks up from the candy corn. Once he notices I haven't joined in, he presses his lips firmly together. "That wasn't a joke?"

"No? Jasper only realized himself a few weeks ago."

His brow lifts incredulously. "The jewelry-wearing, more-dramatic-than-a-whining-baby-pony, long-haired poet?"

"I mean, a straight guy could act that way too."

"Technically, but I also think the odds were in your favor."

I search for Jasper across the ballroom. He stands by his aunt, as commanded by Robby, gesticulating and blabbering in a way that almost comes off heated, like they're having an intense heart-to-heart conversation. Knowing him, though, he must just be speaking passionately about ancient Sumerian poetry's lack of syllabo-tonic versification to distract her. He claims they aren't close.

Still, Principal Grimes nods like she's paying attention. Like she cares.

It pulls a question to the forefront of my mind. "Do you know if Jasper has the same"—I pause, unsure how to phrase this—"values as his aunt?"

"What do you mean?" Robby asks.

"She's the principal. Of this academy."

"Ah. Well, two years ago she took over after the previous principal."

"Jasper's aunt is new?"

"Yup. Before, she was at some private LA school."

Principal Grimes's name likely wouldn't have come up as a camper, but it makes even more sense now why I'd never heard of her. "She's not as strict?"

"Nothing's really changed since she started here. I doubt she'd create and implement the rules we have, but it also seems like she's complicit with the status quo."

"Oh," I say.

"Too harsh?"

"No, you're right." But it's nice, knowing I'm not alone in the feeling. I take another look around the ballroom. A few girls and boys have begun to mingle instead of avoiding contact at all costs from opposite walls. Matt St. Paul, in particular, stands one table away with a girl who holds a striped, lopsided candy wrapper that I remember folding one of my own blackout poems into, her face beet red and her grin wide.

It's working.

A scream cuts through the ballroom, high and shrill. Blaze, who's collapsed in front of the giant plastic cup spider dangling from the ceiling. The letters wrapped in candy foil are spilled across the floor.

"Today's the day," he mumbles beneath his white sheet.

A few chaperones peek over, even with Xavier's massive back blocking their view.

"Need help?" Ms. Nallos calls. She's already walking over. If she picks up just one piece of candy, it'll feel too light to her.

My heart rate skyrockets. I look for Delilah and spot her; she's as wide-eyed as I must be. Gradually, she reaches into her handbag and pulls out three sticks. Three sparklers.

Leaning toward the nearest taper candle on a table, she lights the tips with the flame, then chucks them toward the opposite side of the ballroom. They skitter across the floor as red-and-gold sparks crackle, pulling everyone's attention.

Robby and I use the distraction to rush over to Blaze. As Robby scrambles to shove the candy back into the trick-or-treat bucket, I shake Blaze's shoulders.

"The arachnids' weaponry?" Blaze says, trading frantic looks between the sparklers and the spider behind me.

"Blaze." I snap in front of his eyes. He barely peels his gaze off the spider. "Blaze, give me the trick-or-treat bucket."

"But I must aid STRIP."

"We made a promise—you helped with my love letters, so I assist you on the fated day. Okay? I can handle this spider." I check over Blaze's shoulder. Ms. Nallos is circumventing the chaperone circle inspecting the sparklers in confusion, and Robby has at least half the letters to still pick up.

We're out of time. We need to buy some.

"You know what you can do to aid STRIP, Blaze?" I ask.

"What ho?"

"You got your slingshot with you?"

"Everlastingly."

"Get out that slingshot and knock down that spider."

I reach under Blaze's white sheet and into his tracksuit pants pocket. Once I find the slingshot and marble, I pull them out and shove them into his tiny twelve-year-old hands.

A fire rushes to his eyes. Gripping my shoulder, he rises shakily to his feet and aims at one of the two wires. He shoots, and the marble goes soaring.

The spider shakes, tilts, and comes crashing down. The plastic cups explode, knocking into cocktail tables and classmates' heads.

Every instructor rushes to the cups next, shouting if everyone is safe. Robby and I race to toss the remaining candy into the bucket.

"Mr. Charlie?"

I spring to my feet and spin around, tucking the bucket behind my back. Principal Grimes stands before me in all her glory. Between her usual high-quality pantsuit and blond hair clipped out of the way, she must've stepped out of her office right before the mixer began.

"H-hello, Principal Grimes," I say.

A tug comes at the bucket behind my back. Robby.

"I'll keep passing out the candy...," he says, wandering away with it.

Principal Grimes smiles. "Everything okay over here?"

"Yep! Yeah. Awesome."

She watches the unfolding commotion on the dance floor. "Always an unpredictable mess, these mixers. Although I can't deny I get a bit of a kick out of it."

Those are the last words I expected to hear from her. I don't respond.

"Sorry to intrude on your supercool night," she continues, "but I had been meaning to speak with you."

Because I didn't rank.

"Right," I say, my heart sinking. "I know my Excellence Scholar requirements—"

"I just received word we're no longer applying the ranking system as a metric. Well, as a requirement for our Excellence Scholars at first. It takes baby steps with the board of trustees."

I try to speak. To move. I'm too stunned.

"What changed?" I say, my voice barely a whisper.

"Jasper didn't tell you?"

"Tell me what?"

Principal Grimes sighs in a way that sounds half humorous and half exhausted. "Let's just say he gained the support of a few other students with parents who are vital to our financial donor stability, and they wrote to a certain board of trustees, threatening to release quite the op-ed about the"—she pauses—"antiquated ways of Valentine."

My head races over who he convinced to join—Xavier? Blaze? Did they know this whole time? Is this what Jasper was speaking to her about in the ballroom?

Even after what I told him last night?

"I had no idea," I say.

"He came to me personally after the ranks released at first, but I told him it's up to the board. Although I've never been a fan of the ranks either."

"Really?"

"Yes, but my workload has thrown aside my priorities lately, trying to please the board. I'm admittedly proud of my nephew for causing a fuss. I really should get to know him a bit better, now that we're in such close proximity." She presses a finger to her lips. "Anyhoo, I haven't told him the news that your requirements have changed. I wanted you to know first."

Jasper really did this.

He's why I'm staying.

My chest bursts with a joy I haven't felt since I received my Valentine acceptance letter. I don't even care that my eyes water in front of her. "Thank you, both of you."

I have to tell STRIP.

No. Mom. I have to call her back.

"How is everything else?" Principal Grimes asks. Last time I met with her, stress oozed from her, but tonight, all of that is dampened. Maybe she's felt the pressure of tradition too. Either way, it seems like Jasper taking matters into his own hands had an effect. "I hope your time here has otherwise been satisfactory?"

I could give the same response I always do. Busy. Full of studying.

But everything feels like it's changing. Everyone here is really starting to feel like they're on my side. "Principal Grimes, what's Valentine's stance on transgender students?"

The topic shift shakes her up at first, but then she hums more calmly than I expect. "I only started here recently, but I believe there was one student—we knew much later, postgraduation.

None have made it known to us during, so I assume we've never addressed it as such."

I prepare to once again speak what I swore I never would. My friends won't let me go home. Jasper too. I know that now.

And I don't want to hide. I can stand up for myself. "I had originally requested a single room, but there was a mix-up. This is why I requested one. For privacy."

We stare at each other. "Thriller" starts to play. Again.

Then Principal Grimes nods, albeit unnaturally quickly. "We need to get that part of the guideline package fixed, then."

Is that a good or a bad thing? "Fixed?"

"I'll bring this promptly to the board of trustees at our next meeting. Goodness, getting paired with Jasper must've been a shock! What is this about a mix-up? If it makes you feel better, he's recently gotten a room back in my instructor's quarters, if you didn't know. You should have a space to yourself soon, Charlie."

With how fast both Jasper and his aunt barrel through conversations, it takes a second for me to process.

Am I *dreaming*?

"Thank you. Again," I say, my heart full. "I've heard a few other good ideas from other classmates. They might be worth hearing at that meeting too."

"Oh?"

I glance across the ballroom until I spot Xavier, who slow dances with a totally innocent-looking Delilah despite her previous sparkler crimes. Xavier, however, looks seconds from a breakdown as he holds her, shoulders tensed to his ears. "Like, a coed lacrosse team."

A grin pulls at Principal Grimes's lips. "We can leave space for questions this month."

As she walks away with a polite goodbye, I search the crowds more. Robby is passing a letter to another sister student. Luis stands at a table with Michael in his black suit and orange bow tie, a little too close to just be friendly. London must've also received a letter because she's taken a break from her delivery duties to shyly talk with Griffin Li. Way more couples are paired up now. Talking. Laughing. Finally with each other instead of the gloom and doom we walked into.

The plan really worked.

Then there's Jasper in his white suit and left-down hair and brilliant eyes. He's patting Blaze's back, most likely for fighting so bravely in the arachnid war. Suddenly, Jasper flicks his head my way. The first look I've gotten all night.

Across the sea of bodies, dancing and hugging during the most romantic event of the year, he smiles. Even though I pushed him away.

I made a mistake. A huge one.

Chapter 42
THE IMPORTANCE OF BEING EARNEST
THURSDAY, NOVEMBER 14

Unspoken Guideline 18: Do not sit on the fountain in winter, or your ass will freeze.

Snow hasn't fallen in Au Sable Forks yet, but my breath visibly leaves my lips as I wait out here. I still prefer this to being surrounded by the lovey guck in that ballroom, reminding me how Jasper and I aren't getting the night we deserve.

Any moment, the mixer will end. Jasper will walk out of that ballroom among the crowds. I need to tell him I made a mistake.

But will he listen?

The double doors open, chandelier light seeping into the night. A group walks down the steps, hollering about the fallen plastic cup spider. More follow, wandering toward the residential hall. Ten or so minutes pass, and there's barely anyone left.

Fabric slaps me across the face.

I choke out a very not-hot noise and grab at it.

"You're cold" comes from above me.

Lowering the fabric—a white suit coat—Jasper stands in his white vest and dress shirt, hands tucked into his slacks pockets.

"I'm not cold," I say through a chatter.

Jasper spikes an eyebrow.

I huff and wrap his suit coat around my shoulders. "You didn't have to."

"What are you doing out here?"

I clench my fist against my lap. "I was waiting for you."

Jasper's eyes widen, a light breeze fluttering his left-down hair. His rosy cheeks are already turning brighter. "P.M. wished to speak with me. Apologize, rather, for mistakes he hadn't known he'd made. And explained some others."

"Like?"

"Well, he believed I wrote better love letters for STRIP than him. Better poetry than him, especially after the popularity I found after he featured me online. And I ranked at the top when he knew he wouldn't come close." Jasper's laugh is sour, in a way that sounds like regret.

I don't know what to say at first. "None of that's your fault."

"This whole time, I thought P.M. was overshadowing me, yet he felt the opposite. So much that he needed to leave Valentine to escape me."

"Jasper, that's not true."

He just shrugs, sniffs in the cold air.

"Well, I'm not leaving Valentine," I say.

"Pardon?"

"The board of trustees is getting rid of rank requirements for Excellence Scholars. Because you apparently collected a group of people to convince them. Thank you."

Jasper's face falls into something so unbelievably warm and genuine—everything I've come to know about who he is in the past few months. Years. "Charlie. Charlie, I'm so—" He steps forward, lifting his arms almost into a hug, but then back again like he's lost.

"Why did you still do that for me?" I ask.

Jasper doesn't respond.

My mouth opens. Closes. "Can we talk?"

Still nothing.

"Jasper?"

"I'm sorry, but no."

My heart drops into my toes. After how I reacted last night, maybe I should've expected this answer, but admittedly, I didn't. "Why did you smile at me in the ballroom, then?"

"Because I—" He looks away. "I'm not sure why I did."

"Not being honest with me anymore?"

Then my breath catches in my throat.

Because there's a shine to Jasper's blue eyes now, and it's not the reflection of the lampposts or the crescent moon. "I don't want to talk to you, Charlie, because I'm terrified that whatever it is you're about to say will break my heart again, and I'm not—" He sucks in a shaky breath, and the first teardrop falls. "I'm not sure if I can survive that again. Not when I love you as much as I do."

The words shatter me. "You love me?"

"I never stopped."

So many thoughts zoom through me, but one sparkles brightest. If any spotlights were to shine upon Jasper and me for being together here, he'd make sure I never get hurt—we'd get through it together.

How can I keep thinking otherwise?

"I don't want to break your heart," I say, rising off the fountain and stepping cautiously toward him. "I made a mistake. That's what I was waiting here to tell you. I like you."

That only pulls a bitter smile out of Jasper. He scuffs his dress shoe along the pavement, kicking a gravel chunk. "I know you like me, Charlie."

"Then why do you think I'll—?"

"Because you still don't like me enough to take the risk."

The words are a wound in my gut, but I still gently take his hand and lead him onto the fountain ledge to sit too. "I am honestly a bit scared. But I don't want to be. I want you. I don't know what to do."

He nods a few times, but his expression doesn't change.

A speck of white falls between us, and I look up. Snowflakes flutter through the dark sky. The light from the ballroom doors makes each one flicker.

By the time I look down again, Jasper has slipped his hand out of my grasp. He reaches toward my nose and wipes it. "They like your face."

He likes my face. He told me.

I yearn to lean forward, to touch him and kiss him until we're both burning in the snow, and make him mine. Jasper always claims that writing helps him release his love *and* fears. Things can't be that simple. But Jasper believes so.

"I assume you're staying at your aunt's tonight," I mutter. "But tomorrow. Do you want to write with me?"

Jasper stares. He's so close that I can pick out every wispy eyelash. "Write?"

"Like we used to. At camp? Come with me to the lake. Noon?"

He takes another shaky breath. Prepares to say no.

"Right," I say despite the deepening pit in my stomach. "I under—"

"Okay," Jasper says.

Shock hits me like a punch. It turns to excitement, bursting through me. "Really?"

He nods again. Gradually.

I'll take it. I'll take anything. "Okay. Okay! I'll see you then."

"Comrade, are you out there?!"

We look to the ballroom, where Blaze is running down the steps, then tripping as his white sheet tangles between his feet. He tumbles and hits the pavement in front of us.

Xavier and Delilah stand by the doors, wincing. London isn't with them—she must still be with Griffin, enjoying the night she and everyone else deserve.

"Sorry," Delilah calls our way. "We couldn't find either of you, so we thought you'd—You know."

Gotten caught.

As they join us by the fountain, Jasper pulls his pen out of his chest pocket—of course he brought the pen—and waves the nib their way. "Well, you just put quite the attention on us by yelling that into the night, thank you very much."

Xavier whips out his lucky spoon. The two commence battle. Blaze must've risen back to life at some point because he's lugging himself over Xavier's back now as well, adding his slingshot to the mix.

Delilah sits beside me on the fountain, elbowing my shoulder. "Mission accomplished, by the way. Looks like they'll trust STRIP again."

Jasper stops thwacking Xavier's spoon, his eyes lighting up. "Really?"

We *did* it.

"I can't believe we didn't get caught," I say incredulously.

Which means my guilt should be gone. But the thought of keeping my mistakes from STRIP for the rest of my time at Valentine only turns my stomach more hollow.

"Of course we didn't," Xavier says. "We can figure out anything. We're the smartest guys on campus. And girl."

"Thank you," Delilah says, raising her nose high.

I take a breath. A long one. "You guys."

Everyone stares at me. Waiting.

"I went to the equestrian center with Blaze and accidentally let out the horses." I shrink deeper into myself. "I think the ripped trash bags were my fault too. My ring that got caught on Jasper. Everything was my fault. I'm sorry—"

"Who cares?" Xavier interrupts. He knocks both Blaze's slingshot and Jasper's pen into the fountain basin while they're distracted. Blaze squeals and fetches them. Delilah rolls her eyes.

As if none of them truly care.

"You should," I say, furrowing my brow at the pen-diving lollapalooza. "You almost got expelled. STRIP's legacy would've also been done—"

"STRIP is a unit, bro," Xavier says. "Your screw-ups are our screw-ups. We're a powerhouse of screw-ups."

I look to Delilah, giving up on Xavier. "Your detentions are my fault. Hit me."

Delilah's mouth twists. "Ew. No."

I grab her palm to slap myself with it.

Jasper stops me in time, lowering my hand to my thigh. "If we blamed you, we'd have to blame Blaze for not checking that the gate was locked, knowing you'd never used it. I'd have to blame myself for wearing the bracelet that got stuck to your ring."

"What you're blaming yourself for sounds like your straight-up existence, Charlie," Xavier adds, "and we're not gonna hear that."

All I can do is blink back in shock at everyone—the people who are still my friends. Slowly, it turns to a smile. Maybe STRIP really will always figure things out together.

But I still have a few last things to figure out on my own.

Chapter 43
LETTERS TO A YOUNG POET
FRIDAY, NOVEMBER 15

In the office, Ms. Lyney plays with a gnome's stubby arms on her desk, humming the *Ghostbusters* theme song.

I knock on the doorframe.

She blinks out of her daze. Today, her spirit wear sweatshirt is accompanied by a Valentine baseball cap, red sweatpants, and a pendant necklace of the arrow-stabbed heart crest. She bought out the whole gift shop. "Wasn't the mixer wonderful, Charlie?"

"Yeah."

"This academy is wonderful. All of you kiddos are. So wonderful."

Mr. Stern definitely put a ring in that gnome.

When I first came to Valentine, I would've cringed. I never would've understood that Ms. Lyney can allow herself to be vulnerable with love because she has confidence in herself. Now all I feel is jealousy. "I need to call back my mom."

With a vacant hum, she dials for Mom and passes me the phone. I head into the back room. As the phone rings, I check my watch. Twenty minutes until I meet Jasper at the lake. Unless he doesn't show up.

Worry races through me at the high probability.

"Hello?"

"Hi, Mom."

"Charlie, finally! Hold on, let me stop shelving these books."

A few thuds come over the line. "I saw the email with the final ranks. Have you asked if there's extra credit? Rank Six is so close. We can fix this."

"No, it's okay. The academy is getting rid of the ranks. I'm staying."

"Really?" Mom shouts so loudly that I pull the phone away from my ear. "This is the best news! This will put a huge dent in your stress over there, won't it? But remember, you're always welcome back home anytime if things change."

"Mom, can I talk to you?"

"What is it?"

"Do you think I can't handle this?"

"What do you mean?"

I clench the hem of my coat. "You keep encouraging me to come home like you keep expecting I'll give up on Valentine."

"Oh, sweetie, no. That's not what I mean at all."

"But you're worried, right? That the administration will find out?"

"Of course I'm going to worry."

"Well, I talked to the principal last night, and I told her," I say.

Silence falls on the other end.

"What did she say?" Mom's voice is unreadable over the phone. Never have I wished to see her face more than now.

"She said the board of trustees will take a look at adjusting the guidelines for me," I say. "She even said I can come to her anytime with issues."

"Really?" I can practically hear Mom's brow soaring. "That... I'm shocked, Charlie. I'm so thrilled to hear. You're doing okay after that? That must've been scary."

"To be honest, I haven't had the easiest time since I got here,"

I admit. I don't know why I do, but it seems right, like Mom and I are getting somewhere—and it's like a dam breaking, how good it feels to finally tell her the truth. "But I'm doing better now. I've found support."

"Oh, good. From instructors?"

"A few. And friends."

"Good!" Her voice is calmer now. "I understand what you mean. I didn't have an easy time adjusting to Valentine either."

"What?"

"Mhm. Staying top five was a nightmare for me."

"But you took me here all the time when I was younger. You loved it."

"Well, Valentine is still a wonderful academy. It's such a privilege to go. But those Excellence Scholar requirements—that's a lot of pressure to put on someone your age. Anyone. At times, it was admittedly the worst I've felt in my life."

I fall quiet in my disbelief. Mom's gone through a failing bookstore and a divorce.

"That's why I've been offering for you to come visit home whenever you'd like," she continues. "I remember wishing Grandma and Grandpa would've done the same for me when I desperately needed a break."

"Why didn't you tell me about this?" I ask.

"Well, you wanted to go so badly. I didn't want to worry you."

"I mean, thanks," I mumble on a light laugh. "But don't you always worry about me? How is that fair?"

Mom laughs back. "I also didn't want this to deter you with so many other things on your plate. I wanted to support you like you asked. And you're very capable. But I should've. I'm glad you're doing better."

She's listening. Finally.

The tension inside me dissolves. "Thank you." I check the clock. Ten minutes till Jasper. "I have to meet up with someone now. I'm excited to see you over break."

"Have fun," Mom says. "Oh, and Charlie, last thing: Despite my rockier memories of Valentine, I made many more beautiful ones. Make a whole bunch this year for me."

❧❧

I check my watch as I reach the Dixon Writing Gazebo. Five minutes past twelve. He should be in there, but vine trellises block me from seeing inside.

Nerves throw a rave in my chest as I stand there, unable to move. Jasper and I are really about to spend the whole afternoon alone.

I'm really about to try to write him a love letter.

That's what I've decided. It only seems fair, especially after he's written so many about me. But I'll need to be honest about everything I've shoved down for years. Even with Jasper by my side, I'm still not sure if I know how.

My heart pounds as I finally walk up. The archway comes into view. Then the benches. Then Jasper, scribbling in his journal. The heat lamps are set so high that his peacoat is balled up on the wood planks. He wears a loose dress shirt—no number-one pin on the collar—with only my scarf to keep him warm despite being surrounded by snow.

He *showed up*.

Relief floods me as I knock against a wood pillar. "Can I come in?"

Jasper's head lifts, blond hair whisping across his cheeks. His gaze zaps around the bushes and lakefront like a lost first year. "What time is it?"

"Can't you always tell from where the sun is?" I point toward the sky.

He flicks his pen in the same direction, his bracelet jingling against his wrist. "The finicky heavens decided to be overcast today. So, no, I cannot see the sun."

"About noon."

"Already?"

I step into the gazebo, only to then embarrassingly hover around his bench. Sitting too close is too pushy. Too far away is too awkward. I opt for about a foot's length, set my backpack on the floor, and take out my notebook.

Jasper's pen was moving when I got here, but now the notebook on his lap is blank. He must've flipped the page. He looks at me. "You said you wanted to write?"

That *is* what we came here for. "I suppose."

"Okay." He picks up his pen and dates the top left of his paper in silence. He still doesn't pry about why I've requested this time together, but from the way he's gripping his pen like a lifeline, I can only imagine the number of questions in his mind.

I stare down at my notebook. To write this love letter, I'll need to create the words myself. There won't be an answer I can carve out like blackout poetry.

But this may be the last opportunity Jasper will ever give me.

Placing my pencil to the paper, I inhale, exhale, and write. For the first time, I try to release every ounce of honesty Jasper taught me, every emotion Mr. Stern claimed would bring my work to the next level. I don't second-guess a word despite my brain warning me that I'm too vulnerable, too weak, too illogical. I write everything about romance that I hate. Or, maybe, used to hate.

The church bell towers chime in unison.

I look up. Already?

"Was that the last lunchtime bell?" I ask him.

"Guess we should go," Jasper says, casually filing his red ribbon bookmark into his journal as if what he said is no big deal. But a heavy disappointment weighs down his words. He expected me to do something. And he didn't get it.

I've broken his heart again.

I reread the words on my paper. How can I possibly recite this love letter to a famous poet like Jasper Grimes?

Jasper is standing now, his cross-body bag slung over a shoulder. I grip his blazer cuff. "Wait a sec."

"What's wrong? You look ill."

I rip the letter out and smooth the frayed edges. My hands are shaking so much that I can barely make out my own writing.

"Charlie?" Jasper says.

"ROSES ARE RED."

He jolts back, gripping his chest. "Y-yes, they are."

Too loud. I hide my face behind the paper. Mortifying. "Can I try that again?"

"Sure," he mumbles.

"Roses are red. Violets are blue. I'm disappointed that I met you."

"I beg your pardon?"

"For violets have become the tint of your eyes and your favorite food, reminding me of who fate keeps bumping me into. Now the lies I've whispered to myself are drowned out by the truth"—I take an unsteady breath—"I think I'm falling in love with you."

The waves roll. The heat lamp crackles beside us.

I squeeze my eyes shut. Cringe. So cringe.

Unspoken Guideline 19: Mom was wrong. There are no beautiful memories at Valentine. Only mortifying, terrible, I-want-to-die memories.

Something knocks against me. Jasper, sitting on the bench again, leaning against my shoulder. He buries his face in the crook of my neck. "One more time."

"Huh?"

"One more time. Recite it again."

"What? No way—" I try to shrink away. Of course he's trying to embarrass me. The actual *good* poet. "Jasper—?"

"Charlie." I've never heard his voice this soft before, yet there's something more unrestrained that simmers beneath it, too, making my chest burst in ways I never knew existed. "Just the last bit at least."

"I—" I clench the letter tighter. "Fine. I said, I think I'm falling in love with you."

Jasper pulls away, dimple popped. The sunlight reflected in his blue eyes shimmers as strikingly as the frozen lake. "Thank you. That was a brilliant poem."

Unspoken Guideline 19 (Revised): Maybe Mom was right.

"It's a bit mean," I mumble, readjusting my glasses to distract myself from the butterflies detonating inside me. "And not really a poem. Just a letter."

"That's what makes it brilliant. It's an authentic work by you. About time."

"Hey, it was impossible to write other people's love letters authentically. I didn't know any of them, unlike you." I cross my arms.

Jasper's lip quirks up. "Of course. My apologies."

"This is still scary, though."

"What is?"

"Reciting this letter. I thought that once I did, I'd stop being scared. And I have. Sort of. Because I trust you. With everything. But now it feels different. It feels"—I waver—"good, almost? Exciting? Does this make sense?"

Jasper pulls me closer by the wrist and kisses me.

Instantly, I sink into him, letting my arms wrap over his shoulders, and I feel him smile against me as his hand finds my knee, gently trailing higher up my thigh. There's a hint of bitterness on his lips, probably from the black coffee he drank this morning, and it mixes with the floral notes of his shampoo and fragrance. My head floods with how much I've wanted this again from only one bed away, and for so long.

Finally, I let him kiss me first.

His lips drift across my cheek until he's by my ear, and a chill races through my spine. "Love is never *not* scary. It's a matter of whether you're enjoying that fear."

"I am. I know I am now."

"I am too."

"Really?" I lean back, cupping his rosy face in my palms. "Really?"

"Really," Jasper says.

So much joy bursts through me—too much—that all I can think to do is kiss his cheeks until my lips are exhausted. A final thought hits me, and my body flashes so hot that I must be a thousand degrees. "Our room."

He smirks. "Convenient, isn't it?"

A million degrees. "I—Well. I know you technically just moved back in, but last night, I think I accidentally told your aunt to make sure you stay with her. So I don't know if you can come back."

"You *what?*" Jasper slaps a hand to his forehead and collapses, slumping on the bench. "Charlie von Hevringprinz, you drive me up the wall."

"It was for a good reason! I told her everything I've been hiding."

"Oh?"

"Yeah. She's looking into updating the guidelines package to help me."

Jasper's gaze softens. "I'm happy for you, Charlie. Truly. I have a feeling there's a new, wonderful journey ahead of you."

I laugh, but I still roll my eyes. "No more poetry today. I'm poetry-ed out."

A laugh leaves Jasper, too, his lopsided dimple popping again. He sits back up and squeezes my hand, then kisses me again. "So, no longer roommates."

"No." I scoot closer, laying my head on Jasper's shoulder. "Something much better."

ACKNOWLEDGMENTS

US CREDITS

Literary Agent: Natalie Lakosil and the whole Looking Glass Literary & Media team

Film Agent: Lucy Stille

Editorial: Nicolás Ore-Giron and Connie Hsu

Audiobook Production: Alyssa Keyne and the whole team

Publishing Director: Allison Verost

Cover Design: L. Whitt and Abby Granata

Cover Illustration: Adelle Kincel

Map Illustration: Virginia Allyn

Production Editor: Mia Moran

Production Manager: Alexa Blanco

Managing Editor: Jennifer Healey

Assistant Managing Editor: Hayley O'Brion

Marketing: Teresa Ferraiolo

Publicity: Morgan B. Kane and Molly Ellis

Sales: Shawn Foster, Isaac Loewen, and the whole team

School and Library: Mary Van Akin and the whole team

Social Content: Teresa Ferraiolo, Carlee Maurier, and the whole team

Intern Assistance: Makena Cioni

Primary Emotional Support: Emily Charlotte, M.K. Lobb

UK CREDITS

Foreign Rights Agent: Heather Baror-Shapiro

Editorial: Georgina Mitchell

Acquisitions: Tig Wallace

Publishing Director: Kate Agar

Desk Editor: Jenna Mackintosh

Cover Design: Joana Reis

Cover Illustration: Bex Glendining

Production Controller: Rhys Callaghan

Marketing: Nils Jones

Publicity: Lucy Clayton

Sales: Hannah Methuen, Katherine Fox, Jennifer Hudson, Jemimah James, Emma Francini, and the whole team

Special thanks to the booksellers, reviewers, influencers, and librarians who keep books about transgender teens on shelves. I am two hundred feet away from your home and rapidly approaching to get down on one knee.